Jane,

"Distance i

in the end, I have you."

MW00975752

Torn into
Pieces

XOXO,

Shelby

A Pieces Series Novel

SHELBY REEVES

Photography by Lindee Robinson Photography

Cover Design by Danielle Styles

Formatted by Marisa-rose Shor of Cover Me, Darling and Allyson Gottlieb of Athena Interior Book Design

To all the military men and women who have served or are currently serving our country. God bless all of you.

ACKNOWLEDGMENTS

First and foremost, I want to thank God for blessing me.

My husband- You are my rock and I couldn't go through life without you or Deven!

My parents- Thank you for loving me and being there for me.

Shannon- What can I say that I already haven't? Thank you from the bottom of my heart!

My CS Chicks- You ladies always give the best advice and I'm lucky to have such amazing friends!

To the fellow authors who have helped me and given me advice...Thank you!

To all the blogs that have shared my author page, teasers, and helped promote me...Thank you for helping me get my name out in the book world.

prologue

Alexis

All I can think at this moment is, *this can't be real.* Things like this don't happen to me. But it *is* happening. I am crying so hard I can't breathe. Julie and I are hanging on to each other as we mourn the loss of the one we love. Her son, my boyfriend. He was supposed to come home. A month was all that was left of his deployment. Then I would be slinging my arms around his neck, kissing him as I welcome him home. But now, I won't be doing that, because he didn't make it. He promised me he would come home to me. Dammit, why did he have to go?!

The sergeants are offering their condolences, yet it doesn't help. Nothing will help take this pain away. Ethan was fighting for our country, does that not mean anything? He wasn't a criminal, he was a good person. He didn't deserve to die. Ethan should be coming home to me, to his family.

Julie is squeezing me tight, sobbing with me.

We finally get together, then he is taken from me and from our child. Ethan won't be here to see his first child being born. He won't be here when his child starts hitting all their first milestones.

I think that is what hurts the most. Not only am I carrying the pain for me, I'm carrying it for our baby too, and his family. My heart hurts so much. It's torn, shredded into a million pieces, pieces that only Ethan can put back together.

He should have come home.

I need you to be strong for me while I am gone, okay? I know you can do it, beautiful. My faith is in you. Stay strong, and hold on because no matter where I am, I'll always come home to you.

Oh, Ethan, why did you have to leave me?

He wants me to be strong, but I don't know if I can. I made him a promise, though, and I am not letting him down. I need to not only do this for myself and his family but for our little family as well.

I love you, Ethan. Watch over us, especially our baby.

chapter one

Ethan

With Lex staring at me like she is now, it's hard to not shove her against the wall and kiss the hell out of her. She is so gorgeous standing in front of me with her hair pulled back in a messy bun, leggings, and an oversized t-shirt. Her face is clean of makeup, showing her natural beauty, which is the way I love seeing her.

"What are you doing here, Lex?" I ask her in a low, hoarse whisper.

An anxious smile graces her face, hitting me right in my gut. She knows what she does to me. I'm an open book to her, and part of me hates it because I know I hurt her more often than not.

"I just came to inform you—" she stops short and I noticeably cringe when a perfectly manicured hand touches my arm. Hurt washes away the excitement she once was gracing. When I had opened the door to find Lex standing on the other side, I forgot all about Kate being here. Guilt swarms me as I watch Lex straighten her shoulders and put on a brave face.

Kate, thankfully, put on a robe, instead of just walking out here wrapped in a sheet. It's obvious what Kate and I have been doing. It doesn't help I answered the door in just my boxers.

I haven't seen Lex since I walked away from her the morning after she went to prom. The last text she sent got to me. Thoughts of crashing the prom so I could spy on her popped in my head more than once.

Around ten o'clock that night, Kaylee messaged me, letting me know she and Adam were home safe and sound. So, I figured Lex would be home not long after. When eleven o'clock rolled around I started texting her, trying to figure out where she was. My mind was running with several possibilities. Were they still at prom? Did they go back to her house? Did they go to his? Then my crazy mind started coming up with these horrifying scenarios thinking she went to a party and had been drugged or kidnapped. It was crazy because I knew Brad would keep her safe. After all, he had been helping Adam and I protect my sister, Kaylee, from the little shit who sexually assaulted her.

My vein throbbed and my jaw ticked when the last possibility flashed in my brain. She and Brad were having sex.

I didn't hear from her until she finally showed up at Adam and Kaylee's in *his* clothes. I couldn't handle seeing her dressed like that because it meant what I thought was just a possibility became more real.

"Hello, little one," Kate sneers, jealously dripping from her words. "It would have been nice if you would have called instead of interrupting our…time."

This is seriously going downhill fast. "Kate," I growl in warning.

Alexis scoffs in disgust. "Clearly."

"Kate go back inside for a minute, I need to talk to, Lex."

Kate jumps back, her hand flying to her chest, appalled.

"No, I'm going to go so you can get back to your skank," Alexis says bitterly. Kate gasps beside me but I could care less.

Alexis turns to go, but my hand shoots out, grabbing her wrist. "No, we are talking. Kate go inside." My eyes never waver from Lex's hurt ones. The hurt *I* put there.

She tries to jerk her wrist from my grasp, but I just tighten my hold. She is not going to walk away from me. "We are talking, Lex," I promise her.

Kate snootily walks back in the apartment, shutting the door behind her. Finally!

"Now, you were saying?" I want to know why she showed up at my apartment. Not that I don't want her here, she just came at a bad time.

"You seriously think I'm going to stand here and talk to you after that?"

Okay, let's try this a different way. "Why are you here, Lex? It's after midnight. You know there is a curfew, right?"

She scoffs. "The curfew is for kids who are under eighteen and in high school. I'm neither one, Ethan, remember?"

Of course, I know that. On her birthday, I went out with the guys and ended up with a massive hangover and Kate in my bed the next morning. I told myself just because she was legal now doesn't mean I could go after her. She is still with Brad. I don't want to put her in the situation where she cheats on her boyfriend, ever.

"That still doesn't explain why you show up at my apartment in the middle of the damn night."

If Kate hadn't been here, I'd be pressured to do something I'd regret later. I'd put her in the position I want her to stay away from.

"It's a moot point now. Goodbye, Ethan," she murmurs, the hurt returning to her eyes.

And like an idiot, I let her walk away. No argument ever gets settled between us since it always ends with her walking away upset and me letting her go while my heart slams against my chest.

One day, I will go after her. I will pull her back into my arms and kiss her, giving her what she's wanted all along.

But it won't be tonight, and it definitely won't be tomorrow.

I pull out my phone noticing I have a message from my sister. It was sent a couple hours ago. I race down the steps of my apartment complex not caring I'm in only my boxers.

I guess I'm running after her after all, just not for the reason she probably will be thinking. "Lex, wait up!" I holler just as she reaches her car.

"Leave me alone, Ethan." Ouch. I can't say that didn't hurt.

"I just saw that Kaylee texted me a couple hours ago. She's in labor."

"I know, she messaged me too."

"Why didn't you say something?"

She throws her hands in the air, clearly frustrated. "I assumed you already knew."

"So, that's not why you came here?"

She opens her mouth, then shuts it. Her eyes soften. "It doesn't matter why I'm here."

"Look, we'll finish this later. Come inside and wait while I get dressed."

"What? Are you crazy? I'm not going back in there!"

"Lex."

"Ethan," she mimics my tone.

"We are riding together to the hospital."

"Why?"

"Because it's the middle of the night and you don't need to walk through the parking garage alone."

"I'm a big girl, trust me, I can handle myself."

Knowing I'm wasting time, I walk toward her, wrap my arms around her legs, and hoist her over my shoulder. Her fists immediately started pounding against my bare back.

"Ethan, put me down!"

I ignore her and keep walking up the stairs. She continues to squirm, hit, and yell as I walk back inside and shut the door. I keep walking, heading to my room.

When I walk in, Kate is lying across my bed in all her naked glory. Thank goodness, Lex is facing the other way.

"Kate, you need to leave. My sister is in labor so we have to go." I keep Lex facing the opposite way so she doesn't see Kate's state of dress.

"Are you seriously kicking me out?"

I grind my jaw. "Kate, I do not have time for your shit. My sister is having her babies so I have to go."

She huffs, grabs her clothes, or lack of thereof, and dresses. "Call me later, E," she says seductively as she walks past me. I swear her mood switches gears constantly.

Once Kate shuts the door behind her, I search my closet for something to wear with Alexis still on my shoulder. She is still fighting me, still beating her fists in my back. No doubt she will probably leave a bruise. I'm afraid to set her down for fear she will bolt out the door. This is the closest I will ever be to her for a while so I'm soaking it in. Once we get to the hospital, she will be far away from me.

Plus, I'm kind of enjoying this.

chapter two

Alexis

I'm sitting on the couch next to Kaylee, holding Jackson in my arms. He is so precious with his chubby cheeks, and his round brown eyes. Jackson, as well as his sister, Jasmine, look like they have been dug out of Riley's butt. Anna, Adam's mom, claims there is an old wives tale about it. I'm glad Kaylee has Adam and his family in her life, though. She has been through a lot over the last few years between losing her father, her mother turning into a psycho, and being at Riley's mercy.

"So… I've been meaning to ask you. When you and Ethan walked in the hospital room you both looked…I don't know…upset? I know something happened between the two of you, I just can't place my finger on it."

Ah crap, why did she have to bring him up? I was doing okay until she mentioned his name. "Nothing happened," I say innocently, knowing I'm full of shit.

Unfortunately, Kaylee knows it, too. "Bull crap! I know you looked hurt, so spill it. What did my brother do?"

Besides the fact he ripped my heart out of my chest, threw it on the ground, and then stomped all over it, he pretty much ruined what little hope I had of us getting together.

"Well, come on, tell me!" Kaylee pushes.

I sigh, knowing I won't be able to leave without telling her. "I went over there to talk to him, that's it."

"And?" she presses.

"And Kate was over there." Ugh, I'd like to stab her perfect, make-up caked face.

"What did you talk to him about?"

"I didn't get to talk to him because she walked up. The moment was ruined so I turned to leave and he stopped me. He ordered Kate to go back in the apartment which didn't help any since all we did was argue, and I left. He came barreling down the steps a couple minutes later, informing me of what I already knew. He told me we were riding together to the hospital and went all caveman when I told him no. Ethan carried me back in his apartment like a sack of potatoes and wouldn't let me down until Kate was gone and he had his clothes. End of story." Ethan made me so mad that night. I don't do well with someone giving me orders.

"You still never answered my question. What did you need to talk to him about?"

Good grief, she's relentless! "Fine, I went over there to make sure he felt the same way I do before I called things off with Brad." Yeah, that turned out real well.

"Oh, Alexis, I'm sorry girl! No wonder you were upset!"

"Yeah, no wonder," I mutter.

"My brother is an idiot."

You don't say? I just shrug it off like I do every other time. I thought for a while Ethan wanted me. I could see it, feel the connection between us. Or maybe it has been one-sided all along? I went over there, going to pour my heart out to him, knowing good well it might get stomped on, but I didn't care at the time. At the time, I was confident he would feel the same way. Now? I have no idea. I'm not planning on holding my heart out for him to trample over anymore. No, if he wants me, he's going to have to fight for me. He's going to have to make me truly believe he wants me. For now, I guess things will go back to the way they were, us avoiding each other. It will be easier once cheer workouts start up, and once fall gets here my schedule will be jam packed with practice, classes, and games. There will be no time for me to think about Ethan Harper.

Too bad my heart doesn't feel the same.

My first cheer workout is tonight, which I'm excited about. I'm nervous since I don't know what to expect. I've never met these girls and guys before so I hope I like them. It will make the season easier. I got a cheer scholarship to Western Kentucky University so I jumped on it. Brad got a basketball scholarship to the University of Kentucky which is almost two and a half hours from here. Brad was so excited when he told me he got accepted. A month later, he came to me saying he is going to WKU with me. I eventually talked him out of it because I know UK is where he truly wants to go and he didn't need to give up his dream of playing basketball for the Kentucky Wildcats for me. Especially since their basketball team has not lost a game this season. Though, I'll miss him, I'm so proud of him for following his dream. His practice starts this summer, too, so I'm afraid we won't get to see each other much this summer. Brad swears we will make this work.

I walk into the gym at WKU and I am amazed. This is nothing like a high school gym. I'm blown away by how humongous it is. Though we had a pretty good size gym for a high school, this one is double its size. A few people from the squad are already in the center of the gym, standing on the red athletic logo which is a hand waving a red towel with the letters WKU in white. I toss my gym bag off the side with everyone else's as I walk onto the court to join the few that are here.

A short petite girl holding a clipboard smiles and waves at me as I walk up. She holds her hand out for me to shake. "Hello, I'm Brittany, captain of the squad!"

I beam at her and shake her hand. "Alexis Collins, nice to meet you."

"Welcome and congrats for making the squad. For now, just mingle and we'll get started shortly."

I guess it's a good thing I'm not shy and have no problem meeting new people.

I meet Matt first, who I learn is very outgoing and friendly. He is tall and broad shouldered with dirty blond hair. Next, I meet Alice, who is my height and build. We hit it off quick so I can tell we are going to be friends.

I smile and shake hands with several others until finally Brittany called us over to start practice. Our coach Mrs. Jenny Hamilton stands before us, introducing herself, Brittany, and Jenna, who is the co-captain. Jenna seems to be stuck up, judging by her demeanor. I hope I don't have a problem with her or anyone else this season. I'm definitely not looking for drama.

Tonight, Coach Hamilton goes over the rules, we lift weights for an hour, and then we spend the rest of practice learning our first cheer. So far, WKU seems like it's going to be a good choice.

I walk out of the gym between Alice and Matt toward our vehicles. We are already making plans to meet up and practice. We exchange numbers before saying goodbye. They break away to their own vehicles and I continue my trek to mine.

I stop mid-step when I notice someone leaning against my car. Then, I smile and pick up my pace. My legs are screaming from the leg workout I did tonight, but it's all worth it to be doing what I love.

"Hey babe." I wrap my arms around Brad's neck and capture his lips. "This is a nice surprise."

"I wanted to see how my girl's first night went."

"Oh my goodness, Brad, I had so much fun! I can't wait for our next practice!" I prove my excitement when I jump up and down in his arms.

He kisses me again. "I'm so happy for you, Lex. How about we go celebrate?"

"I'd love that. What did you have in mind?"

"Well, this was a spur of the moment idea. Do you want to stay in or go out?"

"Can we stay in tonight? My legs are sore from working out."

"Of course, my place or yours?"

I think about it a moment. "How about mine tonight. I need to finish packing some tonight anyways."

I decided I wanted to move into my own apartment right off campus before school starts. It would be more convenient for me with class, practice, and such. I also wanted to spread my wings a bit, so to speak. I love my parents, but I want the chance to live on my own. Luckily, they understand and they support my decision.

Brad calls ahead to a Mexican restaurant and places our order so he can swing by on the way to my house and pick it up.

I decide to take a quick shower before Brad arrives with the food since I know I have to smell from sweating so much during practice. I had just put on my pajama shorts and tank top when Brad knocks on my bedroom door. I open it, letting him in with the mouthwatering food.

We spread all of the food out on my bed and talk about our upcoming busy schedules. We want to pack as much time in together as we can before Brad leaves for UK in a couple weeks. I know these two weeks are going to fly by so fast I won't even have time to blink. I will miss Brad while he is away. I know I can't tell him for sure I'm in love with him and I know I had planned on breaking things off with him if my conversation with Ethan had gone as planned, but the truth is, I care for Brad, very much. Do I believe he is the one I want to spend the rest of my life with? Maybe. I feel very strongly for him,

I just don't think it's fair to him to tell him I love him when my heart is torn in two.

"When did you say you were moving?" Brad asks, pulling me from my thoughts.

"I'm going to look at one this weekend and if I like it, hopefully, I can move in as soon as possible."

"Let me know when you're ready to move and I'll help you if I'm able to make it."

"Okay."

We pick a movie off Netflix and relax in each other's arms for a bit before I continue the dreaded packing process. I have a lot of stuff I have to go through. I plan on asking Kaylee if she wants to go shopping with me once I put the deposit down on my new apartment.

I want to eventually get a job so I can start paying for my own apartment and officially be out from under my parents. Slowly, but surely I'm working my way to be independent. People see me as a spoiled rich kid. I am spoiled, I'll gladly admit it. Except when people associate me with that category they believe I'm a stuck up bitch, which is far from the truth. Now, if you put me in a room full of kids who are all about their parents' money then you will see me in that element. I don't like associating with that type of crowd. Thank goodness my parents don't force me to hang out with those uptight pricks.

When the movie is over, Brad hugs me and kisses me goodbye. I stay up a while to make a dent on my packing.

It is going on two in the morning before my head finally hits the pillow.

chapter three

Alexis

It is rolling on noon before I even crack an eye open. I rub my eyes trying to wake up as I shuffle my way to the bathroom to maintain the mess that is my hair.

The smell of coffee captures my attention as I make my way downstairs. Mom is relaxing in her favorite recliner when I walk in the den.

"Morning dear. For a minute I thought you were going to sleep the day away," she jokes and takes another sip of her coffee.

I plop down in the couch that is seated across from her. "No, I can't do that. I need to pack up as much as I can today while I have nothing planned."

Mom gives me a pointed look. "Sweetie, you know your father and I don't mind you living here while you attend college."

I know they aren't exactly thrilled that their only child is leaving the nest, but I want the chance to stand on my own two feet. "I know, mom, but like I told you and Dad, it will be so much easier if I live right off campus and besides I can't live here forever. You know I'll visit as often as I can."

"Okay, sweetie, just promise me that if you ever need us you will call."

"I promise Mom."

I walk over to her and kiss her cheek before I make my way to the kitchen for a bite to eat while I resume packing. So far all I have packed is miscellaneous things. I'm trying to hold off on my clothes and shoes until the very end.

When I am finished eating, I head to my room. With my music cranked up loud, I get to work.

Man, when did I accumulate so much stuff? I have a pile for the things I'm going to leave behind and separate pile for the things I'm going to take. So far the pile I'm bringing with is larger than the leave behind pile.

I feel my phone vibrate beneath my leg so I pull it out to see who sent me a text.

It's Brad.

Brad: How's the packing going?

Me: It's going. What are you up to today?

Brad: The same thing you are

Me: Sucks doesn't it

I finally put my phone down so I can stay on task. My mind drifts back to wondering if I am making the right decision by staying with Brad. Can we really handle a long-term relationship? How long will I have to wait before I see him? Will it be two weeks? Three? A month? And what about my feelings for Ethan? I keep pushing them aside, yet they seem hell bent on not going away. I don't know which direction is the right way to go. Maybe I should just be single for a while because even though I love being with Brad, I'm not in love with him, and I don't know how much longer I can put off that conversation. As for Ethan, I'm not chasing after him. If he wants me he should man up and tell me himself.

I feel my phone vibrate again so I check it. It's Matt wondering if I want to practice learning one of our new cheers. I might as well since all I'm doing is asking myself the same questions over and over without making any decisions. I message him back letting him know I'm game and to let me know when and where.

I finish packing the box I am working on before changing into my shorts and an old practice t-shirt. I'm dressed and ready by the time Matt replies. I slip on the sneakers I only use for cheer, grab my phone, keys, and purse, then I head out the door.

I make it to my destination in no time. Matt, Alice, and I are meeting at a gym in which Matt has rented out the basketball court so we won't have anyone knocking us in the head with a basketball.

"There she is! It's about time!" Matt hollers as I walk toward them.

"Hey now! I was ready to go by the time you replied with where we were meeting. Alice isn't even here," I point out.

"Yeah, turns out she won't be joining us this go round. It's just you and me." I suspect Matt bats for the opposite team, but I'm not entirely sure. He's still cool regardless and at least I won't have to worry about him trying to get with me.

"Okay, so what do you want to do first?" I ask as I start stretching.

Matt joins me in stretching, warming up our muscles. "Well, I thought maybe we can work on our cheer, tumbling, and since you're a flyer, some lifts."

"Sounds good. Let's get started."

He walks over to a stereo in the corner and puts on some music. Rihanna floods the speakers as I do my first back handspring of the afternoon. We spend the next twenty minutes doing some simple back handsprings and tumbles to warm up. Once we are warmed up we move on to the bigger, more complicated moves like a front tuck, roundoff, back handspring, layout twist.

Needing a break, we lay out on the floor on our backs, stretched out opposite ways with our heads side by side.

"You're a natural at tumbling. You landed that last move like a pro. How long have you been cheering?"

"Since I was little girl. My parents signed me up for gymnastics when I was little and I found my favorite part was the floor routine. I've been to so many cheer camps its unreal."

"What's your favorite part about it?" he asks.

"Being in the air, I guess. It feels cool to be the one they toss."

He chuckles. "Sorry girl, but being the one who can hold you up with one arm is badass."

I laugh out loud. "Well then! Who says I can't do that?" I used to be one of the girls who were part of the base. Which, that was before I learned to be a flyer.

"I'd pay to see that. You'd have to bulk up big time."

"One day, Matt. Mark my words." He's right, to be able to hold the flyer up in the air with one arm is pretty amazing.

"Are you excited for this season?"

I stare at the ceiling unsure how to answer his question. On one hand, I am ecstatic. This is my dream and I finally made it. On the other hand, my situation looms over my head.

"Uh oh. I don't like silence. Spill it, Alexis."

"I am thrilled, Matt. Really, I am. I've worked really hard to get here."

"But?"

"Have you ever been in a long distance relationship? Or better yet, has your heart been torn between two people?" I know I've only known Matt a couple days, but he seems trustworthy. He is easy to talk to and cut up with.

"Ah, can't say I have for either of them. Do you have pictures of both of them?"

I turn my head to the side so I can see him, shocked he even asked such a question. "What? Why?"

"Because I want to see what they look like, why else?"

"Fine." I get up, jog over to retrieve my phone from my bag and jog back, reclaiming my spot on the floor. I scroll through my pictures until I find one of Brad and me. "Here is Brad, who I'm currently dating."

"Nice. Okay, next one."

I roll my eyes and scroll down some more trying to find one of Ethan. I know I have one of Ethan and Kaylee in here somewhere. "Here is Ethan and his sister, who happens to be my best friend."

He whistles low. "Damn girl. What's the story with him?"

I sigh audibly. "I like him, but I'm not sure if the feelings mutual. I was at first, but now I don't know."

"So, let me get this straight. You are with Brad who you like, but you also like this other guy who seems to not want the same thing? Wow, what a mess. Who do you feel more for?"

"Easy, Ethan. Brad is amazing, but I don't feel the same way about him as I do Ethan, and it's frustrating because I have a guy who is so good to me and loves me, but yet I'm not a hundred percent sure I'm in love with him." *I'm in love with someone else.*

"That sucks. So what are you going to do?"

"I'm not sure yet. Brad leaves for the University of Kentucky in less than two weeks. Basically, I have three options."

Matt cuts in. "I'm going to pick the third one."

"You have no idea what the third option is!" I point out.

"You'll see."

Ignoring his smirk, I continue. "Option one, I stay with Brad and hope my feelings for Ethan pass. Option two, break up with Brad and hope Ethan decides he wants me. Option three, I let Brad go and be single." To be honest, I don't care for the third option. If I let Brad go, I want to be with Ethan.

"Want to know why I automatically said option three? Nine times out of ten, option three is the last choice you want to make, which means it more than likely is the right one. Here's where option one and two fail. You don't need to stay with Brad when you aren't happy and you don't need to be chasing after a guy, he needs to be honest with you about his feelings. If not, sucks for him. If you want my advice, stay single for a while. Focus on you. Or, there is always me hooking you up with someone."

I turn and punch his shoulder playfully. "Absolutely not!"

"What? I'd set you up right!" he says as he gets up off the floor. He walks over and stands over me. "In all seriousness, I still say option three is your best choice for now." He leans down, holding out his hands so he can pull me to my feet.

"Thanks, I'll keep it in mind."

"Ready for some lifts?"

Glad for the change of topic, I nod and place my phone on the court several feet away so we don't crush it. Matt fixes the music and then we start.

"Don't forget to lock your knees," he instructs as he places his hands on my waist. The first couple times are a fail since I haven't been lifted by only one person. Right now, I'm wishing we had mats. We regroup and try simpler ones. Once we nail those, we go back and try the more challenging one we are having trouble sticking.

"We got this Alexis. Ready?" he encourages.

"Let's do this!"

He counts, then I bounce. "Lock your knees!" he shouts as I'm rising north. I smile when I realize we did it, but it fades the moment I see *him*. Ethan is practically eye level with me. He is on the top level of the gym, leaning against the railing, his eyes bore into me. There is no telling how long he has been up there watching me.

I faintly hear Matt counting before my feet hit the gym floor.

Matt is cheering behind me, but I am silent, gazing up at Ethan who is now making his way down the stairs.

"Hey, why aren't you excited? We nailed it!"

I point in Ethan's direction. "That's why."

"Sweet Jesus," Matt mutters under his breath when he walks out onto the court.

Yeah, sweet Jesus is spot on. Ethan reminds me of a freaking model, not a preppy one, though. He would be one of the 'rough around the edges' types.

chapter four

Ethan

Who the fuck is this guy? Why are his hands on her? I was in the middle of my workout when I heard the guy holler. I didn't think anything about it until I heard her voice. I had to look over the railing to see if I was hearing things. Nope, I sure wasn't.

I brace my hands on the railing, watching them. Who is he to her? A million questions are swarming my mind. I soon figure out he is on the cheer squad with Lex. I watch them, well mainly her, as they start stretching. Her lean body swaying from one side to the other.

I watch her as she gracefully completes each move across the gym floor. Every flip, every twist she owns. I watched her cheer at a couple of Kaylee's basketball games and I would cringe each time she would fly in the air because I was afraid they wouldn't catch her and she'd hit the floor. She never looked scared when they would thrust her in the air.

Workout forgotten, I continue to gaze at her, following the flow of her movements, mesmerized. They can't have known each other long, yet they act like they've known each other forever.

Right now, they are both lying on the court, talking about me and Brad. I know she has feelings for me. It's not like she keeps it hidden from me. She just doesn't understand how hard it is to not to say the hell with Brad and keep her for myself.

I'm at war with myself on how to make us both happy. I hate seeing hurt in her eyes, the hurt I keep putting there. I kick myself all the time after she leaves because I know I could have handled it better.

"Lex," I say in greeting.

She swallows hard before replying. "Ethan," she replies, copying my tone as usual.

Tearing my eyes from her, I hold my hand out to the guy next to her. "Hi, my name's Ethan, nice to meet you."

"Matt," the guy replies as he shakes my hand. So far he doesn't look like a threat.

A few tense moments pass between us before I clear my throat. "I am surprised to run into you here."

"Yeah, it was totally unexpected," she murmurs, her gaze shifting from me to Matt, who is eyeing me cautiously like he's unsure about me.

Another couple tense moments pass. Man, why is it so hard to strike up a normal conversation with her?

I scratch the back of my head. "Well, I will let you get back to it. I just wanted to say hey."

With one long gaze at Lex, I half wave as I back away. Yeah, I feel pathetic right now.

I turn around and head back upstairs. Plugging my headphones in, I try to finish my workout, but Lex has invaded my head so much I can't think clearly. Giving up on finishing my workout today, I grab back bag and leave the gym.

Heading home, I try to get some sleep in before my first night at work tonight. I'm not entirely thrilled to be working all-nighters, but this is the job I have been working towards. I'm one step closer to my dream job. I knew there was a possibility I would be put on night shift when I took the job. It's part of it.

Closing my eyes, I try to sleep, yet even then she is in my dreams, taunting me. Lex is the type of girl that once you have her, you're addicted. My problem is I haven't had her yet and I'm already addicted. She just has the pull that makes you gravitate toward her.

I need to stay away. I will only break her heart. Besides, she has Brad, someone who can give her more than I can. Brad will be able to give her a future. He will be able to give her a happy life and maybe kids if she wants them. I don't know if I will be able to give her that kind of life, and I don't want to rob her of happiness. This is why I don't pursue her. This is why I *try* to stay away from her. Dammit, I trying so hard to fight these feelings for her, but she provokes them. She stirs up all these emotions inside me with just one glance at me, with one smile, and even just a laugh.

I manage to get some sleep in before my alarm starts blaring. Rubbing my eyes, I get out of bed and get ready for my first shift as Officer Harper.

Walking into the station, I walk straight to the Chief Howard's office, nodding in greeting to my fellow officers along the way.

Knocking on his office door, I wait for him to call me in.

"Come in," he barks out from the other side the door.

I walk through the door confident, ready to get started. Chief Howard is an older man, probably around his sixties, with salt and pepper hair. I heard he is a hard ass. I guess he has to be in this line of work.

A short, Asian guy is in the room, seated in one of the chairs in front of the desk. Both men stand to greet me.

I shake the chief's hand first. "Welcome aboard, Harper. I'm glad to have you here. This here is Farris, he will be your partner for the time being."

I shake Farris' hand. "Nice to meet you, sir."

"Likewise," he replies. Farris is as I suspected, several inches shorter than me with short jet black hair.

Chief opens one of his desk drawers and pulls out a badge and gun, tossing them both on his desk. "Here you go, Harper. I've explained to you in orientation on how you should conduct yourself in and out of uniform. I expect you to follow protocol at all times. Always think before you act. Officer Farris here is one of our finest officers we have here in Bowling Green. He will be your mentor so to speak. Now, get out of my office and get to work."

I pick up my new badge and my gun. "Yes sir." With a curt nod, we both hightail it out of his office.

I follow Farris threw a slew of offices and cubicles. "Anything I need to know right off the bat?"

"Uh, not at the moment, if I come across something, I will inform you."

Walking out the front door, I follow him as he walks towards a cruiser. The model we get is a 2015 Dodge Charger Pursuit. Just looking at this beauty, I can tell a base engine which is a 292 horsepower, 3.6 liter V6 engine. I wish they would have upgraded to the Hemi V8 engine which has 485 horsepower and is a 5.7 liter.

Even so, this car is a beast and I can't wait to drive it.

I will be happy when mine is fully restored. A couple more months, if that, and I should have it fully running again.

I slide in the passenger seat and buckle up. Farris shows me the features of the car and how to navigate the computer. It's a lot to take in, but I will get it.

After being in orientation for what felt like forever, I finally get to be on patrol.

Maybe something interesting will happen tonight.

The night passes relatively slow. The only highlight of the evening was a homeless man harassing women when they would walk past him. It didn't help that he had been drinking whiskey either.

Farris and I talked to the man a while. He told us about his downfall. His wife had left him for another man, taking the house, his truck, and everything else he owned. He is still bitter from the fallout, which happened two weeks ago. Clearly, that's why he was harassing the women. Poor chap, I hope he doesn't give up his search of finding a job. I believe he will get his life back on track eventually.

He was passed out drunk by the time Farris and I left.

Farris takes me around the town, showing me the rough parts of town they usually get calls to several times a month. He says the calls they get are usually drug and fighting related.

All in all, I know I will enjoy my job.

Although, I still feel like something is missing from my life, and I have a feeling I know what it is, or rather *who* it is.

chapter five

Alexis

Apartment hunting is hell. Literally, I am forcing myself to keep my hands at my side so I don't pull my hair out. I have been to six apartment complexes today and I still haven't found the right one. Something was either wrong with it or it was too pricey. How hard it to find a one bedroom apartment that is close to WKU's campus? My parents came with me today, and I'm thankful for that. Dad has been thoroughly checking everything in the apartments to make sure nothing is broken, damaged…you get the picture. Mom has mainly been checking out the closet and the bathroom. I believe she thinks those two are more important than the whole thing.

We are at another complex, and this one is a few blocks from campus, which is a plus.

I hear Mom sigh, and I know she is about to say something I probably don't want to hear. "Alexis, honey, we don't have to find one today, or at all really. I'd feel a lot better if you were still at home."

I stop walking and turn to face my mother. I love her to death, but she doesn't understand my need to spread my wings. "Mom, I love you, but I want to do this. I'm eighteen now, and a college student. I need to learn to stand on my own two feet, okay?"

Mom nods weakly, tears forming. She sniffs and wipes them away. Cupping my face in her hands, she tilts my head up just a little bit. "My baby is growing up." Dropping her arms, she pulls me in for a long hug.

Crying is not really my thing. I usually replace crying laughter or being pissed off. It just depends on the situation. If I cry, it must be something bad.

In this situation, I laugh. "Mom, it's a part of life."

"I know, but my only baby is leaving the nest."

I roll my eyes, faking being dramatic. "Oh mom, you know I will come home if I ever need to."

She leans in and kisses my cheek. "I hope so, Alexis. I love you."

"Love you too, Mom."

Mom steps back and takes a deep breath. "Well, let's check this one out."

Mom holds her elbow out so I link my arm with hers and we catch up to Dad. He tends to stay away from emotional stuff. I guess he is who I get it from. It definitely isn't from Mom because she is as emotional as they come.

So far this apartment is working out. It's nice, it's neat, and nothing looks like it will need to be replaced. Let's just hope the price per month is in my price range.

Mom and Dad have finished with their inspections and they are smiling so I guess it's safe to say they approve. It must be good if it passes their inspections.

It's small, compact, but since it will just be me, I don't need anything bigger. The closet is a little bigger than I thought it would be, which, is a plus.

Dad is talking with the owner of the complex, figuring out a price. I just watch Dad's facial expressions to determine the outcome.

I'm keeping my fingers crossed that this is the one because I'm tired of searching. I need a hot relaxing bath after today.

When my Dad looks over at me with a smile on his face, I practically jump for joy. Mom is smiling at me with a teary-eyed grin. I run over and hug them both hard, thanking them.

I'm so excited to go shopping tomorrow before cheer practice. I'm going to be so exhausted, but it will be so worth it to have my own place to call home.

Once the lease papers are signed, I text Brad letting him know I found an apartment, and I text Kaylee letting her that tomorrow, we are going shopping.

I can't wait to see her and the twins tomorrow. I feel like I haven't seen them in forever, even though it has only been like a week.

The whole way home, I am on cloud nine. My parents on grilling me on safety. Be careful of your surroundings, always lock your door at night…yada yada.

Brad replies and asks if I want to celebrate tonight, but honestly I just want to relax, and maybe pack some more. Mainly, relax, though. It's been a long day.

I text him back, wondering if lunch tomorrow is okay instead. Mom hasn't asked if she can go shopping with me, but I imagine she will. Brad agrees on lunch tomorrow so we make plans for tomorrow, just as I sink into the hot water.

I turn my phone on silent so my phone won't disturb me. The bath is relaxing, so relaxing I almost fall asleep in the tub.

I get out and go through my evening bathroom routine before collapsing on my bed. I hope I sleep well tonight because I'm going to need my energy tomorrow.

"Knock, knock!" I yell as I open the front door to Adam and Kaylee's house. They gave me a key in case I would ever need it.

Adam walks in the foyer looking half asleep with Jasmine in his arms.

"Uh, did you sleep at all?" I ask him, laughing at his hair standing every which way.

"Eh, a little. Have you seen my fiancé?"

I throw my head back and laugh loudly, almost disturbing Jasmine. "Oh wow, that was not the reply I was expecting."

I hold my arms out, wanting him to give me Jasmine. He passes her over with a parting kiss on her forehead.

"Don't ask a question like that and you won't get a response you don't want to hear," he smirks sleepily.

Kaylee walks up about the time he replies, with Jackson cradled in one arm, and smacks him upside his head. "Be nice," she chastens. "Hey, Alexis. Give me like ten minutes and I will be ready." She hands off Jackson to Adam then runs off to finish getting ready.

I help Adam finish getting the twins ready for a full day of shopping. I can't wait until they get a little older so they can interact more.

True to her word, ten minutes later Kaylee is ready to go and the Jasmine and Jackson are both strapped in their car seats. I let Kaylee drive since she has the bottom of the car seats buckled into her car already. It would have been a hassle to move them and having to remember to give them back.

Thirty minutes later, we are pulling into the parking lot of our first store. I'm going to be a good daughter and try to watch what I spend. Everything is so expensive these days so it's going to be hard to keep from spending so much. Since the apartment wasn't furnished, I will have to buy all the furniture. I have most of the small stuff, though.

Once we have the twins situated in their stroller, we are ready to go.

I never realized how much cute stuff there is for an apartment. I'm so giddy, I'm excited. Kaylee is matching my excitement, too.

Every now and then we have people walk up to Kaylee and gush over Jackson and Jasmine. I think Kaylee has gone into the "Don't you dare touch my kids," phase. I know because she isn't really smiling, it's a tight smile, one that says she is about to turn into momzilla if they don't back off.

Oh, the joys of being a new mom. Kaylee does have beautiful babies, though, so I'd consider it a compliment.

It's getting close to lunch time so I text Brad and ask him to meet us at Kaylee and I's favorite Mexican restaurant.

I've managed to buy the rest of the small things I need before lunch so now we just have to go shop for the furniture items.

We arrive before Brad so we go ahead and get us a table. The twins are becoming fussy so I help Kaylee by feeding Jasmine.

These two are the cutest babies in the world. According to Kaylee, they have been sleeping well at night. She has lucked out, according to some of the horror stories I have heard.

Brad walks in while I am burping little Jasmine.

"Hey babe," he croons, leaning down to give me a peck on the lips.

Jasmine finally burps so I cradle her in my arms again to give her the rest of her bottle.

"Hey, what took you so long? I figured you would beat us here," I ask him as I look over at him.

He gives me a sly grin. "I had to stop and pick up something. Took longer than expected."

I know that grin, he stopped to get me something. He wouldn't be smiling at me like that if he didn't.

"What did you do?" I ask suspiciously.

Brad winks at me and goes back to looking at the menu. "You'll see."

I roll my eyes laughingly. Typical Brad, always wanting to surprise me.

Brad starts talking to Kaylee, asking about the twins and wondering how she is liking motherhood.

He ends up stealing Jasmine from me after she was done eating, so I take Jackson from Kaylee.

Watching Brad with Jasmine is hilarious. He continuously makes funny faces at her, trying to get her to smile.

Brad will make an awesome father to his kids one day. He'd constantly be making them laugh.

The food was amazing as usual. We are all stuffed to the max, and now it's time to resume our shopping so I can get ready for cheer practice tonight. I'm going to be exhausted by ten o'clock tonight.

Brad and I end up arguing for like ten minutes over who is paying the bill. Unfortunately, he ends up winning. While he does that, I help Kaylee load the twins into the car.

Brad hugs and kisses me goodbye, promising to be waiting on me after practice with my surprise.

Furniture shopping lasts until three- thirty when we decide to call it quits. I only lack a T.V. and an entertainment center so far. I have everything I need right now set to be delivered this weekend to my apartment. Now, I just need some muscle to help me move in.

Kaylee suggests Ethan, and I know Brad will help at the drop of a hat, but having them two working together might not be a good idea.

"I'll call him," Kaylee announces and my eyes almost bug out of my head.

"Don't call him now!"

"Too late," she teases just as he answers the phone. They chat for a couple minutes until she looks at me again. "What time do you need them there?"

"Them? Who's them?" I question.

"Just tell me what time you need them," Kaylee scolds and I stick my tongue out at her.

Rolling my eyes, I tell her, "The furniture is supposed to be there at ten sharp."

She relays the message and then hangs up a minute later.

"Who is he bringing?" I ask with a groan.

"You officially have four helpers already! It will be Ethan, Cole, Zack, and Keith," she exclaims cheerfully.

I groan, hoping they will actually help and not stand around.

"And if Adam and Brad help, which I'm sure they will, you will have six helpers," she continues.

I'm glad I have help, I just wish Ethan wouldn't come and remind me of how much I like him. He wouldn't have to say a word. With him just walking in will remind me how I'm torn.

Ugh! Is this weekend over yet?

chapter six

Ethan

It's moving day for Lex and all of the guys are giving me shit about it, mainly Cole. They just so happened to be with me when Kaylee called and asked if I could help. After being up all night at work, I'm exhausted, but I wanted to help her. I'm running on coffee and Red Bull at the moment. I'm not scheduled to work tonight so I don't have to worry about this taking all day and not getting some sleep.

"Whoa, man!" Cole exclaims from beside me. "Are you that eager to see the princess?"

My brows knit together, confused at what he is meaning. My eyes glance down at the gauges and I notice I'm driving ten miles per hour over the speed limit.

"Princess? I think she would slap you if you called her that to her face," I snap.

"Ouch, and touchy, too," he counters with a laugh. "And yeah, no doubt she would."

As I turn down the driveway to her how, I try to calm my emotions. The guys all whistle low when they see her house.

"And why is she wanting to move out again?" This is from Keith.

"She wants to live on her own," I tell him, hoping that is the reason. I haven't asked Lex why. Really, it's none of my business, but call it curiosity.

Lex and Kaylee are loading their cars down with boxes.

Cole being an asshole, just to piss me off, runs up and hugs Lex. "Hey there beautiful. Nice to see you again," he smirks.

I growl at his endearment for her.

Lex rolls her eyes and shakes her head at Cole, then looks up at me with confusion. "Why are you guys not at my apartment?"

"I was not told to go there. You said to be here at ten sharp." I'm about ten minutes early, but whatever.

"I meant my apartment. The guy is delivering the furniture there at ten." Then Lex starts freaking out. "Oh my God what time is it. He better not leave with my damn furniture."

I grab her by her shoulders. "Lex, calm down. It's not even ten yet, we're early. Where is your apartment complex?"

She's still tense beneath my hands, but she is calming down. "Oh crap, I can't remember the name, but you know where the university is right?" I nod, then she continues. "It's a block or two down from it. On the North side. My apartment number is B10, which is on the second floor."

"Look, the guys and I got this. Just chill, okay?"

"Okay," she murmurs before stepping away from me, out of my reach. She resumes loading her car down.

I introduce the guys to my sister. Of course, they already know about her, they just haven't seen her in person.

"Where are my niece and nephew?"

"Adam's parents are keeping them while we help Alexis. Adam ended up having to help at the shop today so it's just you four."

I want to see them sometime today if possible. "When we are done, I want to visit with them for a few minutes."

"Sure, just meet us back at the house when we are done."

39

The guys and I say goodbye and pile back into my truck. As soon as we are all in, I punch Cole in his arm.

"Shit, man, what the hell?" he grunts, clutching his arm.

"You know what. You do that to just piss me off."

He has the nerve to laugh. "Technically she isn't yours so I can flirt with her all I want."

"Do it, I dare you," I challenge him.

He throws his hands up in defense. "Dude, I'm just playing! Relax man!"

I shoot him a sideways glare then resume focusing on the road. Lex has me acting like a freaking maniac. I'm never this jealous over some girl. What is it about her that drives me to feel like this?

I need to stop while I'm ahead. She's not mine, and she's not going to be. *Liar.*

She has Brad, who she loves. *You don't know that.*

Lex is happy and I can't give her the life she wants. *Yes you can, if you just try.*

I find her apartment complex easily, and to my luck the furniture truck pulls in at the same time.

Ah, shit. We don't have a key.

Pulling out my phone, I call her. She tells me she's going to call her landlord and call me right back.

A few minutes later, her name flashes on my screen. Lex tells me that her landlord is on his way to unlock it for us.

Now, since that is settled, we can start unloading the truck. When the driver raises the door, I'm speechless. That's all she got? All I'm seeing is a couch, a fridge, several small appliances, and a loveseat.

I guess I will be done sooner than I thought.

The guys and I grab the small appliances first. By the time we reach the top of the stairs, the landlord is unlocking the door.

"I thought this truck would be packed full. Where is her TV?" Zack asks what I have been wondering myself.

"Yeah, don't rich kids usually spend money?" Keith questions.

I shake my head. "Lex is not like that."

"Obviously," Cole mumbles.

"I had her pegged as a spoiled little rich brat at first," Keith says.

I fist my hands at my sides, trying to ignore his comment about, Lex. Trust me, if Lex was like that, I wouldn't be so turned on by her.

Lex and Kaylee arrive just as we unload the last item. Zack rests on the love seat while the rest of the guys plop down on the couch, making themselves right at home. I shake my head at them as they stretch out.

Zack pats the empty spot next to him. "Sit down, Ethan. Take a load off your feet."

"No thank you, and you dipshits shouldn't be sitting down either. We have boxes to unload still."

Lex walks through the front door right about that time, her arms full of stuff. I walk over and take some of it from her.

"Let them rest for a minute, Ethan. It's no big deal. Besides, the pizza will be here soon anyway." I follow her and place the items where she sets the rest.

The guys gloat that they were right.

"See, the princess has spoken," Cole smirks.

Alexis glowers at him but otherwise doesn't threaten him.

"And she is treating us to pizza. Can't go wrong with that," Keith adds.

"Can you at least help with the boxes until the food gets here?" I ask, wondering why I even brought them in the first place.

"You heard the lady. We are allowed to rest," Zack revels.

"She said for a minute," I remind them.

I finally get them up and as we are about to walk down to help, the pizza guy arrives.

I pay the guy and take the pizza from him, trying to avoid the drooling, hungry, twenty-five-year-old guys I call friends crowding around me.

"Back off," I snarl, guarding the pizza so they don't eat it all and leave nothing for the rest of us.

"Oh good, the pizza came," Lex exclaims happily, then looks around. "Wait, where is he? I need to pay him."

"Already taken care of."

She sighs. "Ethan, you weren't supposed to pay. The pizza was a thank you for helping me."

I shrug my shoulders and find a table to sit it on. We end up arranging boxes to use as a table.

"You're welcome," I smirk.

She rolls her eyes and announces for everyone to dig in. Lex disappears back out the door. Is she not going to eat?

The guys dig in like they haven't eaten in a week. Some manners they have. They could have at least let Lex get her plate first since she ordered them.

I am about to go search for her when she reappears, carrying a cooler. She looks like she is struggling with it so I move to take it off of her hands.

"Thank you," she says, sounds relieved. "Drinks are in the cooler if you want one," she announces to everyone as they are stuffing their faces.

Like a gentleman, I let her get her food first before piling my plate. Surprisingly, there's a lot of pizza left. I'm sure it will be gone before long, though.

"Where's Brad? I figured he would be here to help his girlfriend." I didn't really mean for it to come out like it did, but oh well.

Lex cuts her eyes to me, not happy with my question. "He's busy moving his own stuff."

No freakin' way. Is he moving here? Is that why she didn't have a lot of furniture?

"You guys are moving in together?" I'm sure my eyes are popping out of their sockets as we speak.

"No, he is moving to Lexington," she replies, not sounding as sad as I thought she would be.

"If it were me, I wouldn't leave my girlfriend behind, just saying." Lord no, I couldn't handle a long distance relationship.

Lex huffs in exasperation. "Not that it's any of your business, but he got a basketball scholarship to play with the Kentucky Wildcats. There is no way, I would make him stay here when he should be doing what he loves."

Wow, I got to give the guy some credit. I wouldn't turn it down either.

"I'm surprised you aren't moving with him."

Her eyes meet mine, soft and pleading. "Everything I want is here," she murmurs, leaving me befuddled by her response.

Lex brushes past me to join everyone else, like another intense moment didn't happen between us.

Why is everything so tense between us? Is it because of my attraction to her? I need to get a grip on my feelings for her. This can't happen, I know it can't, yet I'm still standing here, gazing at her like she is everything I could ever want.

Snapping out of the trance she keeps me in, I walk over to the guys, who are smirking at me. I guess they saw me staring at her. I play it off like it's no big deal when really, it is.

Lex is a goddess, and maybe one day I will be able to tell her how beautiful I think she is.

chapter seven

Alexis

Moving day didn't go as badly as I thought it would unless you count Ethan's interrogation about Brad not being there to help. He's so infuriating at times, Ethan that is.

Matt and I are enjoying this beautiful day by my parents' pool one last time before I officially start living on my own. Brad is moving the second load of his stuff today so I won't be able to see him. He wants to spend the day with me tomorrow so I agreed since I have nothing to do other than to continue unpacking, which is boring.

"You want ice cream?" Matt asks from the lounge chair beside me.

Ice cream does sound amazing. "Yes, I would love some cookies and cream ice cream."

Matt sits up, throws on his shirt, and grabs his keys. "I shall return with your request," he says in a playful tone.

It's quiet, too quiet now that Matt has gone to the store. When it's silent, I start thinking, which can be a good and a bad thing.

Sitting out on the deck overlooking the pool, my thoughts turn to Ethan. As usual, I wonder how he sees me. Does he see me as a friend or something more? Did I take his intentions wrongly when he acted jealous of Brad? Was he just being protective of me because I'm best friends with his sister?

Is he attracted to me on some level, but is scared to act on it? A snort leaves me at that thought. Ethan doesn't seem the type to be scared of anything. He obviously isn't interested in me that way or he would act on it. Wouldn't he? Sighing in frustration, I stand up and decide to go for a swim before Matt returns.

I still haven't decided if I want to work on things with Brad or break it off with him. He doesn't deserve me, I know I should let him go so he can find a girl that deserves him and is better for him than me, but I just don't want to break his heart.

Grasping the hem of my cover up, I slowly pull it over my head before diving gracefully into the deep end of the pool. The water engulfs me and I swim as far as I can without having to come up for air. Swimming relaxes me. It temporarily erases my rather heartbreaking thoughts of Ethan.

When I break free of the surface the thoughts return. Being underwater is like being under a protective barrier. I smooth my hair back and opened my eyes only to find piercing blue ones staring back at me. Am I imagining him here or is it really him?

The intense of his gaze makes me want to duck back under the barrier. "Mind if I join?" he finally asks.

"No." My voice is small, quiet. He takes his cue and strips. Leaving only his boxers, his clothes are discarded beside the chair I was lounging in earlier. My eyes are plastered to him as I watch him take each step slowly. The scene almost seems like one of those that move in slow motion. To say he is in great shape would be an understatement. Of course his job requires him to be fit. I don't want to think about that, though. I don't have a lot of time before he leaves and will be gone for almost a year. There doesn't seem to be an inch of fat on him. His arms aren't bulging, but they are toned and have a thickness to them. His chest and abs look to be a ripped wall of muscle, right down to the core of him.

He is in front of me now. My throat feels dry all of a sudden from his close proximity. Thinking I was about to do something embarrassing, I tried to distract him by splashing water in his face. At first I thought I had irritated him, but then his lips twitched into a smile.

"Oh, it's on now Lex." I swim away as fast I can, trying to get away. I had no clue what he would do. Would he splash me back, dunk me, or what? He catches up to me just as I am about to touch the edge of the pool. His arms curl around me, pulling me back against his rock hard chest. My breath hitches at the contact of his skin against mine.

With his hands on my shoulders, he slowly turns me around so we are face to face. His eyes flicker to my lips then back up to my eyes. His calloused hands trail down my arms to my waist. Water drips from his hair as his compelling blue eyes bore into mine.

"You're so beautiful, Lex," he finally says. Ethan has been staring at me for so long I am starting to be self-conscious. His thumb brushes my cheek, removing the stray droplets of water. "Don't let anyone tell you any different. Will you promise me that?" Why is he talking like I'm never going to see him again?

Swallowing past the lump that formed in my throat I answer him, "I promise." Something flashes in his eyes that I didn't quite catch.

"Good. Will you promise me something else?" he asks as he leans closer, his mouth now an inch from mine.

"Anything," I whisper because I would do anything for him.

"Promise me that you will always be happy. Promise me that when everyone is weak you will be strong." His eyes search mine, for what, I'm not sure. "I need to hear you say it. I need to know that if something happens to me you will be the one to hold everyone together, that you will be the strong one."

I reach up with unsteady hands to touch his face. He closes his eyes like he is savoring my touch. Suddenly, I want to cry. "I don't know if I can, Ethan." How does he expect me to be strong for everyone else when I'm barely holding myself together right now?

"Yes, you can. I have faith in you, Lex. It may be buried somewhere, but it's there. I saw it when everything happened with Kaylee. I saw it then and I can see it now. Like right now, you want to cry so badly, but you're holding it together for me because I asked you to. You're already keeping your promise, but I still need to hear it," he murmurs softly.

"I promise." As soon as the words are out his mouth is on mine. My fingers lock around the back of his neck holding his head in place. He isn't going to run from me, not after I made those promises, and certainly not after this kiss.

When Ethan breaks the kiss. I almost whimper. "I will dream about this moment for the rest of my life."

"Why dream it when you can live it?" I counter.

He sighs and presses his forehead against mine. "I can't, Lex. You don't know how hard it is for me to walk away from you, but I have to do it. I tell myself that it's better this way."

"Why? Because you don't want to hurt me? The moment you walk away from me will be the moment you shatter my heart." I don't like feeling like this, so vulnerable.

"You don't understand, Lex."

"Help me to understand!"

He grabs my wrists and removes them from his neck. "I'm sorry, Lex, so sorry." He kisses my hands and then swims away, taking my shattered heart with him.

I wait until he's gone to let the tears fall. He says I'm strong, yet, right now, I feel weak.

The look on her face when I swam away will haunt me until I die. *It's for the best.* That's what I keep telling myself at least. I'm trying so hard not to be selfish. In a few months, I will be halfway around the world fighting in a war. Maybe, as painful as it is for me to say it, she will have moved on by the time I leave. That way if I don't make it back she will be okay. She won't be hurting. I'm doing this for her.

I quickly throw on my clothes and head into the house. I go to grab my keys off the counter, but stop when I see Matt sitting at the bar, glaring at me. I wonder how much he saw, how much he heard.

I nodded to him. God, it is a bitter pill to swallow to think of her being happy without me.

Matt stands, rounding the counter to face me. "I don't know what your game is, but I don't like seeing her cry. Even though, I've only known her for like two weeks, I consider her a sister to me. If you want her, then man up. If not, then leave her alone. She doesn't need you to get her hopes up, then crush them right after. Make up your mind, Ethan."

I didn't say anything. What else could I say? I did the exact thing I was trying to avoid. I just poured salt into my own wound.

Matt shakes his head in disgust and I watch as he goes out to comfort her. *I should be doing that, not him.*

And I kissed her, what was up with that? I said I wouldn't pursue her if she was with someone, and I know she hasn't broken it off with Brad. I'm an asshole for kissing her while she is taken. I probably just confused her even more.

Deciding I can't stomach to watch him hold here while she cries over *me*, I turn around and walk out.

As soon as I'm in my truck I pull out my phone. After a couple rings, a sultry voice floats through the phone. "Hey handsome. I've been waiting on your call."

"Can you meet me in thirty?"

"Of course. See you when you get here," she purrs.

"See you in a bit, Kate."

When I arrive at Kate's apartment, I almost turn around, but for some reason I don't. *I shouldn't be here*, I think to myself. As usual, Kate is ready and waiting for me when I let myself in.

For once, I wish I could just walk away from her. Kate has this pull and before I know it I'm inside her, giving her what she wants.

In no time, we are finished and I am putting my clothes back on.

"You don't have to leave so soon, you know?" Kate says, sounding disappointed because I'm leaving her. She knows the rules. I give her what she wants, then I leave.

"Don't start, Kate. You know there is no reason for me to stay."

Kate rolls her eyes disapprovingly. "Why, of course, there is. I am the reason you come here, so why can't I be the reason you stay?"

"Kate," I growl in warning. "Don't go there. There is nothing between us other than sex. You know it just as much as I do."

She climbs out of bed and saunters over to me. I used to be so turned on by her, until I met Lex. Lex has shown me what true beauty is.

Kate reaches out to touch me, but I grab her wrists, stopping her before she gets the chance. "Have a good night, Kate."

She huffs, her eyes narrowing. "I don't know why you are being so cold to me, Ethan. We used to have fun, remember?"

I grunt, displeased. She's right, things were fun between us, but then Lex changed the way I see her.

"Night," I reply, ignoring her last comment.

I rush home to jump in the shower so I can wash away the grime. I feel so dirty sleeping with Kate now. Why do I keep going to her place? Hell, why do I even call her in the first place?

Lex is a game changer for me. Kate used to be someone I *wanted* to call, but now I do it because I am sexually frustrated and she will help me even though I can't stand her.

Lex keeps me so wound up these days and it sucks because I can't have her like I want her. No, I want to do right by her. I'm not going to use her like I do Kate, even though it's getting harder and harder to stay away.

What are you doing to me, Alexis Collins?

chapter eight

Alexis

I feel so stupid for crying over him. Mom had always told me that boys were never worth a single tear. I took her advice and used it all through high school. When a guy would break up with me, I wouldn't cry. Even when I went home and the house was quiet because Mom and Dad were not home yet, I didn't cry. Not even when I could feel my heart breaking.

So why am I crying now? What makes him so "special"?

Matt sits down beside me on the edge of the pool and wraps his arm around me. I lay my head on his shoulder and bring my knees up to my chest, hugging them.

Matt lays his head against mine. "It's going to be okay, Alexis. Don't let him get to you like this. He doesn't deserve you if he makes you cry anything but happy tears."

I don't bother replying to him. What he said, I already know, I'm just blinded by my attraction to Ethan to think clearly.

"There is a party tonight at one of the Frat houses. Would you like to go with Alice and me?"

A party, already? Man, they are starting early.

"Sure, I'll go." I need to go out and get my mind off of Ethan anyway.

The thing about Matt I have noticed is that he usually isn't down for long before he turns cheery again. "Well, let's chow down on some ice cream before it ruins and then get ready!"

I'm not sure if a party is a good idea or not, but I'm not about to lie around and mope.

I need to just let loose and have fun. I text Brad, letting him know my plans for tonight.

As I am getting dressed, my phone buzzes.

Brad: Please tell me you are not going alone?

I roll my eyes, *like I, would be stupid enough to do that.*

Me: No, Matt and Alice are going with me.

Good thing he knows Matt is gay or this would be awkward.

Brad: Okay. Be careful and have fun. Text me later?

Me: I will

I lay my phone on my bed so I can finish getting ready. Matt will be here shortly to pick me up. Since all my stuff is in my apartment, I decided I am going to spend my first night there tonight since its right down the road from the Frat houses. Plus, since Matt is driving and he lives just off campus, it would be a lot closer for me to stay at my apartment so he doesn't have to go out of the way to take me home.

I am wearing my best jeans and form fitting blouse with flats. My hair is down, straight as usual. I didn't have time to curl it tonight since the party was kind of sprung on me.

Deeming myself ready to go, I text Matt to pick me up. Even with my heart feeling like a stake has plummeted through it, I smile bravely and wait on the porch for Matt, kissing Mom and Dad goodnight as I pass through the living room.

Matt, thankfully, doesn't mention Ethan on the ride to the party. Although, it doesn't stop me from thinking about him. I make small talk with Alice, trying to distract my brain from what it wants to focus on. *Curse you Ethan Harper for how you make me feel and how you capture my attention, even when I'm hurt and upset by you.*

Clearing my head of Ethan and his ability to mess with me, I square my shoulders and smile like my heart isn't breaking into pieces.

Taking a cleansing breath, I head straight for the bar, needing a drink to get the night started.

After I pop the top on my drink, I chug it, letting the amber liquid glide down my throat. I don't want to worry about my situation with Brad or my predicament with Ethan. Tonight is about clearing my head and starting anew. In the morning, I'm sure I will regret it when I wake to a killer hangover, but right now, I need this night out. Maybe in the morning I will wake up with some answers. Doubtful, but wishful all the same.

Matt and Alice are already on the dance floor, a place, judging by how quickly they migrated there, love to be.

I am just about to join them when a voice rumbles next to me. "If the dance floor is where you are heading, then so am I."

Taken aback by his straightforwardness, I turn in the direction of the unfamiliar male voice.

I arch my brow in question to the strikingly handsome guy standing to my left. He is not as good looking as Brad or Ethan though. Standing at a good six foot, the shaggy blond hair, blue eyed fellow regards me with a megawatt smile. "How did you know that's where I was going?" I fire back. I'm not interested in anything but to have a good time with my friends. I hope he doesn't mind disappointment.

His eyes roam over me, and I inwardly cringe. "Because you were gazing out at the crowd longingly, like you had a strong urge to join them. Am I right? Was that not what you were going to do?"

I just stare at him, giving away nothing. He's right, but I won't give him the satisfaction of knowing it.

"Fine, don't answer me. I'm right because you had just set your drink down and started to walk in that direction."

This guy is getting on my freakin' nerves. Obviously he is arrogant. I can't stand people who think so highly of themselves.

He sticks his hand out and I stare at blankly. "I'm Josh by the way."

My eyes move back up to his face. Disregarding his hand, I reluctantly give him my name. "Alexis." He isn't getting any more info out of me.

His eyes light up like my name turns him on.

I turn and grab my drink off the counter and take a sip of it.

I do my best to ignore him, even when he continues to stare at me.

"Would you like to dance?" Josh asks, gesturing to the crowd of people in front of us.

"Not with you," I state bluntly.

Taking my drink with me, I leave Josh and walk into the throng of people, heading toward Matt and Alice, who are still dancing.

"Hey! It's about time you join us!" Matt exclaims, wrapping his arm around me.

Alice grabs my hand and smiles brightly at me. It's clear they are having a good time.

I down the rest of my drink and set the empty bottle on the floor next to me. I move to the beat, letting go. This is exactly what I need tonight.

I am having a good time when I feel a burning gaze on me, creating a gaping hole in my skin. The moment I look up and lock eyes with Josh's, a creepy feeling crawls over my flesh. I shudder involuntarily and resume dancing.

I need a drink. I excuse myself and grab another drink from the cooler. I guzzle it down and grab another. Between Brad, Ethan, and now Josh, these men are driving me to drink.

I knock back drink after drink, not caring about anything.

When I'm finally done drinking, I step away from the counter to use the restroom, only to fall back into it.

One thing's for sure, I'm definitely drunk. Ugh! Stupid men driving women like me who never get drunk, to drink until the can no longer stand.

I pull out my phone to call Matt to come help me when I notice a text from Ethan.

Ethan: What are you doing?

What am I doing? After the way you treated me earlier, you are going to talk to me like nothing happened?!

I text back some response, not even caring if what I typed made sense.

Next thing I know, he is calling me.

"Hhheeelloo," I answer, meaning to sound sarcastic. Although, I don't realize that when I'm drunk, things sound different.

"Where are you?" he demands with a growl.

"Isn't it obvious, I'm at a party!" Duh! He should know this.

I turn and lean farther against the counter, hoping I have the strength to hold myself up long enough until I sober up enough to be able to walk.

"I know that I mean where is the party at?" Ethan sounds pissed. *Good serves him right!*

"I'm not telling you. I don't want you here, Ethan." It's kind of a lie. My heart is betraying me. In my head, I know he doesn't need to be here, shattering my already broken heart. My heart, though, is not listening. No matter what Ethan says to me, my heart remains the same.

"How are you getting home?" he barks out.

Oh no, he isn't taking me home.

"That's none of your concern." There, that should shut him up.

Josh is suddenly in front of me again. Good grief doesn't this guy take a hint.

"Alexis, would you like another drink?"

I am about to say no and tell him to shove off when I hear Ethan on the other line. "Lex, don't let him get you one, it's dangerous!"

Hearing him be all demanding is all the motivation I need. "Yeah, I'd like another."

I hang up on Ethan, pissed at how he thinks he can tell me what to do.

"I'll be right back." Josh winks at me then disappears to get the drink I don't even want.

Groaning, I drop my head into my hands. *This is not how I wanted my night to go.*

Josh returns sooner than I'd like. If I knew I could walk without face planting, I would ditch him.

He hands over my drink with a smirk I'd like to slap off his face. "Here you go."

Despite not wanting another drink, I take a big gulp of it anyway.

While trying to come up with a plan to leave, I take another large swallow.

Then another, until I place the bottle on the counter when I start to feel sluggish and sleepy.

I go to walk away to find Matt to take me home, not even making it two steps before I fall. Josh catches me and scoops me up in his arms.

"No, put me down. I need to find Matt," I mumble, growing weaker and weaker as the seconds tick by.

What is wrong with me? Then, it hits me like a ton of bricks. "You put something in my drink."

Weakly, I try to fight him. At this point, I wouldn't care if he dropped me, I just want out of his arms.

He never answers me, but he doesn't need to. Now, I wish I would have listened to Ethan in spite of being mad at him.

I try to look around his shoulder, seeing if I can spot Matt or Alice to get their attention. I know what's about to happen. I'm not naïve enough to think he will drug me and leave me alone.

I tense when I hear a door opening and closing, but I'm too weak to fight him. My body has given up.

"Let's have some fun, shall we?"

His words make me recoil in disgust. When he lays me down on the bed, I try to roll off.

Josh jerks me back, pinning me to the mattress so I can't move. "No, no. You aren't going anywhere."

I feel weightless like I'm floating, but still so weak.

I almost vomit when I feel him tugging down my jeans. I fail, attempting to kick him. Even if I did make contact, it wouldn't be hard enough to stun him.

Josh curses under his breath. "Why hasn't it knocked you out yet?"

I keep fighting to stay awake, afraid that any moment I will fall asleep, and there is no telling what will happen to me then.

My shoes and my jeans have already been removed so now he is heading for my shirt. I whimper in protest, trying to move my arms. He curses again and grabs my wrist with one hand, pinning them above my head. As my shirt reaches my chin, there is a loud noise coming from somewhere. *Matt!*

I turn my head to see if it's Matt coming to rescue me, yet it's not only him. Ethan looks murderous as he marches over to us, with Matt in tow. Josh is jerked off of me and on the floor getting his face pound in by Ethan's fist.

I close my eyes and thank the Lord above I'm being saved.

chapter nine

Ethan

Driving home, I contemplate how I am going to deal with Kate. I only have approximately three months left before I'm shipped overseas. Although I'm excited to embark on this new adventure, I'm going to miss my family and Lex. Lex and I hardly see each other anymore and it's killing me. I keep driving the wedge between us and I know I'm close to losing her for good. I miss her randomly showing up at my apartment. Even though it always ends in an argument because Kate happens to be there every time, I long for her to knock on my door. My beating heart skyrockets when I open my door to her standing there. I forget all about Kate lying in my bed every single time because I'm so thrilled to see Lex standing before me.

My friends tell me I'm an idiot for pushing her away and they are right. I have this beautiful girl, inside and out, that wants me and all I keep doing is breaking her heart. I can't stand the thought of making her promises and then not being able to fulfill them. Maybe in ten months I can make her mine. The problem? Ten months is entirely too long to wait and I risk losing her forever. Brad, even though it sucks, I tolerate, since I know without a doubt he is a good guy. I know he'd never hurt her. The thought of her with someone unknown hurts worse than the knife I already inflicted in my own heart.

I park my car in the usual spot and shut it off. Kate's white Nissan Maxima is parked right next to me. I cringe every time I see her car. Hell, even when I see her name pop up on my cell I want to throw my phone out the window or toss it in my blender.

Kate needs to go on. I need to get my spare key back from her, she needs to grab the few things she keeps at my apartment and leave. I'm already stressed because I know she won't go quietly. I know I will be arguing with her for at least an hour, if not longer. I'm seriously dreading this conversation. I wish I never had met her.

The moment I open the door to my apartment, she comes barreling towards me, jumping into my arms like we are actually a couple and she hasn't seen me in a few days. If I had more time to prepare for her surprise attack I would have sidestepped out of her way. I push her away and close the door behind me. Here goes nothing.

"Kate, we need to talk."

She waves me off like it's unimportant. "No time for talking, E. I've been waiting all day to see you!" She reaches for my hand, but I jerk it back out of her reach. She frowns.

"Kate, we need to talk," I repeat firmly.

Kate rolls her eyes and steps back, folding her arms across her chest. "What is so important that needs to be said now?"

I should have done this a long time ago. "This, what we are doing, is over, Kate. I need you to leave."

"I don't believe you, Ethan! You're lying!"

"I mean it, Kate. We are done. Get your things and get out."

Seriously, how harsh do I need to be?

"So we aren't going to talk this out?"

"What is there to talk about? We are not in any sort of a relationship. You know this!"

"You have been calling me a lot lately so I took it as the beginning of a relationship."

I scrub my face with my hands, realizing this situation is far worse than I thought. "Did I ever insinuate I wanted a relationship with you?"

"No," she huffs.

"Exactly, I would have talked to you about it if I wanted to be in one with you."

"It's because of her isn't it? You're going to throw what we have away for some immature high school girl?"

I release a low growl at her insult toward Lex. "Don't you dare insult her. You know nothing about, Lex. Want to know why I'm done with you? It's you. You're clingy, annoying, and you whine like a two-year old."

She rears back, her hand connecting with my cheek. It stings a little, but it doesn't hurt.

"You asshole!"

"I never claimed to be a saint. Now, for the last time, leave."

She stomps around my apartment grabbing her things. If I was smart and thought ahead, I would have already had her things packed and waiting by the door.

"You haven't seen the last of me, Ethan Harper! I suspect you'll call me when it doesn't work out with the brat."

I open the door and motion for her to walk through. She steps out of my apartment then stops and turns. Kate opens her mouth to speak, but I shut the door in her face not caring what she has to say. That felt good. I wait until I hear the click of her heels fade away before backing away from the door.

I turn around to face my empty apartment. Loneliness creeps in and I immediately think of Lex, wondering what she is doing, who she is with, and where she is at. I think about her constantly and sometimes I wonder if I let her in if everything will work out.

I walk over to my couch and flop down on it. I turn on the TV hoping to pass the time. Soon, I am cursing it, throwing the remote on the coffee table. Nothing and I mean *nothing* will take my mind off of Alexis. Believe me, I've tried it *all*.

I pull my phone out of my pocket and scroll through the contacts until I land on hers. My finger hovers over the call button. Should I call her? I wonder what she's doing.

I need to talk to her.

Instead of calling her I settle for a text message. Once I type out my message I hit send and wait. I'd be surprised if she even responded.

What are you doing?

My heart leaps to my throat when my phone vibrates. She responded though I can't make out a word she is saying. Her words are all mixed up.

Calling her it is. Her phone rings three times before she picks it up and my heart plummets. She is drunk.

"Hhheeelloo," she draws out her drunken greeting. I can hear all of the people hollering in the background and the music blaring.

"Where are you?" I ask, upset by the fact she is putting herself at risk.

"Isn't it obvious, I'm at a party!"

I pinch the bridge of my nose. "I know that I mean where is the party at?"

"I'm not telling you. I don't want you here, Ethan."

Well, if that doesn't sting a little...

This is going nowhere. "How are you getting home?"

"That's none of your concern."

"Alexis, would you like another drink?" I hear another guy ask through the phone.

"Lex, don't let him get you one, it's dangerous!" I bark out, praying she listens to me. Worry sets in, drowning me in its waves.

Ignoring me, she tells the guy, "Yeah, I'd like another." Then the line goes dead.

I don't waste another second grabbing my keys and running out the door. More than likely she is at a college party since she isn't old enough to get into a club. *Unless she has a fake I.D...*

I make it across town in ten minutes unlike the normal twenty minutes it would've taken me. It doesn't take me long to find the massive amounts of cars surrounding the frat houses. I march up the sidewalk and through the front door. I scan the crowd for Alexis carefully, but I don't see her. I try calling her phone and she doesn't answer. Something doesn't feel right.

As I make my way through the crowd, I spot Matt and Alice dancing. I fight my way through the crowd to get to them.

"Hey man! What's up?" he yells over the music.

Skipping his pleasantries I ask, "Where is Lex?"

He strains his neck looking for her through the mass of people. "She was just over in the corner talking to...shit what was his name?" he directs the last part of the sentence to the girl he is dancing with, who just shrugs.

"I'm going to find her."

"I'm coming with you!"

He follows behind me as we push our way toward the stairs. It's obvious she isn't down here. That thought alone has my blood boiling.

When I top the stairs I notice at five doors, three on the right and two on the left. I start with the first one on my right. Nope. The next two are occupied, but she isn't in there. I swap over the last door on the left side. I try the door, but it is locked.

"Lex!" I holler as I pound on the door.

"Alexis are you in there?" Matt calls. Still nothing.

The eerie feeling from earlier is growing. She is in there, I just know it.

I hear muffled voices through the door one second and the next I have the door kicked in. My muscles harden when I see Lex lying on the bed with her arms pinned above her head. Her shirt is pushed up to her neck and her pants are discarded on the floor in front of me.

All I'm seeing is red, massive amounts of it. I grab the guy and jerk him off of her. My fist hits his face repeatedly until Matt stops me. When his body slumps I let go of him and turn to Alexis. She hasn't moved. She's just lying there, her body slightly shaking. She doesn't look good at all.

"You take care of her, I got this punk," Matt says, fury lacing his voice.

I wrap my arms around her and help her sit up. "Ethan…I don't feel so good," she mumbles weakly.

He must've slipped her something in her drink, I bet my life on it. I'm just not sure what, and that can be dangerous.

I grab the hem of her shirt and gently tug it down. "Hang on, Lex. Let's get your pants on then I'll take you back to my apartment."

I grab her pants off the floor and start putting them on her. Her hands grab my shoulders to hold herself steady. I grab her hands and help her stand before I pull them the rest of the way up. I cup her face and gaze at her a moment. All of this is my fault. If I hadn't of been an ass to her she wouldn't be here. "I'm so sorry, Lex." I thumb away the lone tear that escapes. Her arms move slowly to wrap around my neck. I pick her up and she wraps her legs around my waist and she lays her head on my shoulder.

Matt moves to my side. "Where are you taking her?"

This guy has some nerve. "She is staying with me, at my apartment."

"Is that such a good idea?"

Is he for real? "Funny thing, Matt, you didn't even know where in the hell she was. If I hadn't showed up, this sick fuck would have gotten away with taking advantage of her. You didn't seem too concerned either when you didn't find her so yeah, I'd say she is safe with me. Nothing will happen to her when I'm around."

I leave the room fuming, carrying her back downstairs through the party, and out to my truck. I open the passenger side door sit her down in the seat. I reach around her to buckle to her up. My hand grazes her cheek a moment before I reluctantly remove my hand and jog around to the driver's side and climb in. She is struggling to keep her eyes open.

I try to drive as slow and as carefully as possible, hoping the movement of the car won't churn her stomach. Occasionally, I'd ask her if she is alright and every time she'd just nod, still out of it.

I grip the steering wheel, anger pulsing through me. I can't shake the thought of it being my fault out of my head.

chapter ten

Ethan

I get her inside and lay her down on my bed. I remove her shoes, letting them fall to the floor. I leave her for a moment to grab a t-shirt and shorts from my dresser. Lex has been drifting in and out of consciousness. Any minute she will be out completely.

"Ethan," she chokes out as she frantically tries to stand. From the sound of her voice, I know what's about to happen. I scoop her up in my arms and run to the bathroom. As soon as she drops to her knees she empties the contents of her stomach. I just hold her hair back out of the firing line until she is done.

I wet a washcloth and gently wipe her face for her. When I am done, I carry her back to my room. I pick up the clothes I had dropped on the floor and change out her clothes for mine. Once she is lying back on my bed, I run into the kitchen to get her some water to take with the Tylenol I am going to grab.

Once she has taken them, I cover her up, pull the desk chair over to the bed and sit across from her. I gather her hand in mine and kiss the back of it.

"I'm sorry, Ethan. I should've listened to you. I knew better than to take a drink from someone I didn't know, but I was so mad at you." Her voice cracks as she speaks. Her eyes bore into mine. "You hurt me so bad and all I wanted to do was to take away the pain, even if it was just for a night." Her eyes glisten with tears.

The guilt comes back full force. I knew all of this was my fault, but hearing her say it makes it unbearable.

"Don't apologize for something I caused. I never wanted to hurt you, Lex, I swear."

What she says next breaks me even more. "Please don't hurt me anymore, Ethan. My heart can't take it," she pleads softly. I want to die right now.

I watch as she struggles to keep her eyes open. "That's the last thing I want to do, Lex." I lean forward, placing a soft kiss to her cheek. "Sleep, beautiful. I'll see you in the morning." Within seconds her eyes close and her breathing evens out.

I keep our hands linked as she sleeps. I'm hurting her in more ways than I can count. I don't intend to hurt her, but when I'm around her I can only think about being with her. I can't think clearly when she is near me. The only thing my brain knows is *her*.

In the morning, we will talk about what happened tonight. It's going to kill me to have to listen to her tell me what happened, but I want to know what this guy's name is. I can't put my finger on it, but I've seen him somewhere before.

I just wish I could remember where I've seen him.

Alexis

The first thing I notice when I wake is my pounding head and my mouth feeling like cotton. The second thing I notice is the bed I am in. *This is not my bed.* Panic sets in when I think about what I had done. One-night stands aren't me, it's not who I am. The third thing I notice is I'm wearing some guy's pajamas. Okay, so maybe we didn't have sex? I'm so confused right now and it's making my head pound harder.

The fourth and final thing that I notice is the hand that is firmly grasping mine. My eyes move from the familiar hand, trails all the way up the tanned, muscular arm until finally my eyes stop on his perfect face. His eyes are red from I'm guessing staying awake all night. Why though? Why did he not go to sleep?

"Hi," I croak through the dryness in my throat. Ethan leans over, grabs the small glass of water off the nightstand and then hands it to me. "Thank you," I reply, relieved that my throat doesn't feel so dry now. A thought suddenly hits me, making me question how I ended up here. I know I didn't go out with him last night. Where did I go? Oh…the party. That still doesn't explain how I ended up here at Ethan's.

"You don't look like you got much sleep." I don't want to let on that I'm clueless as to what happened last night in case we…

"No, I stayed awake to make sure you were alright after what happened," he says breaking me from my thoughts. I didn't miss the coldness that filtered through his voice. What happened last night? I remember going to the frat party last night. "You don't remember do you?"

"Not…" I trail off when images appear in my mind. I was drinking and dancing, trying to get my mind off of Ethan and how he broke my heart. I had ridden with Matt and Alice. I was on the phone with someone then a guy appeared and offered to get me another drink. Whoever I was talking to told me not to take a drink from him, but I did anyway. The guy returned with my drink, I really didn't want or need and then I started feeling bad all of a sudden and I couldn't hold myself up so the guy carried me up the stairs.

A gentle hand caressing my cheek breaks me from me from finishing my nightmare. "Lex, you're okay. I arrived in time to stop him, I swear."

Ethan must've been the one I was talking to. It all makes sense now. I took that drink to be spiteful and it almost got me raped.

"I'm so stupid, I'm sorry I didn't listen to you," I cried.

"You're not stupid, Lex. Yeah. I wish you would've listened to me, but what's done is done."

I drop my gaze to the floor in shame. How could I have been so stupid and took a drink from some random guy? I know better than that. I know all the dangers and repercussions of what happens to girls who do what I did, yet I still did it anyway.

Ethan unlaces his hand from mine and moves to lift my chin with his fingers. "Look at me, Lex." I lift my eyes to his. "Promise me you will never take a drink from a stranger again. I was so worried about you and I had to make sure you were okay so I drove like a madman to the first place I could think of. Thank God I had good instincts or I wouldn't have made it in time."

A tear slips pass the barrier and down my cheek. Ethan quickly thumbs it away. Before I could talk myself out of it, I curl into his lap, resting my head in the crook of his neck. He tenses from my surprise attack, but after a minute his arms finally come around me. He tightens his arms around me, caging me in.

I can feel his heart thumping rapidly against his rib cage. I move my arms around his neck, hoping I wouldn't have to let go. I want this, need this so much. I've wanted him to hold me in his arms for so long so I'm going to savor every second I can like this.

The tension slowly leaves him and he visibly relaxes. He leans his head over on top of mine. Ethan can't tell me he doesn't feel something for me. I want to tell him that too, but I change my mind. I don't feel like arguing with him and plus I'll ruin this moment.

"I almost punched Matt last night."

I lean back and gape at him. "What? Why?"

"Because when I arrived I couldn't find you and when I saw him I asked him where you were. He couldn't find you either, but he didn't seem worried about it. Then he had the nerve to question me on why I am taking you here," he replies bitterly.

"Matt was just looking out for me."

He laughs humorlessly. "Oh, he was looking out for you all right."

I lay my head back on his shoulder. "He doesn't like you, you know." Matt doesn't like Ethan because he is always stomping on my heart and making me cry.

"So? Right now the feeling is mutual."

"He is a good guy, Ethan. He just made a mistake."

"A mistake where you could have been seriously hurt. Think about something, Lex. If I hadn't of shown up the guy would have succeeded and who knows what would have happened to you after that. And I would eventually be in jail for killing the sick bastard."

I shiver in his hold. I can't thank Ethan enough for saving me. I don't blame Matt though since he is not my babysitter. Matt is not at fault here, I am.

Placing my hand on his cheek, I turn his gaze to mine. "Thank you for rescuing me."

His eyes drift down slowly to my lips before raising them back up to my eyes. "You're worth saving, Lex. I wouldn't hesitate to rescue you."

Kiss me darn it!

If I knew he wouldn't push me away I'd kiss him first.

He keeps gazing at me like he is contemplating it. I wish I knew what he is thinking about right now.

Ah hell, screw it. With my hand already cupping the back of his neck, I bring my lips up to his, crushing his mouth to mine. I almost moan at the contact. After the shock wears off, he is kissing me back. His hand moves to my hair, cradling my head.

I've never felt so much fire, so much passion from a kiss. All the pent up feelings rush back, overwhelming me. I have wanted to feel his lips against mine since the moment I realized he wasn't a creepy stalker, but Kaylee's half-brother.

I shift in his lap, placing my knees on either side of him. My hands fist his shirt bringing him closer.

68

Ethan pulls away, both of us panting like we just ran a marathon. "Lex," he murmurs hoarsely.

I see the regret swimming in his eyes. "Don't you dare say what I think you're going to," I say, shaking my head.

He sighs and his gaze falls to the floor. "You shouldn't hav—"

I push off his lap and search for my things. I'm not going to listen to him say it shouldn't have happened. I power on my phone and pull my hair back while I wait for it to load up.

Behind me, I hear Ethan get up from the chair. "Lex, you don't understand."

"Oh I understand completely, Ethan, you regret kissing me. Why, I'm not sure, but I don't want to hear some bullshit answer. You can pretend all you want, but I know you want me Ethan, and I'm not talking about just sex. Deep down you want a relationship with me, yet for the life of me I can't understand why you keep pushing me away." He just kissed me yesterday for crying out loud!

My phone is up so I send a text to Matt asking him if he can pick me up. Hopefully, he will respond. If not, I will just call Adam and see if he can come get me.

I spin around to face him, finding it hard to look him in his eyes. "It's complicated."

"Talk to me, Ethan! Tell me why! You've kissed me before and it wasn't a big deal!"

He shakes his head. "Can you please just let it go?" He pushes past me and leaves his bedroom.

I grab my handful of things and follow him out. "Okay, fine, but know this Ethan. I kissed you because I know you wanted me to just as much as I wanted to. You can deny your attraction to me all you want, but that kiss we shared was the best kiss of my life."

I leave without another word, hoping Matt is out front waiting for me. I check my phone and notice Matt has messaged me. He will be pulling up in a few minutes.

I am hoping Ethan will run out of his apartment and apologize. He felt something when he kissed me or otherwise he wouldn't have kept kissing me back.

I sit on the sidewalk until Matt pulls into the parking lot. With one last glance at Ethan's apartment, I slide into the passenger seat of Matt's SUV. Ethan is staring at me through the window of his apartment, his gaze impassive.

Matt frowns at me. "This is exactly why I didn't want him taking you home with him."

He squeezes my hand comfortingly as the first tear falls down my cheek. The ache in my heart keeps growing.

"Are you going to be okay?"

I think he is asking about more than just Ethan. "Yeah, I'll be fine."

"Would you be up for fattening ice cream and sappy romantic comedies?"

"With you? Always!"

His face lights up as he restarts his car. "Well let's go shopping for the ice cream binge we are about to partake!"

chapter eleven

Alexis

Matt and I waste no time digging into the tubs of ice cream we bought when we arrive at my apartment. This is our second day in a row we have binged on ice cream, and I have no shame. I picked out my favorite, Cookies and Cream and Matt picked out Rocky Road. I decided I wanted to watch an ugly cry movie so we pop in, *P.S. I Love You* and relax on the couch. I'm also still wearing Ethan's clothes. Even though I am hurt by him, I can't bring myself to change.

"So what did the asshole do this time?" Matt asks as he takes a bite of his ice cream. After yesterday in the pool and this morning, Matt really doesn't like Ethan.

"I don't feel like talking about it just yet." I reach over to steal a bite of his since I haven't tried Rocky Road before and he pulls it back out of my reach. "Hey!" I protest.

Matt shakes his head. "Uh huh girl. You want a bite of this you have to start talking."

I stab my ice cream with my spoon in agitation. "Fine, we kissed and then he said he regretted it."

"Asshole," he grumbles. "Did he initiate the kiss or did you?"

"I did," I mumble.

"Ah, there is your problem right there. Most guys don't like you to take charge. A guy like Ethan likes to be in charge so if you make the first move he feels weak."

"I think it's stupid. I wasn't taking charge of anything. The attraction is there so I just went for it." I don't regret making the first move because one of us has to, otherwise we'll never get anywhere. My only regret is giving him a chance to think.

"By kissing him, you took charge, Lex."

Matt holds a spoonful of ice cream up, rewarding me for answering his questions. Hmm, I might have to buy that flavor of ice cream next trip.

"How do you know all of this?" I ask, remembering his reply.

He rolls his eyes dramatically like I should already know the answer to this insane, confusing riddle. "I'm a guy, duh. How else would I know this stuff?"

"Okay, then explain to me how he kissed me, just yesterday, remind you, and it not be a problem?" That's what I really want to know. It makes no sense to me at all.

"He initiated the kiss. If you had of kissed him instead of the other way around, then you would have had the same outcome then as you did this morning."

I massage my temples with my fingers. All of this is confusing and stupid.

"Look, Alexis, how about we continue to binge on ice cream and sad movies and forget about his stupid ass. Sound good?"

It would work if I could forget about him, but a guy like Ethan is hard to forget even if I wanted to. "I don't want to forget about him, Matt. I've fallen for him, and right now it seems one-sided, which sucks for me, but I know he cares for me too."

"I think he does, too, even though he has a shitty way of showing it," he grumbles.

I eat my ice cream in silence, contemplating why he can kiss me, but yet I can't kiss him? All he is doing is frustrating us both, hurting us both. Can't he see that he is breaking his own heart, too?

Matt leaves a little while later to go run some errands. I glance around my box filled apartment, deciding I better get a move on with the unpacking. Might as well get started since I have nothing else to do.

I spend the next two hours unpacking boxes, putting things where they need to go.

I feel a little accomplished now that I have unpacked a lot of boxes.

A knock on the door startles me. I'm not expecting anyone so I'm curious as to who it is.

I crack the door first to make sure whoever it is, is not a stranger. It's only Brad, and the second I see him, it clicks. I never called him last night. Really, I was out of it so I couldn't anyway, but still. Brad doesn't look happy as he walks past me, into my apartment.

I keep quiet, letting him speak first.

"You never called me," he grumbles gruffly, staring down at the beige carpet. "Why?"

Um, I really rather not tell him what happened last night or this morning. Standing in front of him, under his scrutiny, I feel guilty, ashamed.

I open my mouth to speak, but he cuts me off. "Save it, I already know."

Wait-what?

"I called you last night, only you didn't answer." Oh shit, I know where this is heading. "Ethan," he scoffs as he says his name. "...filled me in. I knew you shouldn't have went. I'm mad because you didn't call me this morning. It should have been me who took care of you, Alexis, not another guy."

Like I had a choice? "I should have called this morning okay, but it slipped my mind."

I cringe, knowing it was the wrong thing to say. How can someone forget to call their boyfriend?

"Slipped your mind?" he sputters in disbelief.

"Even if I did call, telling you all that would have been hard."

"You don't think worrying about you all night was easy?" He steps closer. "What about knowing you were at another guy's house, in his bed? That was hard!"

He closes the space between us, cupping my face gently. "I love you, Alexis, and I'm sorry I wasn't there to protect you from that happening. Where was Matt by the way? Shouldn't he have been the one watching you, protecting you?"

"Matt is not my babysitter." Good grief, first Ethan, now Brad.

"No, he is not, but still, he should have been keeping an eye on you!"

Throwing my hands in the air out of frustration, I yell, "Would you just stop!"

"You know what, I think we need a break," he says in exasperation.

This is my chance to break things off, yet for some reason I don't end it. "I think we do, too." Agreeing to a break was not something I considered doing.

His gaze drops to the floor. "You know, I fell hard for you, but I feel like my feelings haven't been returned a lot of days. You need to figure out what you want. I want you, but something is going on between you and Ethan. I have an idea, but I'm not going to assume. You decide what you want and then we will talk and hopefully work things out. Until then, I hope your first semester goes well."

I flinch when the door slams behind him. He's right, I *do* need to decide what I want, or rather, who I want.

Rather than being upset, I'm pissed. Ethan had no right to answer my phone. I go to grab my keys off the counter when I realize my car isn't here. So I pick up my phone send him an angry text.

Me: **When were you going to tell me Brad called? Or were you not going to mention it hoping he wouldn't tell me? You are an asshole! You had no right to answer my phone. He should have heard what happened from me!**

I'm so angry I could scream. This is twice he has done this to me.

Ethan: **Lex, I felt like he should have known. I'm sorry I didn't tell you. I had planned on telling you when you woke up this morning and well, I forgot.**

Me: **How could you forget to tell me something that important?!**

I mean seriously!

Ethan: **You made me forget, Lex. When you kissed me, it was all I focused on.**

I don't understand him at all. He lets me kiss him, regrets it and wouldn't explain why, and now he acts like he never regretted it at all.

Me: **You're so confusing you know that?**

Me: **And irritating**

When he doesn't reply I keep going.

Me: **And damaging**

Me: **Oh, we can't forget clueless**

Okay, maybe I'm being a little harsh, but I'm upset over the whiplash he is giving me.

Ethan: **Are you done degrading me?**

Me: **Nope, not even close. You can't just say things like that and expect me not to be hurt and confused.**

Guys obviously don't care about girls' feelings anymore.

Ethan: **Once again, it's your fault, Lex.**

Me: **Oh really? Do tell, because you wouldn't give me an explanation this morning. I'm not taking the blame for anything until you tell me the reason you're holding back with me.**

He must have clammed up again because my phone has not buzzed in the last twenty minutes, and I'm still standing here like an idiot waiting for his text.

Deciding I didn't want this conversation to end without an explanation, I call a cab and give the man directions to Ethan's apartment. I'm taking a risk doing this, a huge one.

When the driver stops, I pay the fare and climb out. I march up the steps, determined to make him talk to me. I just want to know why. Why does he shut me out? Why doesn't he want to pursue a relationship with me? Why does he continue to leave me hurt and confused? I have questions that deserve answers.

My fist bangs on his door and my foot taps as I wait impatiently for him to answer the door.

The door swings open and he is stunned to see me. *Surprise.*

Closing his mouth, which fell open when he noticed me, he swallows hard. "Lex," he breathes like he has missed me like he hasn't seen me in months.

I waltz right into his apartment like I own the place. I spin and cock my hip to one side, folding my arms across my chest. "I came here for answers, Ethan. I think you owe me that much."

Ethan looks lost like he can't decide if he wants to give me what I need or not.

"It's not hard, Ethan. Just tell me," I plead.

When he finally does reply, it sounds forced. "I can't."

"Why?" I demand.

He blows out a breath. "It's complicated, Lex. You wouldn't understand."

"You keep saying that and I don't understand why. Maybe if you trusted me enough to tell me this wouldn't be a problem, yet you assume I automatically won't comprehend what it is you want to tell me."

He is silent as he stares at me impassively. I guess he is gathering is thoughts.

When he does speak again, it has nothing to do with the conversation we were having.

"How did you get here?"

"Quit changing the subject!"

He sighs and sits in the nearest chair. "I don't know how to put it," he mutters.

With my anger slowly diminishing, I walk over to him and kneel in front of him. "Ethan, I want to understand. If you don't have real feelings for me then be honest. I want to know why you are giving me whiplash. One minute you are kissing me and the next you act like you don't want to have anything to do with me, and then you act like nothing ever happened."

I cover my hands with his, feeling the callouses and the roughness of his skin.

Ethan brings his gaze up to mine, and I study his features. Reaching up, I run my finger along his strong jaw over to his full lips. His breath hitches when I run my finger across them.

Ethan sucks in a breath and abruptly backs away from my touch. "Lex," he says in a low, hoarse whisper. "You can't touch me like that and expect me not to want to lose control."

I want him to lose control because maybe then he will get past the walls he is hiding behind.

"Please, Ethan," I beg for him to tell me, to give me answers.

He shakes his head and my heart plummets in my chest. "No, not while you have a boyfriend and not when I'm about to leave."

Tears threaten again, but I back away like he just burned me. When it's clear he is going to say anything else, I pick myself up off the floor and go to leave.

I pause at the door, the uncomfortable silence is deafening. The tension is thick, I don't know if a knife could even slice through it.

"If you want it to be this way, then fine. Don't text me, don't call me, and don't even look my way if I am near you. Have a nice life, Ethan Harper." I close the door behind me, resisting the urge to slam it.

I guess it's time to put Ethan in the past. It's time to close the door on my heart to him and move on. I just need to throw myself into my classes and cheering and be done with it. Maybe Brad and I can be friends. There are too many decisions that need to be made and I feel like just saying screw it all and be start over fresh.

As I wait for the cab to come pick me up, I try to figure out where I go from here. I need to give Brad the space we both need. He hit the nail on the head when he said I needed to sort my crap out. Those weren't his exact words, but that's what he was implying.

I need some advice.

When the cab arrives, I give him directions to my former home, the home I shared with my parents. Mom will know what to do, she always does.

chapter twelve

Ethan

After Lex walked out of my front door, I called up Farris and asked if he wanted to squeeze a workout in before our shift tonight. I will be dog tired by the middle of my shift since I won't get a nap in, but oh well.

I need to relieve some stress in the weight room for a couple hours. My back is against the weight bench as I breathe through my last rep. I'm pushing myself harder than normal today and Farris has picked up on it.

"Geez, Harper, go easy on yourself," he chastens, which only fuels my need to continue.

When my arms feel like jello, I finally stop.

"What's with you today?" Farris asks as I wipe the sweat pouring off my face with a towel.

"Nothing," I snap, then regretting it. He doesn't deserve to be on the receiving end of the anger I have pent up. "Sorry," I grumble in an apology.

He hands me my water bottle as a peace offering. "Do you want to talk about it?"

"You'll laugh."

"Ah, if you think I will laugh then I already know it's going to be about a girl." He sits down on the weight bench across from me, a sly smile etched on his face. "So, who is she and what did you do?"

I toss my towel at him then abruptly stand, feeling the need to pace. "What makes you automatically assume I did anything?"

He shrugs. "Just a hunch."

I walk over to the railing and grab it, squeezing the bar with my hands.

"She's so irritating at times and she doesn't know when to stop," I growl thinking of Alexis trying to get me to open up. She was relentless earlier. "She kept trying to get me to confess my feelings for her earlier and I wouldn't do it." I shove off the rail and go back to the weight bench.

"And why don't you. I mean you clearly feel something for her."

"Because…it will change things." Our lives will change and I'm afraid of the change not turning out like we want it to.

"It can't be that bad of a change."

I grip my water bottle tightly in my hand. Thinking about the future, not knowing what is going to happen is scary. I'm faced with the unknown and I am afraid of breaking her.

"It will be good at first, and then, maybe bad, who knows."

Farris chuckles, I don't. He doesn't understand the hidden meaning. "You are being cryptic you know that?"

I know, it's what I intended on. "Some things are better left unsaid, Farris."

"Have I seen her before?" he asks to change the rather dreary subject.

"I don't know."

"Well, tell me about her. What's her name? What does she look like?" Man, he is rattling off questions like he thinks I'm going to spill every piece of information I know about her.

With a sigh, I pull out my phone and find one of her with my sister. "She's the girl with the black hair."

When he whistles, it takes all my willpower not to punch him. I wish I hadn't of shown him a picture of her. He better not get any ideas about pursuing her because I will put a stop to that real quick.

"She's pretty man."

No, she's more than pretty, she's gorgeous. Pretty is not a strong enough word to describe Lex's beauty.

"Don't even think about it," I bark out. First Cole, now Farris. What is it with all the guys trying to get with Lex? They know how I feel about her.

Farris holds his hands up innocently. "Whoa man, don't take things the wrong way."

I lay back on the bench, feeling the urge to push myself harder. The desire, the irritation, and the longing are all pent up inside my flesh, wanting to be set free. I desire her in ways I shouldn't, she irritates the hell out of me, and I long to lay my heart out on the line for her. She wants me to reveal my feelings to her, yet I'm afraid when it's all said and done, I will end up passing a lifetime of hurt down to her. Lex wouldn't understand. She says she will, but I believe she will be blinded by her attraction to me that she wouldn't really listen to what I am saying. Maybe I am going into all of this the opposite way I should be. Going into war, preparing to die is not how I should be thinking. I want to come back and see Lex waiting for me. I am just trying to prepare for the future *if* somehow I don't make it back.

Shaking my head, trying to get rid of the depressing thoughts, I finish my last rep.

My arms are aching tonight. I've overdone it tonight, big time.

"So, have you come to a conclusion?" Farris asks, catching me off guard. He must read my expression because he adds, "You were thinking pretty hard the whole time you were pumping iron so I just assumed you were trying to come up with an answer to your rather complicated predicament."

"Unfortunately no. Besides, she's off limits no matter how much I want her."

Farris stares at me with a puzzled look. "Boyfriend," I say as a way of explanation.

Farris laughs deeply, obviously not believing me. My suspicions are confirmed when he says, "Yeah, okay. And I am rich."

"I'm serious. His name is Brad. They went to high school together."

His laughter dies when he realizes I'm telling the rather heartbreaking truth.

"Huh, didn't see that coming."

I just grunt in agreement. I don't see how Brad and Lex are still together. Not when she has made her feelings known to me and especially with Brad moving off to college.

Noticing the time, Farris and I hit the showers to get ready for a long night.

It's official, night shift sucks. Time is already dragging by and I have only been on the clock for an hour.

My phone buzzes in my lap and I briefly wonder who it's from as I unlock my screen.

Lex: You're still an ass

There is no denying her statement. She has every right to call me an ass because that is what I have been to her.

Me: You are still beautiful

There, it's time I try to right some of my wrongs.

Lex: Bastard

I chuckle lightly at that reply, earning a questioning look from Farris. I ignore him and continue my somehow playful and degrading banter with Lex.

Me: Intoxicating

Lex: I know I have told you this several times today and yet, you still don't seem to get it. YOU ARE CONFUSING!

Me: Have I told you how irritating you are? I think I have, but I will tell you again. You get under my skin, Lex, and it scares the shit out of me.

Lex: And you don't scare me? Ethan, you have the power to wreck me, completely shatter me. I never cry, yet with you, when you stomp all over my heart, I bawl my eyes out like a freakin' baby.

My heart clenches from the sting of her words. I don't hurt her deliberately, I swear.

Me: I don't do it on purpose, Lex

Lex: Enlighten me then. Answer my questions.

Ah, crap. Not this again.

Me: You know my answer to that. Besides, I thought I wasn't supposed to be talking to you?

Lex: Have a good night

Sighing in frustration, I toss my phone on the dash. I can tell Farris wants to comment so I beat him to it before he gets the chance. "I don't want to hear it, Farris."

He chuckles and I let my head fall back against the headrest.

"I wasn't going to utter a word."

Shaking my head in disbelief, because I'm positive he is lying, I punch his arm, warning him to keep quiet.

"Dude, you need to get her out of your damn system or something. You are violent when she gets to you," he grumbles, rubbing the sore spot I'm sure he has.

"Tried that and it didn't work."

Farris whistles low. "Maybe you just haven't found the right person yet."

Lex is the girl for me, I just can't have her…yet. I don't need to search when I have the perfect goddess in front of me.

"Then what do you suggest I do?" I shouldn't have asked that question because Farris *loves* women. I may not know much about him yet, but that I do know.

Every shift he always talks about his conquests on his off days.

I fight the urge to text her back, explaining myself, relinquishing what she wants to hear, but I don't.

Farris just flashes me a sly smile, which clearly means trouble.

"Just wait until we are not on the clock, Harper. I'm going to show you a good night on the town."

The rest of the night, in between calls, I think of Lex, wondering if I tell her will things work out in our favor or will my original prediction take over?

She is still in my head when I arrive back at my apartment around eight in the morning. When my head hits the pillow and I close my eyes, she's still there.

The rational part of me wants to decline Farris' offer, but the other part wonders if I should take him up on it. Maybe a night out to clear my head is what I need. A drink or two wouldn't hurt. After all, it's what Lex tried to do a couple nights ago.

I have a strong feeling that no matter how much I drink, how numb I get, Lex will still be in my head, taunting me with her exquisiteness, reminding me how badly I want something I can't have.

chapter thirteen

Alexis

I walk through the front door of the house I have shared with my parents since I was born. It's relatively quiet, with faint sounds of murmurs coming from the den. My whole life I have been given everything I could ever want. I just batted my eyes at my Dad and he got me whatever I asked for. Mom, however, I had to work a little harder to get her to crack. The moment I turned sixteen and was handed the keys to my brand new car, the one I still drive, I began only asking for things I really needed, not wanted. Watching all these other snobby kids my age demand for something made me pause and think about how I was treating my parents. After that, I started becoming responsible. If I wanted something, I would clean or help with something around the house so that I earned it. I have the best parents I could ever ask for. They are understanding, forgiving, and open-minded when I tell them about my ideas. At one point, when Kaylee and I considered going away to college, they were understanding. Dad has conditions, which weren't outrageous. Mom even helped me start searching. I know they are relieved to have me here, attending a local college. Sometimes I wish I would have still applied to a university out of state, but then I think of leaving Kaylee and the twins, my parents, and even Ethan. I would miss them too much.

Walking into the den, I find Mom on the phone. I wait patiently for her to finish, sitting quietly on the leather couch next to her. She gives me a polite smile as she finishes up her conversation.

When she is done, she hangs up the phone and pulls me into a long hug. "How is your day going, dear?"

I give her a tight smile. "It could be better."

"Oh? What's bothering you?"

Here goes nothing. I haven't really talked guys with my mom, so this is a first, but we talk about a lot of other stuff, some personal, so naturally I thought of her first. "Well, first off, I guess I should tell you that Brad and I are taking a break."

I suspected Mom to be shocked because, well, she loves Brad, yet she's not which is confusing me. *Great, first Ethan, now Mom.*

"Why are you taking a break?"

How can I tell her I went to a party, was drugged, and woke up at Ethan's apartment? "Um, well, we got into an argument and he said he needed a break."

Mom gives me a look except I am not sure how to read it. "May I ask what the fight was about?"

"Brad thinks there is something going on between Ethan and me and he wants me to figure it out."

Mom leans back in her seat and crosses her legs. I can tell she is thinking, it's just what she is thinking kind of scares me.

"Is there something between you and Ethan?"

"Kind of, I'm not really sure. He's kissed me and then left. I kissed him and he flipped out. I don't really know, Mom." Mixed signals are all I'm getting from Ethan. I need more of an explanation from him, which he won't give me for some odd reason.

Maybe he is still trying to decide if he wants me. He may be the one confused. I'm not indecisive about Ethan, I know I want to be with him. My head and heart are even on the same page with that. What I am unsure on though is what to do with Brad. I'm not in love with him like he is me, and I definitely have stronger feelings toward Ethan, and yet, I can't seem to cut ties with Brad.

"Hmm…I see. You need to ask yourself if you even want to be in a relationship with Brad. Do you care about him enough to want to continue with what you have?"

"That's where I am stuck," I groan.

"Okay, let's try this a different way. I know how he feels toward you because I've seen it, but with you I'm unsure. Alexis, you have to answer these honestly. You don't have to answer these out loud if you choose not to."

I nod and then she begins her questionnaire.

"Does your heart speed up when you are near him?"

Sometimes, I think.

"Do you automatically smile when you see him?"

Most of the time.

"Do you still get butterflies just thinking of him or hearing him say things?"

Sometimes.

"When he is away, do you find yourself missing him?"

Not really.

"And finally, when Brad told you he wanted a break, how did you feel?"

Kind of relieved, but then I felt a pang of sadness. I didn't cry, though, like I have over Ethan.

"Okay, what did you come up with?"

Sighing, I tell her my conclusion. "He's told me he loves me, but yet I haven't said it back and it's been a few months now. I'm not in love with him, and at first I thought maybe it was just too soon for me. When he told me he wanted a break, I felt pretty much relieved because I don't want to be the one to break up with him. I don't want to be the one to break his heart."

"I knew you didn't love him, it was written all over your face. Like your answers were. Even though you didn't say them out loud, I still knew because of your facial expression."

Well, I guess that's that. It's time I relinquish Brad and set him free. I didn't deserve him at all, and I'm surprised he is just now catching on. I mean, we haven't had sex or anything and we have been together since late fall.

Mom sits up and places her small hand on top of mine. "Honey, Brad is an amazing guy, but he is not for you. If he was, you wouldn't be here questioning your decision. Ethan is Kaylee's brother, right?"

"That's him," I reply, my voice soft.

"Tell me about him," she urges.

I want to question her, but I don't. "Well, he works for the Bowling Green Police Department and he is in the Army, which he gets deployed in November. He's intimidating, he's confusing, but he is also sweet when he wants to be." Ethan joined the Army right out of high school and has been overseas twice already.

Mom has a huge grin on her face when I finish. "What?"

"Nothing, it's just when you talk about him, your face lights up. Ethan is obviously your choice."

I nervously tuck a strand of hair behind my ear. Why am I shy all of sudden?

"He is, and I know he likes me, but he's holding back and I can't, for the life of me, get him to tell me why."

"Maybe he is afraid?" Mom suggests.

I haven't thought of it like that before. "Afraid of what?"

"Dating, messing things up…honey, this list is endless."

I find it hard to think of Ethan being afraid, but I guess everyone is afraid of something.

"And he won't tell you because he is scared," Mom adds.

Ethan scared to tell me? "I don't understand, Mom."

"Ethan could be scared of what he feels for you, and he won't tell you because he is afraid of how you will react. What if he puts his heart out there and you stomp on it?"

"Oh, I guess I didn't think of it that way."

"Honey, just give him some time, okay?"

I smile graciously at her. "Thank for listening to me and for the advice, Mom."

Mom holds her arms out and I lean into her embrace. "You are so welcome, Alexis."

She kisses my cheek then leans back.

I knew coming to Mom was the right choice. I'm going to continue to give Brad the space he wants and needs. I still want to think on it some more before I make my final decision.

With my decisions made and my head clear, I head to my apartment to get ready for a long night of practice.

chapter fourteen

Ethan

"Yeah, boy! It's time for my man to have some fun!" Farris cheers in greeting as I walk down the steps from my apartment to his car. I just laugh and shake my head at his outburst. I never know what to expect from him. Farris is just full of surprises.

"A Lexus, really Farris? I figured you were a truck kind of guy," I tease him when I notice what kind of vehicle he is driving.

"Hey now, this car does amazing on gas and it has power, Harper. Don't knock my car."

I chuckle and slide in the sleek black car. "So where are we going, my friend?"

A wicked smile forms and in my gut, I'm thinking, *tonight is going to start off fun then turn into hell.*

I don't like it when he smiles like that because it usually means I'm going to wake up with some chick in my bed and a killer hangover to go along with it.

Cole has given me several of them smiles so I know firsthand what it means. Usually, instead of some random chick, it would be Kate.

Seeing how I've deleted her number out of my phone, I don't see myself calling her tonight. I'd get some random texts from a number which I assume is hers because she is begging for me to come back. I just delete them and go on about my day.

"Harper, get ready for the night of your life!" he hoots and hollers in the driver's seat while I resist the urge to cringe.

Yeah, I do not like the sound of that at all.

Farris pulls into a local bar parking lot and parks. He rubs his hands together in anticipation before climbing out.

Begrudgingly, I follow him out. *Pace yourself,* I coach myself. Getting drunk off my ass is not what I really need. I get too….happy when I am drunk. Hey, at least I'm not an angry drunk like some people.

The bar is dimly lit with all the neon lights glowing. There is a huge crowd of people dancing to the music the DJ is playing.

Farris and I walk up to the bar and the first thing Farris does is flirt with the bartender. Eventually, I get to tell the girl my order and soon I am downing it.

"So," I start, placing my empty bottle on the counter. "What's your first name, Farris?"

"Jay," he replies.

We order another round and I slow my pace on this one.

"What's your story?"

His face is grim as he picks with the paper on the bottle that's in his hands. "Nothing much to tell."

Ah, I am smart enough to know he doesn't want to talk about it.

His face morphs back into the Farris I have seen since I walked out of my apartment. "I'm going to talk to that pretty little lady over there."

He pats my shoulder and makes a beeline to the girl he picked out in the crowd.

My phone buzzes in my pocket again. I am disappointed to see it's Kate again.

E, why are you ignoring me?

Good grief, what do I have to do to get rid of her?

Me: Kate, for the last time, quit texting me.

Kate is relentless. I should have listened to the guys a long time ago when they told me not to mess with her.

You miss me, I know you do.

Uh, no I don't.

Me: If I missed you, you would know it.

I down my second beer and turn back to the bartender, needing something stronger. Whiskey might do the trick.

I look down at my phone again when it buzzes.

Where are you? Can we just hang out like old times?

Hang out? When have we ever done that?

Me: Kate, you and I both know we haven't done anything other than sex. Lose my number.

At this point, I am contemplating changing my number, or blocking her.

I knock out two glasses of whiskey, pleased to see Kate hasn't replied yet.

I curse when my phone buzzes again. I spoke way too soon.

You always come back to me

Nope, not anymore.

Me: Not happening, Kate

I turn around, searching the crowd for Farris. When I spot him, I laugh. He is dancing, if you call it that, with the girl he picked up. He spots me laughing and makes some inappropriate gesture.

I laugh harder and down the rest of the whiskey.

A skinny brunette walks up to me, wearing a dress that is next to nothing. She is cute, but not gorgeous. "Hey handsome, want to dance?"

I shouldn't, but I'm feeling buzzed and right now, all my rationalization is gone.

I pocket my phone then smile at her. "Lead the way," I hold my hand out in gesture to the dance floor.

She grabs my hand and tugs me along behind her.

Somehow, we end up next to Farris. "Hey, hey! It's about time, Harper!" He winks and slaps my shoulder before turning his attention back to the girl he is dancing with.

I soon figure out the girls are friends. Farris probably is in on her asking me to come dance with her.

I shake off everything I am feeling, just living in the moment. The whiskey is hitting me hard now. I am freely running my hands over the girl's hips and backside.

I vaguely hear Farris ask if I want another drink. I order another whiskey, I think, I really don't remember because the girl has turned and is now rubbing her backside against me. Brushing her hair to one side, exposing her neck, I lean down, pressing my lips to her skin.

Her skin is not as soft, or as velvety as Lex's, but still feels good all the same.

My fingers dig into her flesh as she continues to grind her hips. I'm only enjoying it a little bit, but I am too far gone to care.

I thank Farris when he returns with my drink I so desperately need. I am about to take a sip when I feel my phone vibrate in my pocket. I almost ignore it, but what if it is an emergency?

I should have known who it would be, though.

Where are you Ethan?

Me: None of your business

I pocket my phone again, determined to ignore it the rest of the night.

With the whiskey flowing through me, I dance for another couple songs before we find a table and sit. The girl, whose name I haven't asked for yet, flops in my lap instead of the empty seat next to me. I don't force her to move even though I should.

The girl twists, straddling me. I bring the glass up to my lips, leaning my head back to take a sip. The chick leans down and begins kissing my neck. Her lips don't feel as soft as Lex's and I am not getting turned on as quick as I would if it was Lex in my lap. Lex. Man, I need to quit thinking about her. Tonight is supposed to be about getting her out of my system, and yet, I'm here comparing her to the girl in my lap.

Lex consumes my mind all the time so why did I believe it would only take one night to forget about her? Oh, right, Farris gave me that idea. His confidence spoke volumes so I believed it would happen. And I was wrong.

I need to get this girl off my lap. I tell her I need to use the restroom. She gives me a seductive smile and climbs off my lap. I stagger toward the bathroom, relieved to see it is empty.

I feel a lot better when I walk back out of the bathroom. I lean against the wall and pull out my phone. I scroll through my contacts and pause on Lex's name.

Not really thinking, I press the call button and place the phone to my ear.

She picks up on the fourth ring, sounding half asleep. "Ethan?"

Her raspy voice hits me square in the gut. "Why can't I get you out of my head?" I slur. "You are like permanently etched into my brain, Lex. I want you, okay? There, I finally said it, but I can't have you and it's killing me."

I turn and lay my forehead against the wall, waiting for her to say something, but I am only met with silence. I am about to hang up when she finally speaks.

"Ethan, we will talk about this later. Where are you?"

"I'm with Farris at a bar," I slur, my voice sounding worse.

"Which bar?"

"Uh, the one on Main Street. Can't remember the name."

There is another long pause.

"I'm coming to get you, Ethan." Then the line goes dead.

I stare at my phone for several minutes wondering why my plan just backfired, whatever my plan was.

I punch the wall then walk, not very gracefully, back to where Farris and the girls are seated.

I plop down in the extra seat next to Farris. The girl I danced with earlier frowns then sips on her fruity drink.

I pat Farris on the back. "Man, I just totally messed up."

Farris whips his head over to me with a knowing smile. "You called her didn't you?"

I look at him, stunned that he knew what I had done. "How did you know?"

"I'm not stupid, Harper. Now, what happened?"

"I said some things to her and it resulted in her saying she was coming to get me."

Farris shakes his head, but he is smiling. "It's cool, man. I will catch up with you later."

Farris seems calm and collected while I am spinning and not really caring what I am doing. It's the whiskey.

I stand, shakily and walk in the best straight line I can toward the exit.

Outside, I stand against the brick wall and wait for Lex.

A few minutes later, a car pulls up in front of me and stops. Lex gets out of the car and walks over to me. My mouth falls open at the sight of her in sleep shorts and tank.

"Why are you not wearing different clothes," I slur, trying to stand. I end up losing my balance and fall to my right.

Lex must have super human strength because she catches me before I hit the ground. "Nice catch. How strong are you?" I ask, glancing down at her arms to look at her muscles.

"Not strong enough," she grunts, walking me to the car. My arm is around her neck and I am leaning into her.

Lex opens the passenger side door and I fall in, hitting my head on the middle console. "Shit," I curse, placing my palm to my forehead when my head starts to throb.

I finally get situated and almost swallow my tongue when Lex leans over me to buckle me up. Her chest is right in front of me, and I can see down her shirt.

"Nice tits."

Lex scowls at me and backs out of the car. "Don't you dare think about throwing up in my car."

"Yes ma'am," I salute as she slams the door.

Lex stomps around the car and slides in. Even in the dark, I can make out how short her shorts are.

"Nice legs," I compliment.

She ignores me and pulls out onto the highway.

chapter fifteen

Alexis

It's a hard task to haul a drunk Ethan up a flight of stairs. He weighs a freaking ton. Okay, maybe not that much, but it sure feels like he weighs that much. The whole ride to my apartment Ethan groaned, from what I was sure was his stomach being nauseated, and he would continue to compliment me. It pissed me off that drunk Ethan can tell me all of these things, but sober Ethan can't. I should have taken him home to his own apartment and let him sleep it off, but I was afraid he would choke on his own vomit so I just brought him to mine. I know I will regret this in the morning when he wakes up.

I open the door to my room and walk over to my bed, letting him fall on to it. I pick up his legs, one at a time, to remove his shoes before attempting to straighten him up so I can have room to lay down.

His eyes are closed though I don't think he is fully out yet.

He pats the empty spot next to him and murmurs, "Lay down with me, Lex. I want to hold you."

I shouldn't, I know this, but I can't resist him.

Crap, he is laying on top of the covers. I lift his legs again to free the covers.

I end up having to roll him on his side to get the rest of the covers out from under him.

Ethan sits up suddenly, struggling to remove his shirt. Sighing, I help him remove it.

He throws himself back down and covers up. Removing my sandals, I climb into bed, trying to keep some distance between us. Maybe he has already forgotten his recent comment.

I gasp when his arm latches around my middle, pulling me back so his chest is pressed against my back.

He nuzzles my hair and for a second I swear I hear him inhale like he is smelling my hair.

My suspicions are confirmed when he mumbles, "You smell good."

No sooner than he says that, he is out. I lay quietly for a moment, listening to him breathe.

Eventually, I close my eyes and drift off to sleep in Ethan's arms, a place I have always wanted to be.

I wake up to someone pounding on my door. I manage to remove Ethan's arm from around me and roll out of bed without waking him. I grab my robe hanging on the back of my door and hastily put it on.

I peek through the peephole to find Brad standing outside. Great, just what I need this morning.

I unlock the door, opening it half way. "Hey," I murmur, not knowing what else to say.

"Hey. I, um," he clears his throat. "…I just came to tell you that I am heading to Lexington this morning."

I just nod because what am I going to say?

"How are you?" he asks, filling the awkward silence.

"I'm good."

He blows out a breath. "Listen, Lex, I love you, and I miss you, all right? I don't know if I will be convinced that there isn't something going on between you and Ethan, but I am willing to give us another shot." He rocks back and forth on his heels for a moment before reaching forward to grab my hand. "I guess what I am trying to say is that I don't want to leave with a rift between us. So, what do you say? Do you want to break up or do you want to give us another try?"

Do I want to stay with Brad? I know I don't deserve another shot, but with him standing here on pins and needles, looking sad, I want to tell him yes. But then, I think of Ethan in my bed asleep, *or at least I hope he is,* and it makes me want to cut my ties with Brad.

I really don't want to hurt Brad, though, because he is such a sweet guy.

I smile at him and watch his shoulders sag in relief. "Another shot it is."

I'm going to try to be a better girlfriend to Brad if it will work, I don't know, but I am going to try. That means, no Ethan.

Brad engulfs me in a hug, kissing my cheek, then my lips.

"I'm trying to work on the "I love you" thing, okay. It's just that those are really powerful words and I don't want to say it and not mean it."

"I got you, but just know that I will continue to say it regardless."

He wraps his arms around me, hugging me hard. "I've got to go," he sighs. "I will text you in a bit. As soon as I get my schedules and stuff, I will start planning a visit to come see you."

"Okay, be safe."

"Love you," he murmurs, then kisses me once more before leaving.

I wave at him as he walks down the stairs. When he is out of sight, I turn and walk back into my apartment. I let out a shriek, jumping back into my front door when I see Ethan sitting on the couch. He is staring down at the floor, his jaw tense, and his eyes raging.

I have no idea how long he has been sitting there, listening, but I imagine he heard more than enough.

"So, that's it? You are just going to get back together?" Ethan asks sullenly, his eyes never leaving my beige carpet.

"I don't know what you want me to say, Ethan." It's pretty obvious he is not going to pursue me so I just need to try again with Brad.

He lifts head up, his eyes finding mine. "Why didn't you tell him no?"

I fist my hands at my sides. "I didn't because I know nothing between us will change, Ethan. I've already made my move and was shut down so now it's your turn. You decide what happens between us. Besides, Brad is a great guy."

"Why didn't you just take me back to my apartment, Lex?"

I knew I would regret this come morning and I was right.

"I thought about it, but I wanted to make sure you were okay. You're lucky I didn't drop you trying to carry you up the stairs. You are not exactly light."

I see a hint of a smile on his lips, but as soon as it's there, it's gone.

"Well, thanks for the concern, but I am fine," he hisses.

Taking a better look at him, I notice he is fully dressed, seeming ready to go.

"I guess I will take you home then."

"Don't bother. I will just find my own ride."

I roll my eyes dramatically. Ethan is one frustrating piece of work. "Be serious, Ethan. First, you need to eat something. I'm surprised you didn't puke your guts up all night."

I head straight into the kitchen and start pulling out ingredients to make pancakes. I figure Ethan would just walk out since he is so determined to leave, so when he walks into the kitchen and starts helping me with the pancakes, I almost drop the mix.

As I am whisking the batter, Ethan sprays the skillet with the non-stick spray and turns on the heat.

"How many do you want?" I hope my voice doesn't sound as breathless as I feel with him standing right next to me.

"Depends on the size, but usually I eat four."

"Four it is then. Would you mind making some coffee?"

Ethan nods and turns around to the coffeepot, giving me room to breathe.

"Why were you and Brad on a break?" he asks, and the question makes me angry, but I shove it down, not wanting to fight.

"You are to blame for that."

He grunts in what I'm sure was disapproval.

So I explain, "Because you being nosy, answered my phone and told Brad something he should have heard from me. If anything, you should have woke me up and let me talk to him."

Ethan bursts out laughing. "Yeah, okay. Exactly how would you have been able to make clear concise sentences?"

I clench my fist around the pan, resisting the urge smack him with it. "You could have just ignored the call."

"I figured it was the right thing to do."

"Well, it wasn't."

Ethan doesn't reply to my comment, instead, he changes the topic. "So, what are you doing today?"

Okay, this I can answer without wanting to resort to violence. "Not much, although, I do have to get my things ready for the first day of classes in the morning."

"What are you majoring in?"

Ah, the question my parents tend to ask me a lot. I don't have a precise answer for it yet.

"Um, I'm not sure. Right now, I am just taking my general education classes until I decide. I am thinking about majoring in Elementary Education."

Ethan seems to think about it for a moment. "Huh, didn't peg you for a teacher."

"I love kids and I love watching them learn new things."

Ethan just stares at me like I've grown two heads all of a sudden. "What?"

Shaking his head, ridding himself of his thoughts, he replies, "Nothing."

"No, seriously, what were you thinking?" Probably not a good question to ask. He may something totally unexpected which would bring back the anger that has dissipated.

"I am just surprised is all. It's kind of hard picturing you as a teacher."

I'm not surprised by his comment. I'm sure he isn't the only one who thinks that, but going through all the possible majors, elementary education stands out the most to me.

"Like I said, I haven't fully decided."

The pancake I am cooking is done so I add it to Ethan's plate then pour more batter in the pan to start making mine.

Ethan walks up and begins dressing his mouthwatering pancakes with butter and syrup.

I am so distracted by him for a millisecond that I almost poured too much batter into the pan.

"I didn't say you couldn't do it or that you shouldn't go for it, Lex. You need to do what you want, not what people think you should do."

"I know that, and I will."

I watch as Ethan shoves mouthfuls of pancake in his mouth. "There are delicious," he says with his mouth full of food.

I laugh softly, turning my attention back to my own food to make sure I don't burn it.

But, I grab without looking and my hand touches the scorching hot pan. I yelp and jump back, clutching my burning hand.

I mumble some kind of half cuss, half regular words under my breath.

Ethan automatically sets his plate down and turns off the burner on the stove.

I turn around to turn the faucet on wide open. I cringe when the cold water makes contact with my skin. I try to keep my hand open, but my fingers keep curling from the pain.

Ethan is suddenly standing over me, holding my hand in his. "You really need hot water, it takes the burn out."

I look at him like he has lost his ever loving mind. "Are you crazy?!"

"I'm dead serious. It won't be scalding hot, just warm water."

I bend over and rest my head on my arm on the counter. "Just do it," I half grumble, half whimper. It's going to burn worse now. I hope he knows what he is doing.

"Okay."

The moment the water turns warm, I flinch and my hand instantly balls up into a fist.

Ethan pries my hand open and holds it flat so it is directly under the stream of water.

Oh my God, this hurts so bad!

"I don't see how this is helping," I whine, wishing he would stop this torture.

"Trust me," he murmurs. The soft tenderness of the voice has me thinking that those two words are meant for another situation entirely.

Finally, he relinquishes my hand from the water. I grab a towel and start patting my hand dry.

"Do you have any ointment or gauze?"

"No, I don't."

"Okay, where are your keys? I'm going to buy some."

He wants to drive my car? "I can drive."

Ethan pinches the bridge of his nose. "Be reasonable, Lex."

"Fine, but I riding with you."

His eyes take in my clothing. "Are you going to change?"

I look down at my robe. Yeah, I probably should do that.

"I'm going," I grumble.

"Need any help?" he smirks.

Instead of slapping him, I give him the bird and walk out of the room.

Changing clothes with one hand is as hard as it looks. I'm pretty sure if recorded me, I'd go viral instantly. I end up doing some weird looking dance to get my shirt over my head.

I slip on my sandals and breathe, before stepping out into the living room, grabbing my keys on the way out.

"Ready?" I ask Ethan, who is sitting on the edge of the couch.

He takes one look at me and bursts out laughing.

I glower at him. "What is so funny?"

It takes him a minute to calm down so he can actually form words. "Did you not look in the mirror before walking out here? Your shirt is on backwards and your pants are twisted."

Horrified, I glance down at my attire, noting he is right. With an agitated sigh, I stomp back into my room to turn around my shirt and fix my yoga pants.

This time, I do look in the mirror, making sure everything is in order before I walk back out.

"Now, I'm ready."

Ethan gives me a playful smile. "Are you sure?"

"Yes, you ass."

"Well then, let's go."

Ethan holds the door open for me to walk through and shuts it behind him. I lock my apartment, making it is secure.

As we walk to my car, Ethan places his hand at the small of my back. He even goes as far as opening the passenger door for me. I got to give him credit, even though he acts like an asshole most of the time, he is really a gentleman.

"Thank you," I murmur as I slide in, careful not to bump my injured hand.

I'm actually glad he is driving because no doubt I would have wrecked.

I think about cheer practice and wonder if Mrs. Jenny will make me sit out. I frown at the thought.

As Ethan backs out of the parking space, I swear I catch a glimpse of a girl who looks like Kate, parked two cars down from mine.

That's absurd, why would she be here?

I brush it off and relax back in my seat as Ethan drives us downtown. I don't know what is going on between us, but whatever it is, it feels nice. I want to hold on to it for as long as it lasts. Soon, things will go back to how they were, us arguing, and I'm not ready for him to pull away from me.

chapter sixteen

Ethan

"Get this one," I tell Lex, pointing to the cream she needs for her burn.

She picks it up and looks it then puts it back on the shelf.

"What are you doing?" I question her. I just told her the right stuff to get.

Her eyes scan the shelf. We have been standing in the same aisle for the past fifteen minutes because she hasn't made up her mind yet. "I'm looking at what's here. I can't just pick the first one I come across."

Rolling my eyes, I pick up the one I told her to grab in the first place. "This is what you need, I promise."

She looks from the cream in my hand to me. "Are you sure?"

"Positive."

She takes the product from my hand and we finally leave the aisle with both the gauze and the cream for her burn.

Lex and I walk over to the checkout and I lay the items on the counter. I start to pull out my wallet when Lex stops me.

"I'm buying these."

I ignore her and pull out my wallet.

"Ethan, I know you heard me. It's my stuff so I will buy it," she says, more firmly.

Feeling frustrated at her persistence, I turn toward her. "Is shopping with you like this all the time because, if so, I pity everyone who shops with you."

She punches me weakly in my shoulder using her left arm. Her right arm is her good arm, which is the arm with the burnt hand.

I pull out my debit card and start to swipe it through the reader when her hand suddenly comes down and smacks my card out of my hand.

"Seriously?" I grumble as I pick up my card. When I straighten she has already swiped her card and is putting in her PIN number. I shake my head and apologize to the cashier. "My apologies ma'am."

She just laughs and waves me off, "I always need a little entertainment while at work."

The cashier hands Lex the receipt while I grab her bag of two items that took almost thirty minutes to get. If I had come alone, I would be almost back to her apartment by now.

Women, I will never understand them.

As I am driving us back to Lex's apartment, her stomach growls. "What are you hungry for?" I ask her, my eyes already scanning the different restaurants along the highway.

"Um, IHOP sounds pretty good right now. At least I know, I will get my pancakes if we eat there."

"IHOP it is."

I end up having to turn around and go back a couple blocks, but it takes only a few minutes.

I make Lex wait before going in so I can apply the ointment and wrap her hand before we go in.

"Thank you," she murmurs when I finish.

I bring her hand up to my lips and kiss her fingers. "You're welcome," I reply, my voice low and hoarse.

It was a bad move on my part since all it did was make me fall a little farther for her.

I drop her hand and climb out of a car that is too small for me. I hope I didn't just give her any false hope because when it is all said and done if I pursue her, she would be the one with the broken heart. I hate that there is a chance of me not returning, but this is the reality of the career I chose.

I push those depressing down and focus on now, on today, and on the fact that I am having breakfast with Lex.

I keep my hand on her back as the hostess takes us to our seats. I pull out her chair for her when we reach the table. She smiles at me appreciatively.

We place our drink order and start scanning the menu to see what we want to eat.

To strike up a conversation, I go with, "So, how is practice going?"

"Good."

I nod, trying to come up with something else to ask her about.

"How are you liking your new apartment?"

She peeks over the top of her menu. "I love it. It's just right off campus so really I can walk a lot instead of having to fight for parking."

"You need to be careful, Lex. Be smart. Don't walk alone, and don't walk home at night, especially not alone."

"Yes, *Dad,*" she sneers, but she needs to understand.

I close my menu and lay it flat on the table. "I don't care if you only have walk a thousand feet home, don't do it."

"Okay, I got it," she replies in an aggravated tone.

Apparently she doesn't watch the news much or The First 48 or otherwise she might be understanding.

The waiter comes back to take our order and his eyes start lingering a little too long on Lex. *Back off dude!*

Lex either is oblivious to the way his eyes train on her or she just isn't acknowledging him.

When I think he is finally done, his eyes drop to her burnt hand. "What happened to your hand?"

Lex looks a little surprised he asked, as am I. "Oh, I uh, burnt my hand on the pan trying to make pancakes. No big deal." She waves him off, her face turning beet red like she is embarrassed.

"Ouch, have you taken care of it properly? I'm a med student so I could take a look at it for you if you want."

Are you fucking kidding me? "*I* took care of it," I growl.

The waiter's head whips over to me like he forgot I was sitting here. He regains his composure quickly, trying not to look intimidated, but it was too late because I saw it.

"If that completes your order, I will turn it in so they can get started on it." His eyes shift from me to Lex. I think he is being more careful about not gazing at her for too long.

Just as he turns to walk off, I glance at his name tag to find out his name. If he told us earlier, I don't remember it.

When he is gone I look back at Lex to find her glaring at me. "What?"

"Why were you so rude to him?"

Really? Did she honestly not notice? "Because he was staring at you way too long and he was obviously flirting with you."

Lex scoffs as she rolls her eyes dramatically. "Are you for real right now? You are not my boyfriend so back off with whatever caveman crap you are doing."

"Caveman?" I chuckle, making fun of her. Leaning forward, I keep my eyes locked on hers. "Regardless of whether or not I am your boyfriend, he still shouldn't be looking at you like he was. Even if his look meant the same as mine, he doesn't even need to think about it."

She leans forward, her arms resting on the table, mocking my stance. "Oh really, what makes you so special?"

"I never said I was special."

"Okay, let me rephrase the question. Why isn't he allowed to look at me and you are? Neither of you are dating me."

"Because he isn't good for you."

Lex scoffs again and leans back in her chair. "And how would know you he isn't?"

"Because, the look he was giving you is different from mine. When he looks at you, he is imagining you as his next lay. When *I* look at you, it's the total opposite. I see your true beauty."

I hear her breath hitch, and I mentally kick myself for revealing so much.

Lex closes her eyes briefly, and when she opens them she looks hurt. "Ethan, why do you keep saying stuff like that to me? Do you really even mean it or is this part of some game?"

"I mean every word, Lex. You are not a game to me."

"Then why do you not take that next step?"

I sigh and run my hand over my face. She wouldn't understand if I told her.

When I don't respond, she takes the hint.

Finally, our food arrives so I can dig in. Thankfully, Brett, the waiter, leaves without acknowledging, Lex.

Lex is pissed and she is taking out her frustration on her pancake.

"What did that pancake ever do to you?" I ask, looking for a death wish.

She ignores me like I never even spoke to her.

When Brett comes back with the bill, we both reach for it. Luckily, I snatch it up first.

Lex scowls but surprisingly doesn't argue.

I pull out my card and place it with the check.

As we are waiting for Brett to come back, we get an unexpected visitor.

"Harper! Man what's up?" Farris greets as he walks up. When his eyes shift to Lex, I know immediately that I would probably end up punching my partner. "And who is the pretty lady?"

Sighing, I introduce them. "Farris this is Alexis, Alexis, Farris."

He holds out his hand for her and she shakes it. "Nice to meet you," she says in a sweet sounding voice I don't think I have ever heard. It's probably because I usually either piss her off or make her cry.

Farris grabs a chair from a nearby table and sits down with us. "Harper, last night was so much fun. We should go again sometime. Alisha was bummed that you left."

I really shouldn't be having this conversation in front of Lex. She is already mad at me enough as it is.

Alisha must have been the girl I was dancing with.

"You can dance too, brother. I'm going to be honest and tell you that I didn't think you had it in you," Farris continues.

My eyes shift to Lex and I know she is putting all of the pieces together.

"Why didn't you tell us that you left? How in the world did you even get home?" What is he playing at? He knows Lex came and picked me up. Unless he was too drunk at the time to remember.

I look back at Farris. "I don't really remember much." I'm actually being quite honest. I remember bits and pieces of last night. I remember dancing with Alisha, talking with Lex, and explaining to Farris that she was coming to get me, but after that everything kind of goes fuzzy. I don't see how Farris likes to go out as much as he does.

Out of the corner of my eye, I see Lex's shoulders slump. She abruptly stands and says, "I'm going to the bathroom."

As she is walking away, I catch Farris staring at her ass. I deliver a hard punch to his arm to knock him out of his trance.

He curses under his breath as he rubs his arm. "I take it she is the girl who has you so wound up?"

I want to lie, but he will see straight through it. "Yeah," I grumble.

Farris whistles. "She sure is pretty. No wonder you can't stay away."

Pretty has nothing to do with it. It's the way she carries herself.

"I'm surprised to see you out and about so early," I mutter, changing the subject.

"Yeah, well she kind of kicked me out this morning."

I tried not to laugh, but I couldn't hold it in. "Ouch, Farris. Did the door hit you on the way out?"

"It was either that or get shot by her boyfriend. Personally, I would rather the door hit me than a bullet."

"Really, Farris?"

He holds his hands up innocently. "I swear I did not know until she was rushing me out the door."

I look over in the direction of the bathrooms to see if Lex is on her way back yet. I don't spot her at first, but when I do, I slam my hand down on the wooden table and abruptly stand, almost knocking over my chair.

Oh hell no, I thought the douche, Brett got the hint. I guess he didn't. So now it's time to remind him.

As I walk away from the table, I hear Farris say, "Oh shit."

"Oh shit," is right. I know she isn't *mine*, but I am still going to protect her.

Neither of them notices me until I am standing right next to them. I want to throw my arm around her to stake my claim, but I can't, so I keep it tucked to my side.

"Lex, we need to go. Also, don't you need to call your boyfriend?" I just pulled a dick move, yet I could care less.

Lex gives me her usual scowl while Brett doesn't seem fazed. This asshole is ruining the good morning I was having.

Lex gives him a small wave then steps away. I glare at him as I imagine pinning him against the wall and letting him know just what I think about him. Instead of doing what I figure would be fun, I continue to stare at him angrily. "Stay away from her," I warn him.

The guy scoffs. "Yeah, okay, and what is the big bad brother going to do about it?" he mocks, pissing me off more.

I step closer to the guy, fisting my hands at my sides. I am so close to punching him. "Not big brother, not even remotely close.

I'm going to say it again, and you better listen to me. Stay away from her or I will throw your ass in jail."

When the guys' eyes widen a fraction, I know I hit a nerve. I bet this guy has been arrested before. Either that or he is doing or has done something illegal.

He regains his unprovoked expression. "For what? I haven't done anything except talk to a pretty girl. Besides you aren't even a cop."

I fish out my badge from my wallet to prove him otherwise. I hold it to where he can see it. "You see, that is where you are wrong. I could slap sexual harassment on your ass. Or maybe I could dig further and find out what you are really doing." I take a moment to assess him. He is skinny, as his clothes look a little big for him. "Drugs? Burglary? Oh, the possibilities. You see, it wouldn't take much to catch you snorting or smoking something you shouldn't be. Hell, maybe even catching you having a case of sticky fingers. It would seriously make my day, so go ahead and talk to her. I dare you."

I am practically bullshitting my whole speech. I don't have a clue if he does any of those things or not. His reaction will tell me all I need to know.

As suspected, I see him swallow hard, and I catch him trying to hide his shaking hands.

"You don't know shit," he counters and I literally laugh in his face.

"I know more than you think, Brett." I glance down at his hands again. "Your hands are shaking which means one of two things. Either you are itching to go get high or you are scared shitless right now because I figured you out. I'm guessing it's the latter since you are starting to sweat, judging by the perspiration on your forehead, and the fact you keep swallowing hard."

He is starting to crumble under my scrutiny, I can see it. "Do we have a deal?" My voice is hard, cold.

He nods, gulping again.

"Good."

He scurries off to the kitchen. I turn around and head back to our table to see Farris giving me a nod of approval and Lex pouting.

Farris smiles widely. "Dude, you scared the daylights out of him! What did you say to him?"

"I just told him to stay away from, Lex. I figured out that he has a drug problem and a possible stealing problem."

Lex whips her head over to me. "How?"

"I really didn't know, but I had an inkling from just looking at him. I pretty much just accused him of it, but then his expression changed to shock for like half a second. That's when I knew."

"Damn boy, that's what I am talking about!" Farris exclaims a little too loudly, gaining the attention of others around us.

Lex and I both glare at him. "Oh, my bad," he says quickly, realizing his mistake.

Once the bill is paid-Brett actually came back to the table-I walk Lex out to her car with Farris trailing along behind us.

Once she is in and the car door is closed, I turn to Farris. "See ya tonight?"

"Yeah, have fun with her. She doesn't seem too happy."

Gee, I wonder why? "She will get over it."

I slap his hand in goodbye, then walk around the front of the car.

This afternoon is going to be interesting.

chapter seventeen

Alexis

I am so glad I didn't schedule an early morning class. Even having to get up at eight am is rough for me.

Yesterday, after we left IHOP, Ethan drove to his apartment. He still argued with me about driving home, but I ended up winning and drove myself home. Ethan took my reaction to the waiter all wrong. The guy creeped me out, big time. I am actually glad he came over to save me from him. Brett stopped me as soon as I stepped out of the bathroom like some stalker. Ethan's hurtful words are what made me scowl at him.

Brad called and we talked for about an hour. He seems to really like it at Kentucky so far. He is already making plans to come see me next month. Kaylee's wedding is coming up and thank goodness they planned it before the season starts for Brad and on my off week for football. In less than two months, my best friend will be married. In three months, Ethan will be leaving for Afghanistan. My heart drops at that thought.

Calculus and Biology are going to kill me this semester. I have to keep my grades up or otherwise I am off the squad. *This semester is already starting off well.* As football season is gearing up in the next three weeks, I don't doubt we will be practicing longer.

I'm going to be busy this semester, so busy, I hope it keeps me from thinking about what is going on between Ethan and me. Brad, I have been thinking about, though. I know what I should do, and I am not entirely sure why I keep putting it off. Maybe it's because I don't want to see him hurt.

The plus side of being so busy is I won't be seeing Ethan much, if at all. I will be able to think clearly without him clouding my decisions.

I really need to go see Kaylee and the twins again. I miss those little boogers.

My first two classes of the day are done and out of the way. I scheduled my two toughest-Calculus and Biology- first thing in the morning and back to back on purpose.

It's lunch time, and I am meeting up with Matt and Alice, so we can eat together but I'm running a few minutes later than planned since my last class ran over.

I quickly grab some food and search for them in the cafeteria.

"Alexis!" I hear Matt yell my name so I turn in the direction of his voice and spot him instantly.

I smile at them as I walk over to where they are sitting.

"Hey, guys!" I greet as I sit down.

The smile at me in return. "How were your first two classes?" Alice asks. Of course, she would. Out of the three of us, she has the most brains.

"Oh, you know, boring as ever," I groan as I start digging into my food. "I hate Math and Science."

"Yeah, they can be tough. If you need help, I'm your girl."

I'm sure I will be calling her real soon. "You might be rethinking that statement by the end of the semester," I tell her in utter seriousness.

She smiles at me appreciatively. "Nonsense."

"So how was your weekend?" Matt asks, and I wish he hadn't, though, because now Ethan is front and center in my mind.

"Okay," I mumble.

Matt narrows his eyes. "What happened with, Ethan?"

How did he know it was about Ethan?

I stare at him apprehensively. "Can you read minds or something?"

Matt laughs. "Uh, sorry to disappoint you, but I don't have that power. I'm just good at reading people's expressions. Whenever something happens with Ethan you pout."

"I do not pout!"

Matt gives me the "really?" look.

"Okay, fine, I pout. Sometimes."

"Glad you owned up to it. Now spill. I want details so I can kick his ass."

Rolling my eyes, I tell what happened this weekend. "Well, he drunk dialed me, basically asking me why he couldn't stop thinking about something he wants but can't have. I ended up going to get him and bringing him back to my apartment."

Matt cuts me off. "I'm going to stop you for a second. That is where you messed up. He should have gone to his *own* apartment, not yours, but carry on."

Matt is right, I know he is because I told myself the same thing, I just didn't listen.

"So anyway, he is a sweet drunk, I will tell you that much. The next morning, Brad showed up-"

"Oh, this is going to be interesting," Matt cuts in, earning a smack from Alice, who I thank appreciatively.

"Are you done interrupting me?"

"Maybe," he replies with a wink.

"Anyway, as I was saying before I was so rudely interrupted. Brad showed up, wanting me back-"

"Okay, I'm going to interrupt you again. What do you mean "wanting you back"? I never knew you guys weren't together?!"

This time, Alice joins in. "Yeah, I didn't know either."

"Okay fine, long story short, the night I was at Ethan's after the party, Brad apparently called and Ethan told him what happened. Brad came to my apartment after you left, Matt, and said we needed a break. I agreed, so now, back to my original story. Brad and I talked and he didn't want to leave with us not in a good place so he asked me if I wanted to give us another shot, and I said yes."

I know they want to interrupt me again, so this time, I beat them to it. "Save all questions for the end, otherwise, I will not get to finish the story."

They grumble some response, so I continue. "Brad left and I walked back inside to find Ethan sitting on the couch. He didn't like the fact that we are trying to have a relationship again. We fought about that for a few minutes then I made pancakes in which I burnt the crap out of my hand. We ended up going to get some stuff for the burn, then we went to IHOP and ate, where Ethan ended up going all psycho on the waiter because he was flirting with me. Ethan's partner showed up and started talking about their night out. Apparently, Ethan had plans to go home with some girl until he called me. It has just been a mess."

As soon as I finish they start firing off questions. "Did Brad know Ethan was there?" "Why did you give Brad another shot?" "What was the waiter doing?"

I hold up my hands to stop their relentless questions. "Whoa, whoa, one at a time!"

I try to answer their questions the best I could, but the "Why did you give Brad another shot" question had me stumped.

"Look, Alexis, you have hardly talked about Brad to us. I barely know the guy! It seems he isn't the guy for you," Alice says, catching me off guard.

Then it hits me like a ton of bricks. I *have* to break it off with Brad, even though it's going to hurt him. "He isn't," I whisper, voicing my realization.

"Then why are you with him?"

Sighing, I tell her, "Because I am afraid of hurting him. He is such a sweet and charming guy, Alice. I don't want to break that part of him."

She regards me with a sympathetic look. "Either way, he is going to be hurt, but the kind of hurt is what makes a difference. The longer you string him along, the more hurt he is going to be."

I groan, dropping my head in my hands. Breaking up with Brad has to happen, I know this.

Placing my hands on the table, I push back and stand. "I need to go to Lexington," I say as a way of explanation. I hastily gather my things and take off.

"Be careful!" Matt hollers as I rush off.

I rush back to my apartment and drop all of my books on my unmade bed then run back out. After I make sure my door is locked and secured, I dash back down the steps, only to come to a halt.

I stare at my car in disbelief, trying to conjure up who could slash my tires in the few seconds I ran inside my apartment? I don't know how it's possible?

Still in shock, I reach in my pocket for my phone and fumble it for a second. Luckily, I don't drop it.

I dial Matt's number, praying he isn't in class yet.

When he answers, I sigh in relief. "Matt, I need your help. Can you come to my apartment?"

"Sure thing," he replies without hesitation.

I sit down on the sidewalk as I wait for Matt to arrive. My mind is still reeling about who could have done this.

It takes Matt no time to get here and he notices it right away. "What the hell?"

"I know, I don't understand it either."

Matt crouches down to inspect on of the tires. "This is serious, Alexis. Have you filed a report?"

I shake my head. "No, and I don't want to."

Matt stares at me for a long moment, then stands. "Well, what are you going to do now?"

"I need you to take me downtown. I have a friend who owns a shop that can fix this." Speaking of, I need to call, Adam.

I call Adam and give him the rundown on what has happened to my car. He says he will bring his tow truck over so he can haul it back.

"So much for heading to Lexington," I mutter under my breath.

Matt walks over to me and drapes his arm over my shoulders, side hugging me. "It's going to be okay, Alexis."

chapter eighteen

Alexis

Adam is a lifesaver. He had my car towed and brand new tires put on in no time. Kaylee and the twins happened to be at the shop so while I waited for my car, I was able to catch up with her, and love on her adorable babies, who are also my Godchildren.

I wish I visited her more often than I have been, but with her being newly married, I wanted to give them some space. They did, however, invite me over for dinner tonight, which I gladly accepted, until this very moment.

I am blankly staring at this truck sitting in the driveway in front of me. Adam didn't mention him going to be here tonight.

My forehead rests against the steering wheel as I concentrate on breathing steady. "You can do this. It's just, Ethan," I chasten myself. I give myself another little pep talk before exiting my car.

When I reach their front door, I take a deep breath then ring the doorbell.

Thankfully, it is Adam who opens the door. "Hey! You made it!"

What? Did he not think I would show?

He opens the door wider. "Come on in. You arrived just in time, Alexis. We are all in the kitchen."

I force a smile and follow him through the living room into the kitchen. My nerves skyrocket when I see Ethan holding Jasmine. And, of course, the only empty chair is next to him.

I sigh and walk around and the empty seat, which I wish was on the opposite side of the table.

Ethan doesn't acknowledge me at all, which hurts. But, it's what I want, right?

Kaylee and I instantly talk about how my classes are going for a few minutes. Then, Adam has to go and open his mouth, "Hey, Alexis, I saved those tires for you in case you needed them for evidence."

I shoot him a look telling him to shut up, but it is too late.

Now, Ethan decides to acknowledge my presence. "Evidence for what?"

"Nothing," I say quickly, hoping he will drop the subject, but alas he doesn't.

"Apparently it isn't nothing."

"It's nothing, Ethan, drop it," I repeat firmly. The last thing I need is for Ethan to be involved in another aspect of my life.

Just when I think the conversation is over, Adam opens his mouth again. "Wait, you didn't file a report did you?"

"No," I answer through clenched teeth. "And I'm not going to."

I almost did, but I don't think it will do much good.

Then Kaylee has to put in her two cents. "I agree with Adam, Alexis. You don't need to just drop this."

My fork clatters against the plate when I roughly drop it. "It's not a big deal, okay? Can we just leave it alone? I don't want to talk about it anymore."

I resume eating as Ethan asks about the non-important incident again. "Will one of you please tell me what is going on?"

I alternate pointing my fork between Adam and Kaylee. "Don't you dare," I warn them.

Kaylee stares at me, her eyes full of worry. "Alexis, please," she pleads.

Having enough, I stand up, the force almost knocks over my chair. "What is the point of filing a damn report when nothing is going to come of it?! Excuse me if getting my tires slashed doesn't scare me as much as you think it should!" I throw my napkin down on the table and storm out. I need a breather.

I slam the front door behind me, inhaling the night air. I sit down on the granite steps and tilt my head up toward the sky. Out here, things are peaceful compared to the war raging inside me.

I hear the front door creak open and the sound of it clicking shut. I know who it is by the way the air changes around us. It's tense, thick.

"I'm still not filing a report," I grumble.

He doesn't respond to my statement right away. He sits down next to me on the steps and gazes up at the sky with me.

Right here, at this moment, I want nothing more to be his so he can wrap his arms around me and hold me tight. Too bad all I can do is vision it instead of live it.

I hear him shift, letting me know he is about to address the non-issue I don't want to talk about.

"Lex," he murmurs, and I know it's coming. "Why won't you tell me what is going on?"

I drag my eyes away from the stars above to look in his eyes, which is a mistake on my part because they suck me in. Suddenly I'm lost in the softness of his eyes. I manage to break contact before Ethan notices. Clearing my throat, I find my voice. "Because, like I said, it's not a big deal."

He is becoming agitated because I won't tell him, but it doesn't bother me. It's really none of his business.

Ethan moves to crouch down in front of me. My breath hitches when I notice how close his mouth is to mine. A few inches and his lips will be on mine, something my heart is longing for.

He places his hands on top of mine and draws me in again with his eyes. "Despite what you might think, I *do* care about you, Lex. Your safety matters to me, so yeah, it is a big deal to *me*. Will you please tell me?"

I soften at his words and how sincere he looks. "Fine, but I'm still not filing a report, got it?" He nods so I tell him. "Earlier after lunch with Matt and Alice, I drove home. I was only in my apartment for maybe thirty seconds at most because I just dropped my books off since I wouldn't need them in Lexington. When I went back out all four of my tires had been slashed." His jaw hardens at my words, but I continue anyway. "I don't understand how they managed to do it in a matter of seconds or how I didn't hear it, and it's baffled me all afternoon."

Ethan is quiet, although, his eyes haven't wavered from mine. "And you didn't file a report because?"

I snort. "Because what information would I have? Who could have possibly seen them if they completed the task that fast? The stupid report would be useless. The investigation wouldn't last long enough to find any evidence either so what's the point in going through all of that?" I lower my head, breaking our contact once more.

His eyes search mine for a long, tense moment. "That is completely understandable, Lex, but what I don't understand is why you didn't want me to know." The hurt in his voice is evident, making me suddenly feel awful for keeping it from him.

"Ethan," I sigh. "Can I be honest with you?"

I hear him swallow hard, but he nods anyway.

This may be tough for him to hear, I know, yet it's something I need to say. "I didn't want you to know because you already consume me too much. If I had called you, you would have pressured me into filing a report. And don't say you wouldn't because you would have," I rush out quickly when he opens his mouth to protest. "Look, I don't know how you feel about me, but I know how I feel about you. You need to get your shit together and quit playing games with me. I get so much whiplash from you, it's unreal. One minute you act like you want me, then the next time you see me, it's like a switch has flipped."

He retreats when I go to stand. He is staring at me with an unclear expression.

I walk down the steps and stop right in front of him. "Until you can give me an honest answer, I don't want you to contact me or randomly show up where I am at until you know exactly how you feel about me."

When I am around him, I am so caught up in him, I lose control. This way, he can stay away, giving me the space I need, and not show up and break my heart in the process.

Reaching up on my tip-toes, I place a soft kiss to his cheek. "Bye, Ethan."

I walk to my car without looking back. I hope Ethan listens to me and figures out his feelings.

Then hopefully, we will both be happy in the end.

chapter nineteen

Ethan

"She said that to you?" Cole's eyes bug out like mine almost did that night. Lex has guts to open up like she did, but that is Lex, though.

"I can't say that I blame her," Zack quips, causing me to shoot daggers at him. I thought he was my friend? Isn't he supposed to sympathize with me?

"I agree with Zack, Ethan. You have been back and forth with her too many times. What did you say to her?" Keith inquires.

I shrug one shoulder. "Nothing."

"And why the hell not?" Cole scoffs, hitting me on my shoulder.

I chug the rest of my beer and slam the empty bottle on the counter. I called the guys out tonight for a good time, and yet, we are all discussing the reason for my so-called night out.

"Because, in case you have forgotten, she still has a boyfriend," I grumble, wanting to change the topic.

Keith punches my arm. "Dude, you had the perfect opportunity to tell her how you feel and you blew it."

I did, but she is still someone else's girl, it wouldn't be fair to her or Brad.

"She mentioned she was heading to Lexington," I reply bitterly.

Zack places his hand on my shoulder, giving me a little shake. "So? How do you know she wasn't planning on driving there to break up with the guy?"

His question made me ponder. It is possible that was her plan. I guess I will never know.

I order another beer, hoping this night will get better.

Three hours in, my night is finally looking up. Keith, Cole, and Zack have all found their hook-ups for the night. I lost count of how many beers I have had, but I know it's almost in the double digits.

I search the crowd for a girl of my own, but all I see is Lex. Damn it. I need to get out of here.

I say bye to the guys, then hail a cab to take me home. They were disappointed I didn't stay, but whatever.

Contemplating on what to do when I arrive home to an empty apartment, an idea pops into my head. I am about to regret my next decision. Before I back out, I pull out my phone and dial her number.

"Ethan!" Kate shrieks when she answers, and I cringe.

"Hey, Kate." *I shouldn't do this, I shouldn't do this.*

"I just knew you would call me, baby."

Skipping conversation, I ask her to meet me at my place then hang up.

At least I will get some relief tonight, even though she is on the verge of crazy at times.

True to my word, I regretted calling Kate and I think she can tell I don't want her around.

She is dressing-thank goodness-and I walk out of the room without uttering a word. Guilt is clawing at me, but I force it down.

I hear her feet pad along the carpet as she enters the living room. She sits down on the sofa next to me.

"What's wrong, E?" She tries to lean on my shoulder, but I shrink back. Kate appears shocked, but she masks it quickly.

"Nothing, Kate." My words are short, clipped.

Kate huffs then gets up and gathers her keys and phone. *Good, she gets the hint.*

"Why did you invite me here, Ethan?"

Because I was trying to fill the void in my chest, that is the size of Texas. Funny thing, Kate only filled it for a few minutes. Tonight was a mistake, a stupid one on my part.

"I made a mistake calling you, Kate," I tell her, my tone bitter.

She gasps, no doubt appalled. Kate is fuming. "Tonight was not a mistake. You called me for a reason, Ethan, and I know it is because you miss me."

Huh? Miss her? Yeah, right. I snort, earning a glare from Kate. "You are out of your mind if you think that is why I called you."

Kate throws her hands in the air, not happy with my response. "I can't think of anything else!"

I shoot off the couch and march over to where she is standing by the door. "The only reason I called you tonight was so you can fill the void in my chest, nothing more, nothing less. It was definitely a moment of weakness and stupidity on my part." My words are harsh and my tone is gruff. Kate doesn't understand you if you talk all nice to her, and most of the time, she doesn't get anything you say, mean or not.

"Why her, Ethan? Why not me?" she whimpers like a little puppy. She even goes as far as giving me the sad eyes. Kate can act, I give her that.

"Easy, I don't want you, not like I want her. I don't see you in that way, Kate."

She flinches like I slapped her. I am totally unprepared for her hand connecting with my cheek, but I deserve it.

Kate wanted the truth, well, she got it. She marches out the door in tears, slamming it behind her. Good riddance.

I shuffle to the shower and get the water as hot as I can handle it. I scrub every inch of my body to rid it of Kate's perfume and all the places she touched me.

Resting my head on the tile, I release a frustrated breath. Alexis talks about me needing to get my shit together, yet, she needs to choose between Brad and me. She is just as confused as I am, it seems.

Stepping out of the scorching hot shower, I towel dry my body before throwing on some boxers and falling onto my bed.

I need to be well rested for my shift tomorrow night.

Too bad when I close my eyes all I see is Lex breaking down in front of me, all because I called the one girl who could drive the wedge the rest of the way between us for good.

I breathe as I push through my reps during my workout. Nickelback is blasting in my ears, motivating me. As of right now, I bench press two hundred-seventy-five pounds, and I am working on three hundred.

Farris should have been here by now. Really, he should have beat me here. I sent him a text asking him where in the hell he is at, and so far he hasn't responded.

I place the bar on the rack and sit up, my face drenched in sweat. I left my damn towel at home by mistake so I guess I will just borrow one from the gym and use it until I leave. Standing from the weight bench, I squirt some water down my throat as I head toward the storage closet to retrieve a towel.

My phone buzzes in my pocket as I turn down the hallway. It's Kate…again. What am I going to have to do for her to get the picture? *Maybe you shouldn't have called her last night, dumbass.*

I ignore her text and open the storage closet door only to shut it back instantly.

"Damn it, Farris!"

Just what I wanted to see, Farris's naked ass.

I can hear him laughing through the door. Bastard.

I lean up against the door, waiting until he is done with his little adventure.

It wasn't five minutes later when the door opens and they walk out with no shame on their faces. Farris is on the verge of laughing again by the way he is smiling.

I glower my eyes at him. "Dude, what the hell?!"

Farris holds his hands up. "What? It's exercising!"

I shake my head and against my better judgment, step inside the storage closet and snatch a towel off the rack.

"That was not the kind of exercising I had in mind when I invited you to my work out."

Farris smiles slyly. "Technically, it is considered a workout."

Farris says goodbye to the girl in typical Farris fashion, which is tongue in mouth and hands on the girl's ass.

She walks away, swaying her hips purposely.

I give Farris a hard look once more and head back to finish my workout before work.

"Harper, how can you say no when it is offered to you?" he asks in a drop dead serious tone.

"I worry about you, Farris."

Thankfully, I don't have to hear Farris talk about his closet adventure for the rest of time we are at the gym.

So far tonight has been relatively slow and it's only nine o'clock. Tonight is going to be long and dull. Especially, if Farris doesn't close his trap about that girl he hooked up with earlier. I thought he was done talking about her when we were back at the gym.

The radio crackles, gaining my attention. The dispatcher reports a break-in at Hampton Drive Apartments. *Shit, that's Lex's apartment complex. B 10, Lex's apartment.*

"Farris step on it," I bark out.

"Dude, chill out, I am." He flips on the lights and speeds through the traffic.

Why do we have to be on the other side of town?

I sincerely hope Lex isn't there while all of this is going down.

Feeling worried, I yell, "Drive faster, Farris!" as he weaves in and out of traffic.

"Harper, I am already doing ninety!"

Finally, almost ten minutes later, Farris pulls to a stop in the parking lot of the complex. I jump out and run up the stairs. When I reach Lex's apartment, I pull my gun out of the holster and aim it inside. Hell, this place is a mess. The door has been kicked in and everything is in shreds, pieces, and piles on the floor. Nothing looks to be still standing.

I clear each room in her small, one-bedroom apartment before walking back onto the balcony.

"Anyone home?" Farris asks me when I walk back out.

I walk over to the rail and look down at all the cars parked. I sigh in relief when I don't see her car.

"No, she's not here. Thank God," I breathe.

Farris looks surprised. "You know who lives here?"

"Yeah, this is Lex's apartment."

His jaw drops. "No way! No wonder you were rushing me! Well, where is she?"

I rack my brain, trying to remember what she does on Monday nights.

Then it hits me. "Cheer practice. We need to get her."

We turn and walk down the stairs just as another squad car pulls up.

We fill him in on what we know and he heads up to search for clues.

I drive the short distance to the Western Kentucky University gym, parking right next to Lex's car.

The side entrance is locked, but lights are on everywhere so this has to be where they enter. When I hear music start up, I know I have the right door.

I bang on the door loud enough for someone to hear. A woman peeks around the corner, then straightens, and walks toward us. She opens the door and lets us inside, locking it behind us. Good to know they take safety precautions.

"What can I do for you gentlemen?" the middle-aged lady asks.

"I'm officer Harper and this is officer Farris. We need to see Alexis Collins, ma'am," I tell her.

Her expression turns to confusion. "May I ask what for? She isn't in some sort of trouble is she?"

I shake my head, assuring her. "No ma'am, her apartment was broken into not long ago."

"Oh dear. Okay, right this way. My name is Mrs. Hamilton by the way."

The hallway takes us right to the court. They are in the middle of a routine, with Lex looking like she is about to be lifted into the air by Matt when the music is cut.

I see Matt whisper into her ear. I don't know what he says, but whatever it was it earns him an elbow to the gut.

I can see the fear in Lex's eyes. She knows we are here for her.

Mrs. Hamilton calls out her name and I see Lex momentarily freeze. She seems hesitant but steps forward anyway. Farris and I follow behind Lex and Mrs. Hamilton, disappearing around the corner into the hallway.

We stop just outside the office Mrs. Hamilton came out of earlier. She turns to Alexis. "Sweetie, these gentlemen need to talk to you. If you can't make Wednesday's practice I will understand."

Lex looks at me with so much fear that it makes me want to pull her into my arms and comfort her.

I gaze at her with sympathy. "Lex, someone broke into your apartment. It's completely trashed."

Lex takes the news the opposite of what I was expecting. She doesn't burst into tears I like assumed, she becomes pissed and takes off. I have to run to catch up with her.

I jump in her car with her just in time before she takes off.

Tonight is starting off just peachy.

chapter twenty

Alexis

Cheer practice is going great. I have the routines down, the cheers mastered, and Matt, who is my lifting partner, and I have perfected our stunts. Jenna and I are sort of getting along, and by that I mean, I want to gouge her eyes out with a fork. She gets on my everlasting nerve. It's obvious she doesn't like me. I'm not entirely sure why either. Maybe it's because I don't take any of her crap. Yeah, that could be it. I don't fear her like most of these girls do. No, I stand up to her.

Jenna watches me closely as we perform a routine. I know she is just trying to point out a missed step or something. She's just waiting for me to screw up so she can bring it to everyone's attention. Too bad I know the routine like the back of my hand.

We are in the middle of one our dance routines when the music is suddenly cut. I was in the middle of being lifted in the air. Luckily, Matt catches me and sets me on my feet.

All the air leaves my lungs when I see Ethan standing next to Mrs. Jenny with Farris standing beside him. Oh no, this can't be good. I hope nothing is seriously wrong. It's the only reason I think he'd be here. Ethan wouldn't just crash practice just to see me. No, he'd be waiting by my car. After I told him to stay away, I know he wouldn't show up without a real reason.

"Well, look who it is, Mr. Hot Stuff has come for you, Alexis. And he looks mighty fine in that uniform, too," Matt murmurs in my ear.

He grunts when I elbow him in the gut, but he is right. Ethan looks good in his uniform.

When Mrs. Jenny looks at me, my fear is confirmed. "Alexis, dear, I need to see you for a moment, please."

Great, now everyone is going to think I'm getting arrested.

Matt pats my shoulder as I walk toward the guy who makes me want to bang his head into a wall so I can knock some sense into him.

As I pass Jenna, I see a satisfied grin on her face. She will probably spread a rumor around about me know. It's cool, though, rumors don't bother me like they do most people. I just smile and go on with my life. I have no time for drama nor do I want to be a part of it.

I swear you can hear a pin drop as all four of us walk off the court. Mrs. Jenny and I are in front with Ethan and Farris behind us.

When we are out of earshot from the group, Mrs. Jenny stops walking and turns to me. "Sweetie, these gentlemen need to talk to you. If you can't make Wednesday's practice I will understand."

What in the world is going on? I don't like the way she is talking to me.

I look at Ethan, confused, and now a little frightened.

"Lex, someone broke into your apartment. It's completely trashed," Ethan gazes at me sympathetically.

Okay, this is not as bad as I was beginning to think. Still, someone broke into my apartment, and probably took most of my possessions.

Brushing past them, I head to my locker to grab my gym bag which has my keys and all inside. Snatching it up, I run out of the locker room into the hallway, not stopping as I run toward the exit.

I hear Ethan curse behind me. "Lex, wait up!"

Ignoring him, I continue to run to my car. I quickly toss my bag in the backseat after grabbing my keys from the side pocket. I slide in at the same time Ethan slides in the passenger seat.

"What do you think you're doing?" I ground out. The more I think about the break in, the more pissed I get. Having Ethan around is not helping either.

Ethan gives me a pointed look. "Did you seriously think I was going to let you go alone? Hell no. What if the perp is still around the vicinity?"

Rolling my eyes, I turn onto the highway toward my apartment complex. I almost walked to school today, but I had errands I needed to run before practice.

A minute later, I am parking my car in my normal spot. I jump out of my car, slamming the door and run up the stairs to my apparently trashed apartment.

"Dammit, Lex! You can't just walk in alone!" Ethan barks out as he runs to catch up to me.

I ignore him again. I am a woman on a mission at the moment.

My door was wide open, displaying the mess the intruder made. An officer is inside, surveying the damage, searching for evidence.

"Wait, right here. Let me go talk to Bryan right quick."

I stand at the door as Ethan wades through the mess, making his way to Bryan.

Ethan was right, my home is trashed. My furniture is turned upside down, my belongings are everywhere. Whoever it was clearly had been here a while to make this big of a mess.

Ethan finally tells me I can come in. I would have walked in despite what he said just to piss him off, but I didn't want to mess with an investigation if they were even doing one. I don't see the point, it's not like they will be able to find the suspect. Just like my tires, the case will just be another unsolved mystery.

I step through the mess over to Ethan.

"I need you look to see if anything is missing." He is in full police mode now. Strong and determined.

Sighing heavily, I take a look around. "I really don't think I'm going to be able to tell if something's been taken with it like this. Now, once I get to cleaning, I can probably point what was stolen."

Ethan is about to reply when Farris interrupts him to inform him he is going to ask the neighbors if they seen or heard anything.

I don't think that will help either, but whatever.

"Just humor me, please," Ethan says, acknowledging me, then turns and walks off.

Rather than acting on the thought of slapping him across his perfect, handsome face, I glance around the room, wondering where to start.

Heading into the kitchen to get trash bags, I stop mid-step when I notice the even bigger mess in the kitchen.

"REALLY?!" I yell in frustration. They didn't just trash the kitchen, oh no, that would be too simple. The assholes knocked over my fridge and emptied my cabinets. All of my food is in a heap on the floor.

Ethan and Bryan walk up behind me, I guess they heard me yelling.

Bryan whistles low. "Either this burglar was looking hard for something or just did it because they could."

I turn to Bryan, and in complete seriousness, I ask, "If a miracle happens and you catch this asshole, can I punch them in the face or knee them in their man parts? Better yet, can I take a baseball bat to them?"

Bryan laughs likes he thinks I'm joking. Ethan isn't laughing because he knows I am utterly serious.

Bryan's laughter fades when he sees Ethan and I are dead silent. "Oh, you were actually serious? As much fun as it would be to watch, I can't let you do that."

Bummer, I was looking forward to smashing their face in for wrecking my apartment.

I find the garbage bags over in the corner under the Mountain Dew two liters. Snatching them up, I get to work cleaning up the mess the burglar should be cleaning. Bryan and Ethan go back to what they were doing before I interrupted them. Farris walks back in with the news I expected. They had no leads and no good description of the guy since it is dark. All they could make out was black clothing and what they think was blonde hair.

I'm busying picking up the remains of my belongings when I hear Bryan shout for Ethan and Farris. I drop the garbage bag and follow Ethan, who was in my bathroom, in my room, with Farris right behind me.

Bryan is staring at my bedroom wall with a perplexed look. "Guys, this wasn't a regular break in, this person has it out for you."

Clearly, if the word 'Whore' painted on my wall in red paint was any indication.

Farris and Bryan fire off a round of questions. Who do you think would do this? Do you have any enemies? A crazy ex? Did I piss anyone off?

I hold my hand silencing them. "Guys! Enough questions, please!" I rub my temples, trying to process their gazillion questions. "No, I don't know who would do this. No, I don't have any enemies that I know off or a crazy ex. My boyfriend wouldn't hurt a fly, and as for pissing people off, I do sometimes, but none who would do this."

I'm sure I piss people off daily, but none of them would trash my apartment all to hell and leave an insulting message on my wall.

Ethan stares at me with a confused look on his face. "Lex, how are you not upset about this?"

"I'm pissed off, not upset. There is a difference." Crying would not solve anything. Being mad may not either, however if it did, it just might land me in jail because if I find out who this asshole is, I will make them wish they had turned themselves in. I might be a girl, but I pack a mighty swing with a bat. Oh, and I have been taking lessons on how to shoot a gun. Speaking of guns, where is mine? I run to where my bedside table is toppled over and straighten it. Yanking out the drawers, I empty what little is left inside. When I don't see it, I start searching the area around it, throwing stuff in every direction.

"Lex, what the hell are you looking for?" Ethan grunts as I toss a book in his direction. Okay, I may have done that on purpose.

"My gun," I say like it's normal for me to have one.

"Your gun?" Ethan questions, like it's the scariest thing in the world. "Since when do you have a gun? Better yet, why do you have one in the first place?"

Giving up my search, I straighten and spin around to face the guys. "My daddy thought it would be best if I had one at night in case of an emergency. And yes, I know how to use it. Dad's been teaching me how."

All three guys look like their eyes are about to bug out. Why is it a shock to know that I have a gun and I know how to use it?

"Wipe those looks off your faces boys. Shock doesn't make any of you look attractive." I smile and wink at them as I walk passed them.

My father isn't going to be pissed that my gun is gone because I'm not going to tell him about the break-in. The moment I tell my parents they will force me to move back in with them and lock me in my room. They are loving and protective, but sometimes they are over protective. I know they love me, but there is no reason to make them worry.

I go back to the living room to resume my cleaning. Everything in my apartment is destroyed. Papers? In shreds on the floor. Furniture? On their backs, their sides, or broken. TV? Well, the screen is in pieces in the floor. Everything is either broken or shattered in the floor.

I need a cigarette and I don't even smoke.

All three guys walk back into the living room. Ethan says goodbye to Bryan. I shake his hand and he tells me if he has any information he will notify me. I seriously doubt he will find out more than what he already knows, but maybe we will get lucky.

"Lex, have you called your parents yet?" Ethan asks.

"No, I have not and I don't plan to."

Pinching the bridge of his nose, Ethan questions my decision, "Don't you think they need to know?"

I shake my head, wondering why it's such a big deal to him. If I don't want to tell them then it's my decision, not his. "I'm sorry, but I don't want to be locked in my room for the rest of my life because they are too afraid to let me out."

Ethan curses under his breath. Good, I get on his nerves about as much as he does mine. "Have you at least figured out where you are staying tonight?"

No, I haven't, but Ethan isn't going to want that for an answer.

"I'm working on it," I lie. I figure I can stay with Matt or Alice. I don't want to intrude on Adam and Kaylee.

"You need to be figuring it out. This isn't a game, Lex, this is your life!" Ethan yells, like I'm a five-year-old needing scolding.

"Yes, it's MY life! I will go where I want to and do what I want to do. You have no right to order me around. Just because your sister is my best friend doesn't give you that right!" And just because you're hot and you look good in that uniform doesn't count either.

Ethan softens a little though he doesn't show any remorse. "I don't do it because you're Kaylee's best friend."

I fold my arms across my chest. "Then why?"

He opens his mouth opens, then closes abruptly, not saying what he was about to. I probably don't want to know what he was about to say.

"If you need a place to stay, call me."

Ethan walks out of my apartment without uttering another word.

Farris looks uncomfortable as his eyes shift between the door and me. He clears his throat. "Have a good day, ma'am."

"Bye, Farris."

The door clicks closed and I'm left alone with a messy apartment. I guess I better get to work.

chapter twenty-one

Alexis

I manage to get my door to close. It won't stay, I know, but at least it prevents people who are walking by from staring. People are so nosy. It has taken me three hours to get the kitchen picked up and cleaned. One room down, three to go. This is going to be a long night.

Before it gets any later, I call and order a pizza. My stomach is growling though I am trying to get as much as I can clean. Tomorrow, I will talk with the landlord about when my new door will arrive. He came by earlier to inspect the mess. Although, he claims he is going to do a little investigating himself, I doubt he will be able to figure who the person responsible is.

I also need to go buy groceries since my cabinets have been wiped out along with the fridge. I'm going to either need a shot of something strong or tons of coffee to help me get through this night.

A light knock on the door startles me. I wade through the mess and peek through the peephole.

I open the door to Matt holding coffee in one hand and Chinese takeout in the other. "Oh my god, I love you!"

He smiles as he steps inside. "Figured you need this. Mrs. Jenny told me what happened." He whistles as he takes a glance at the giant mess.

I fix the door back like I had it, then follow Matt in the kitchen. "You're a lifesaver, you know that?"

Matt smirks as he empties his hands, placing the food on the now clear table. "Just remember that when I cash in. So, where is the hot cop?"

I shoot him a glare. "I don't want to talk about him. All I want to do is stuff my face with this delicious food and get wired up on coffee so I have enough energy to finish cleaning."

"Well, let's get started."

The pizza I forgot I ordered arrives a few minutes later. I stick it in the fridge for later.

Matt and I scarf down our food and chat for a few minutes before he leaves me to my coffee and cleaning. I turn on some music to help keep me awake.

Since the kitchen is done, I move on to the living room. I have no idea what I am going to do with my broken furniture. I guess replacing it is another errand to add to my list.

One of my favorite songs starts playing so I move to the beat, picking up as I move. I dance my way to the closet in my bedroom to retrieve the vacuum.

In no time, I have the living room clean, except for my furniture mess which needs to be trashed.

It is going on two in the morning when I hear another knock on the door. This time, it's Ethan.

He gives me a tight smile and walks inside my halfway cleaned apartment. "Wow, you've really been working."

"Somebody's gotta do it," I retort.

Ethan chuckles. "Your new door will be here around nine."

"How do you know that? *I* wasn't given the information!"

Ethan places his hands on my shoulders. My stomach flutters from his touch alone. "Relax, Lex. I called your landlord and asked."

Why couldn't the man tell me earlier?

"I came to see if you wanted to take a coffee break. Want to ride with me?"

Coffee with Ethan? Should I? Is it a good idea? "I didn't know you drink coffee."

His lips curl into a smile. "There is a lot you don't know about me. What do you say? Are you up for some coffee?"

Needing a break and another round of coffee to help me stay away, I agree to go with him.

"How did you know I'd still be up?" I ask him once we are settled in my car. "And how did you get here?"

"Farris dropped me off. He is meeting us there. And I didn't know if you were up or not. Not until I saw the lights on."

"Were you that confident I would go with you?"

Ethan laughs. "I didn't know what your answer would be. I was just hoping you would agree."

"And if I didn't?" I challenge him.

"I would have called Farris and made him turn around."

He must have thought this through.

The smell of coffee greets me as I walk inside Starbucks. I inhale the mouthwatering scent, instantly relaxing.

I order a double shot espresso, hoping it keeps me awake for a while. I pull out my wallet to pay, but Ethan intercepts, adding his order to mine and pays for both. Normally, I would argue, but I am too exhausted.

"Thank you."

"You are more than welcome, Lex."

I find Farris sitting at a table near the window. "Hey, Farris," I greet as I sit down.

His smile is bright as usual. "Alexis, nice to see you again. How is the cleaning going?"

I groan. "It's going."

"How much do you have left?" Ethan asks.

"Just the bathroom and my bedroom."

He nods and takes a sip of his coffee.

"How do you guys stay awake all night? I am exhausted!"

They laugh at me, but I am being serious. They don't seem tired at all and here I feel like I am about to fall over.

"It's not easy, especially on slow nights," Farris answers. "But, I have been doing this longer than he has."

"You get used to it eventually."

I take a large sip of my drink then fold my arms and rest them on the table, along with my head. I close my eyes, resting only for a minute.

I feel a hand brush my hair back. It has to be Ethan. The touch feels too intimate to be Farris.

"Lex, why don't you go sleep at my apartment? You can finish cleaning tomorrow." Ethan offers.

"I can't," I mumble. "I have class to attend, along with furniture and groceries to buy."

"What time are your classes?"

It takes me a second for my tired brain to think. "Ten, eleven-fifteen, and two."

"And when were you planning to sleep?" Farris asks, sarcasm lacing his words.

I don't think I factored sleep in when I planned all of this.

"Just come back to my apartment and sleep, Lex. I won't be in until around eight, but I will make sure you are up in time for class."

I mutter some kind of response to him.

Sleep, I need lots of it.

Ethan

"Dude, she is out." Farris laughs as Lex softly snores. "One look at her and you could tell she was exhausted."

I continue to run my hand over her hair, preventing it from falling in front of her eyes. "I'm going to drop her off at my place before we go back on patrol."

Farris nods and starts clearing the table while I lift Lex into my arms.

I carry her to her car and place her inside. I make sure I buckle her before climbing in the driver's seat.

The drive is short since we aren't but a couple miles from my apartment. I try not to wake her when I transfer her from her car to my bed.

She stirs and stretches when I lay her down. Thankfully, she doesn't wake.

I pull the comforter up to her chin and drop a kiss to her forehead before backing away.

Farris shakes his head as we walk out into the night. "You have it so bad," he teases.

I don't deny it because I know the pull she has on me is strong.

"Do you think she will still be there when you come back?" Farris asks the question which is currently swimming in mind.

It's a tossup, really. If she wakes before I get back, I have no doubt she will leave. On the other hand, the cards will be in my favor if she is still asleep when I return.

"I guess we'll see, won't we?"

Farris laughs. "I bet you fifty bucks she will still be there. She won't be asleep, though."

I scoff at his absurd bet. "And what makes you think she won't bolt the moment she wakes?"

Farris shrugs a shoulder, not revealing his reasoning. "Scared, Harper? How about I raise the stakes? A hundred dollars."

"Fine, a hundred bucks. I still say she will leave." Lex didn't even want to stay at my apartment in the first place. What makes him think she will stay?

Farris winks. "Trust me, man. I know women."

A call comes through from the dispatcher, ending our conversation.

I hope tonight flies by. The image of Lex in my bed has me thinking things I shouldn't. Nothing I do will drive away my attraction her. If anything, I fall harder for her.

Lex and I both have things to sort through. I can only hope this ends with both of us happy...together.

chapter twenty-two

Ethan

The moment my shift is over, I rush out of the station. Farris is laughing behind me, but I could care less.

Will she be happy to see me? *If she's even there...*

I breathe a sigh of relief when I see her car is still parked in the same spot. I trek up the flight of stairs, wondering what I will find when I open the door.

I pause outside, taking a much-needed breath before I turn the knob and walk inside.

What the fuck? I surely didn't expect to see Kate sitting on my couch. How did I not see her car? *Because you were too focused on Lex.*

I don't address Kate until I check my room for Lex. To my relief, she is still sound asleep.

"What the hell are doing here, Kate?" I ask, venom dripping from my words.

She stands and saunters over to me. "I came to see you, silly. However, I am surprised *she* is in your bed."

I pinch the bridge of my nose. "How did you get in here?"

"You gave me a key, remember?" She reaches out to touch me, but I intercept, grabbing her wrists.

I forgot I gave her my spare key when we started seeing each other frequently. "Give me back my key and get the hell out."

She frowns, sticking her bottom lip out. "E, why are you treating me like this?"

"You know why, Kate, so don't act stupid. It's not attractive at all."

Kate stomps her foot like a toddler. "You are just going to throw me out like trash?!"

"That's what you are." I don't condone being mean to women, but Kate has pushed me too far.

She tries to make a pass at me again. I block her next advances just like the first two times. "Can we hook up for old times' sake?"

"No. Get out."

She huffs and finally leaves.

My phone buzzes in my pocket as she slams the front door.

It's Farris.

Farris: **Where's my hundred bucks?**

Me: **She's still sleeping.**

Farris: **Damn! I was looking forward to taking your money.**

Me: **Better luck next time.**

I pocket my phone and open my bedroom door. Lex is lying on her stomach, the covers kicked off of her. I smile, silently laughing at the sight.

I empty my pockets and start undressing. Maybe I can get a shower in before she wakes.

I rush through my shower, a cold one I might add. I notice she hasn't moved when I walk back in my room with a towel wrapped around me. I quickly throw on some boxers and some jeans. If I had thought about it, I'd have stopped and picked her up some coffee and breakfast on the way home.

Glancing at the time, I notice it's going on eight-forty-five.

I walk over to the side of the bed and sit down on the edge. Like last night, I brush her back from her eyes. "Lex," I murmur. Nothing.

Leaning over, I whisper in her ear. "It's time to get up, beautiful."

This time, she groans as her arm searches for the comforter. Giving up when she can't find it, she rolls over, facing me.

Man, she is hard to wake up. If she didn't have class, I'd let her sleep.

I shake her gently and she responds by slapping my arm.

I pick up my phone and open up one of my apps. She is going to be pissed at me.

I hold my phone close to her face and press a button.

When the sound of a horn blares, she screams and shoots up in the bed, her arms flying.

I couldn't help but laugh. Setting my phone down, I take in her appearance. Her breathing is heavy, her hair disheveled and she still looks amazing.

She looks to me and if looks could kill, I'd be dead. "Why'd you do that?!"

"I'm sorry, but you weren't waking up and it's going on nine."

She huffs and climbs out of bed. "I hate you!"

Lex glares at me as she walks across the hall to the bathroom. I take the time to make a pot of coffee for us. It's going to be a long day for me.

I can feel Lex's stare burning into my back. "Like what you see?" I smirk over my shoulder.

When the coffee is ready, I pour us both a cup in cups to go. I turn around to find Lex's cheeks flushed. Her hair is now fixed and pulled back.

"Thank you, for the coffee, and letting me stay," she murmurs when I hand over her cup.

"It's not a problem. Let me finish getting dressed and I will meet you at your place."

Her expression morphs into confusion. "Why do you need to go to my apartment?"

"I need to make sure your new door is put in and I'm going to finish cleaning your apartment for you."

"Ethan, you don't need to do that."

"I know, but I want to. Besides, I will have plenty of help so we can knock it out quick." I sent a text to the guys asking if they could come help me early this morning. All three of them give me shit, but said they could help.

"Okay." Wow, I figured she'd put up more of a fight.

"Also, give me a list of what furniture you want to replace and we'll go get it."

She sighs and rubs her temples. "Ethan, I'll settle for letting you finish cleaning, but I draw the line with the furniture. When will you get to sleep? Come on, you just worked all night?"

"Don't worry about me. We need to go if you are going to make your class on time."

"Fine."

After making sure she has everything, we leave my apartment.

When we arrive at Lex's place, her new door is being installed. While Lex is getting ready, the guys arrive.

"Good lord, somebody did a number in here," Cole says, taking in the room.

Keith follows behind him. "Yep, we have our work cut out for us."

I had given them a rundown of what happened when I messaged them.

Zack assesses the damage. "Not as bad as you originally described."

"That's because she cleaned most of it last night. All we have to do is take out the broken furniture and clean her bedroom and bathroom."

Lex hops in the room while trying to put her sock on her foot. Her backpack falls off her shoulder on the floor.

"Thank you guys for doing this for me. My second class lets out at twelve-thirty so I will pick you up something to eat. I think there still might be something to drink in the fridge that isn't destroyed." Lex runs around her apartment grabbing things, looking stressed.

I grab her, stopping her. "Lex, don't worry about us. Relax, we got this." Her shoulders slump. "Go to class. I will text you if we need anything."

She gives me a tight smile, straightening her shoulders. "Okay, I'm going."

I let go of her arms and she spins around to pick up her backpack.

Cole smirks. "Leave it to us, princess, we are pros."

Lex cracks a smile.

"Go learn something, shorty." Keith only calls her shorty because she is the shortest of the four of us.

"You guys are the best." Lex flashes me a smile before waving at the guys and walking out the door.

I don't realize I am staring at the door until Zack shoves me. "Dude, you are so in love with her!"

"Am not. I'll admit I *really* like her, but I don't love her."

He shakes his head in disapproval. "Whatever you say."

Needing a change of subject, I ask, "Can we get started? One of you grab the other end of the TV."

And so our day of cleaning has started. I pondered Zack's words for most of the morning. I really liked, Lex, but I knew my military career would keep us apart. Would she stay while I was gone all those months? What if we get into a relationship and she decides she couldn't handle it? More importantly, I couldn't risk hurting her if something happened to *me*.

By the time lunch rolls around, we had all the broken stuff taken out and her bedroom almost cleaned. Cole cleaned her bathroom in no time since it wasn't very big while we started on her room.

My phone buzzes in my pocket.

Lex: **What are you guys hungry for?**

Me: **We aren't picky.**

Lex: **Okay then, I will just run by Taco Bell and get the big boxes of tacos. Drinks?**

Me: **Just pick something.**

I pocket my phone and holler at the guys. "Hey, Lex will be here soon with food!"

I shake my head when I hear appreciated responses from the guys.

As soon as Lex arrives with the food, the guys surround her. "Back off or I will eat all of these by myself!"

Cole, Zack, and Keith look at one another, shocked by Lex's comment. I, however, laugh and take the food from her.

I'm happy she doesn't take their shit.

chapter twenty-three

Ethan

It's been a whole month since I've seen, Lex. With her school and practice schedule, she has been swamped, according to Kaylee. On the bright side, I finally finished restoring my car. This car turned out to be everything I wanted it to be. She looks and runs like a dream. When I first bought the car, it was in really rough shape, but I couldn't pass up the opportunity. Dad told me when I was younger that when I got older, we would restore a car together. I was maybe eight at the time. I loved cars as much as he did. After he died and I lost contact with Kaylee, I didn't have the time between the Army and searching for my sister.

But none of it matters now, Kaylee and I are closer than ever and as for losing Dad, I miss him every day, but I know he is watching over Kaylee and me.

Turning the key over, I smile when I hear the rumble of the engine. It feels so good to drive this car again. This beauty finally gets to leave the shop.

Adam called me earlier to ask if I wanted to meet everyone for dinner tonight. Everyone, including Brad. It's going to suck seeing them together, but my need to see Lex overpowers the feelings I get from Brad with her. Either way, I'm already dreading tonight. Maybe, just maybe, tonight will be fun.

I park my car across the street from the club we are meeting at tonight. Adam's parents are watching the twins so Adam and Kaylee can have a night out. Oh, did I mention I will be the fifth wheel? Kaylee has Adam, her soon to be husband, and Lex is with Brad, leaving me alone. I'm only here so I can spend time with my sister and Adam, and to see, Lex.

I spot everyone seated at a table mid-way in. They all greet me, except the one person I wanted to see.

The seat at the head of the table between Brad and Adam is the only spot open. As soon as I sit down, the waitress comes over takes my drink order.

I catch Brad smiling at Lex, and at that moment, I damn well knew tonight was going to suck.

Seeing Brad with Lex ignites feelings that I don't normally feel with a girl. Each time he looks her way, let's his fingers graze her skin or lean in close to her, I want to march over to him and shove him to the ground. I'm torturing my damn self by watching it all happen. I keep telling myself to look away, but I don't. Maybe I'm waiting on him to slip up so I can jump in and rescue her like some damn knight in shining armor. Or maybe it is so I can catch her occasional glances at me. Her eye flick to mine every now and then, and every time she looks quickly away when she notices me watching her. I watch her body language change when she looks at me, to see her reaction. The first time she caught me, a hint of a smile grew on her face and her cheeks heated. After that, she would either, nervously tuck a strand of hair behind her ear and look away, or she would wring her hands together in her lap.

Right now, she is squirming in her seat, her right hand is rubbing her left arm. I can see the goosebumps across her skin, which tells me one of two things. She is either cold or she is turned on. I personally think it's the latter. Scratch that, I know it is.

Someone taps my shoulder, forcing me to look away from Lex and her captivating beauty. Whoever it is better have a damn good reason for disrupting me.

A tall, perky blonde is all smiles as she waits anxiously for me to acknowledge her presence. There is no question about what she wants, it is written all over her face. I'm genuinely shocked that all she did was tap me on my shoulder. Any other girl would sink their spray-tanned arm around my shoulder or make some upfront comment.

"Can I help you?" I ask in a nicer tone than I wanted.

Her eyes light up, happy that I have given her some attention. "I think it's more along the lines of what can I do for you?" Clearly, she is more brazen than I originally thought.

In my peripherals, I see and hear Lex start choking on her water. A smile itches to form, but I remain unfazed by her less than sexy approach.

The last thing I want is for the girl to believe I am smiling at her.

I can feel Lex's burning intensity against my skin. She's watching, waiting for my answer. I don't want this girl. The girl I really want is pushing her chair back from the table as we speak. Out of the corner of my eye, I see her walk away, heading for the bathroom.

"I'm good," I reply, releasing the coldness I wanted to begin with. Let's hope she gets the hint. Most girls never do, though. Take Kate, for example, she still texts and calls me.

The girl scoffs and replies, "Sucks for you, it's your loss."

As the girl walks away, I stand to go confront, Lex. She needs to know I don't want just any girl, I want *her*.

"I'll be right back," I tell everyone else, then walk away. I pray Brad is not watching which way I am heading.

Lex is walking out of the bathroom when I approach her. I grab her hand and pull her behind me as I walk us away from the crowd. I find a quiet spot in a dark corner and spin her so her back is against the wall. I place my hands against the wall on both sides of her face, caging her in.

"E-Ethan, what are you doing?" she stutters.

She stares up at me, her hands on my chest. "You don't know how much I miss you. No one else compares to you, Lex."

Bringing my hand up, I caress her cheek. She leans into my touch, closing her eyes. "I miss you, too, Ethan." When she opens her eyes, she locks her gaze with mine. "But, we aren't going any further until you tell me why you are holding back."

Stunned, I can only stand there and let her walk away from me. Telling her would change things and the change is what scares me since I don't know if it will be a good or bad change.

Composing myself, I head back to the table, masking my emotions. I can't blame anyone but myself. If I want to tell her, lay my heart out there, but I'm afraid of getting it stomped on.

The rest of the night, she ignores me. I glance at her every now and then to find her looking off somewhere. She looks happy despite our short conversation earlier.

I think Kaylee is catching on to me glancing at Lex because she is scowling at me. I toss back the rest of my drink, then stand. I say my goodbyes then walk away.

They all said goodnight to me, everyone but, Lex. She kept her head down and didn't utter a word to me. I guess I deserve it, but it still hurts.

chapter twenty-four

Alexis

The next couple weeks pass in a blur. Between putting the finishing touches on Kaylee's wedding, school, homework, practice, and games, I've had little sleep. Matt, Alice, and I have been studying together when we can. It helps a lot because I would be falling asleep while writing my essay. I seriously don't know how I'm juggling all of this. The only good thing that has come out of my packed schedule is I haven't had much time to think about, Ethan. I meant what I said that night at the club. I'm tired of getting my heart broken by him. With the way he was looking into my eyes, I knew he was about to kiss me. Then, he would regret it like he always does. As much as I didn't want to stop the kiss, the ache in my heart would be worse.

My arms are pinned above my head, my shirt is bunched up to my chin. Where is Matt? I need him to save me.

"Don't worry, it will all be over soon."

My body is too weak for me to fight him. His hands roam the length of my body. I am repulsed by his touch.

Only this time, no one comes to stop him. This time, he finishes what he started, leaving me feeling used and dirty.

My eyes fly open, my harsh breathing filling the room. Not once since the party have I had a nightmare about Josh. Why now?

Something at the end of the bed catches my eye. A figure. *Josh.* I lean over and flip on the lamp to find nothing. Phew, it was just a hallucination.

I switch the lamp off and lay back down. To my dismay, sleep never comes. I toss and turn for an hour before getting frustrated. Crawling out of bed, I throw on some comfortable clothes. On my way out the door, I grab my backpack and keys. Good thing Starbucks is open all night.

It's one in the morning and I am pulling up at Starbucks with the plan of staying here for a while.

I order my coffee and find a comfy spot to study.

I am deep in Calculus with a voice startles me.

"Lex?"

I gasp and drop my book. Looking up into brown eyes, I try to catch my breath. "Ethan, you scared me."

His eyes glance over my appearance. "You look exhausted, Lex. What are you doing here at four a.m.?"

It's four o'clock already? "I couldn't sleep so I came here to study. I didn't realize I had been here so long." I start packing up my things, dreading going back to my apartment.

"I'll walk you out."

Ethan places his hand on the small of my back as we walk out. When I reach my car I place my bag in the passenger seat and walk around.

"I'll see you around."

"Bye, Lex."

I give him a small wave and slide into my car. I turn my key over and nothing happens. It doesn't crank nor does it make a sound.

Sighing in frustration due to the morning I am already having, I get out of my car.

"Pop your hood," Ethan instructs. I'm glad he hasn't left yet or I would be stranded.

I pop the hood and wait for him to diagnose the problem.

"Your wires are shot." I walk to the front of the car to see what he is talking about. "They have a short in them because they aren't connecting properly."

"Great," I mutter.

He lowers the hood. "Adam can fix it. I don't know how long it will take, though. I'll call him later."

"Okay."

A voice crackles through the scanner in his car. Ethan leans over and listens for the information.

He responds then straightens. "I'm going to drop you off at my place since it's right down the road and on the way."

I quickly grab my backpack and hop in the cruiser with Ethan.

I grab hold of the door as he flies down the highway. I let out a breath when he turns into the parking lot. He parks the car, then hands me a key. "I will be back in a few hours."

"Be careful."

He nods and I climb out of the car.

Knowing Ethan will wait until I am inside safely, I run up the stairs and let myself in.

I drop my bag in the floor by the door and shuffle to his bedroom.

This time, sleep finds me easily. I fall asleep surrounded by the smell of Ethan's cologne.

The smell of bacon greets me the moment I open my eyes. Throwing the covers back, I sit up and rub my eyes.

I check the time and notice it's going on nine. The thought of skipping my first class is sounding really good. I try to remember if I have a test or anything important this morning. I walk into the living room and dig around in my bag for my schedule. No test. *I am definitely skipping this morning.*

The luring smell of coffee has me shuffling to the kitchen.

Ethan turns and smiles at me. "Morning. How did you sleep?"

I slept really well. I didn't have another nightmare. "Good."

I pour myself a cup of steaming coffee, adding a cream and sugar.

"Good grief, Lex. How much sugar are you going to put in there?"

I stop pouring and stir the contents. "It tastes better this way."

Ethan shakes his head. "I called Adam and he will tow your car and fix it. He isn't sure how long it will take, though."

"I guess it's a good thing I live in walking distance from campus."

Ethan sets a plate of mouthwatering food in front of me. "What about practice?"

"I only have practice tonight. Friday we leave for our first away game."

Ethan stops eating. "Where are you going?"

"Bloomington, Indiana. We will be back Sunday, I believe," I say.

He gives me a stiff nod. "Just let me know when you are ready and I will take you to class."

"Actually, I'm not going to my ten o'clock class."

I take the last bite of food, then walk over to the sink to rinse my plate off.

"Oh?"

"Nope, I plan on going back to sleep."

"Do you want me to take you back to your apartment?"

My breath hitches. "No," I say a little too quickly.

Ethan gives me a questioning look. "Is everything okay?"

Clearing my throat, I try to keep my voice normal. "Yeah, things are fine. Why do you ask?"

Ethan shrugs. "Because normally when I suggest that you come to my place you automatically say no."

Crap, I was hoping he wouldn't catch on.

I need to come up with a convincing excuse. "Why would I make you drive out of your way to my apartment?"

"It's not out of my way. Besides, you will need to stop there anyway, right?"

"Not today. I already have my books for those classes," I lie.

"Okay."

Leaving the kitchen, I walk into the living room and plop down on the couch. I grab the blanket off the back of it to cover up with.

Closing my eyes, I try to sleep, but I only end up tossing and turning again.

I start to turn over again when I am lifted in the air.

"What are you doing?" I ask Ethan as he carries me through the apartment.

"You are not sleeping on my couch."

He lays me down in his bed, on the side I woke up on this morning.

"Where will you sleep then?"

He smirks and walks around to the other side and crawls in.

I turn on my side so my back is to him.

I hear him move around, and then I feel him behind me. "Wake me up when you are ready to leave," he rasps in my ear.

I gasp when his arm wraps around my middle. Slowly relaxing, I close my eyes, finding sleep to come easy.

I wind up sleeping through all of my classes. Wrapped in Ethan's arms, I feel comforted, safe. He makes my heart race and relaxes me at the same time. This will not last like I want it to so I am going to make the best of it. In the end, I know I will only break my own heart, but I want to live in this fantasy for as long as I can. A piece of my heart becomes his each time he melts my heart.

His arm is still snug around me, his back pressed against mine.

My phone vibrates on the nightstand. It's probably Matt wondering where I am.

"Hey," I whisper into the phone. I don't want to move out of Ethan's embrace nor do I want to wake him up.

"Why are you whispering and where the hell are you?"

Oh boy, how am I going to explain this to him? "Um, I'm at Ethan's."

"That doesn't explain why you are whispering."

"He's asleep."

Matt grows quiet. I know he has mixed feelings about Ethan with the way he has hurt me in the past. "So you skip class to play house? I don't understand?"

"It's hard to explain," I reason. I haven't even fully explained it to, Ethan.

"I've got loads of time since my bestie stood me up for a hot cop."

I softly laugh, careful not to disturb Ethan. After working all night, I know he needs his sleep.

Slipping out of Ethan's embrace, I tiptoe out of the bedroom.

I relax into the plush couch and begin explaining to Matt how I ended up at Ethan's.

"I woke up from a nightmare about Josh and I started hallucinating. No lie, Matt, I swore I saw him standing at the end of my bed. I tried to go back to sleep, but I couldn't. I end up going to Starbucks around one in the morning. That's where Ethan found me three hours later. I go to leave, but my car wouldn't start, which is why it is currently sitting in the shop. Ethan had a call come in so he couldn't drive me back to my place so I agreed to come here.

"I was so tired from being up almost all night so I decided to skip class. Ethan told me to wake him up when it was time for me to go to class, but Matt, if I leave here…" I pause and swallow hard. "Right now, I am not sure I want to go back to my apartment."

I hear him sigh. "I get it, Alexis. I'm sorry Josh tried to take advantage of you, but you can't let him get to you, understand? You know, I have space for you here at my place."

I smile. "Thanks, Matt. I'll probably take you up on it."

I whip my head around when I hear a noise come from behind me. My eyes grow wide when I see Ethan leaning against the door facing.

"Um, Matt, I will talk to you later." I hang up before Matt can ask why. Matt will be wanting an explanation later.

"I'm sorry for waking you," I murmur as he steps further into the room.

Ethan sits down next to me. On the inside, I am anticipating him making me leave. I don't know what he is about to say, but judging by how quiet he is at the moment, I don't think it will be good.

He brings his eyes up to mine. "Why didn't you tell me the real reason you agreed to stay?"

Swallowing past the lump in my throat, I turn my head, unable to answer him.

He gently grasps my chin, turning my head back so I have to look at him. "Don't be scared to tell me anything, Lex. If something is bothering you, I want to know, okay?"

My breath hitches as Ethan leans forward, kissing the corner of my mouth. He pulls back, letting his thumb brush over my lips. Without a word, he stands and walks out of the room.

I exhale slowly, wondering what is becoming of us. Something is shifting between us and I don't want to stop it.

Ethan walks back in the room and places a key in my palm. "Whenever you feel like you need to, use it. Middle of the night, early in the morning, I don't care. Will you promise me you will use it?"

I glance down at the single silver key in my hand. This is not how I envisioned this talk going. Bringing my eyes up to his, I gaze into his soft brown ones. "I promise," I murmur.

Another piece of my heart just became his.

"Good. Would you like to talk about it?" he asks.

Shaking my head, I bring my knees up to my chest. "There isn't really much to say. I mean, I was shaken from the dream. When I woke up, I saw him there or imagined him there at least."

I stare at the wall in front of me. Josh is the last person I want to think about. I'm having issues with an anonymous person that is trying to make my life hell and it's annoying me that they aren't quitting.

Ethan rises from the couch and holds out his hand. Gingerly, I place my small hand in his large one. He pulls me up and I fall flush against him, my other hand on his bare chest.

His hand comes up to my cheek, his thumb brushing my skin. "Lex, you know I didn't get to be there to stop Riley from hurting my sister, but I can help you. You are important to me."

I am lost in his eyes, my mind screaming for him to kiss me. I want to feel his lips on mine again, only this time, I don't want him to walk away from me.

chapter twenty-five

Alexis

Ethan is whispering sweet nothings in my ear while his hands travel down my sides, stopping when he grasps the backs of my knees. He lifts my legs, one at a time, wrapping them around his waist. My legs instinctively lock around him, inviting him deeper. I let out a small gasp when he does just what I want. I need to feel him, all of him. He flexes his hips in a rhythmic motion, diving deeper with each calculated thrust.

Ethan releases a low growl as my nails rake down his back, my fingers feeling every couture of his muscles.

I manage to open my eyes long enough to gaze into his piercing brown ones. Ethan brings his hand up to my cheek, his thumb padding over my heated skin.

Then, all of a sudden, Ethan's figure morphs into Brad's. Brad is staring down at me, except he doesn't have the same longing look Ethan had. No, he looks hurt.

"It should be me, Alexis."

The words are hung in my throat. Swallowing hard, I am unable to tear my eyes away from him.

"I trusted you. How could you do this to me?"

Do what to him? Oh, Ethan. My heart cracks hearing the pain in his voice.

This is exactly what I didn't want to happen. I don't want Brad to hurt, he doesn't deserve to be heartbroken because he is too good for me.

"You're breaking my heart, Alexis. I love you so much, please, don't do this," he pleas, searing the cracks, opening them further. His voice, an audible whisper.

"I'm so sorry," I murmur.

My eyes fly open and I shoot up in the bed. I'm drenched in sweat and with tears rolling down my cheeks, and with an ache in my chest.

The dream only confirmed what I had feared all along. My feelings for Ethan aren't going anywhere and Brad is going to be hurt. God knows I want Ethan, so bad, yet, I'm so tired of the games his is playing. He either wants me or he doesn't, it's that simple.

Glancing at the clock, I notice it's time for me to get up and get ready for class. I have been staying at Ethan's all week since I am too scared to go back to my own apartment. Ethan is softly snoring beside me so I decide not to wake him. All week we have been spending time together like we are a couple, except without the kissing and all the intimate things.

Adam had my car fixed two days ago so thankfully my impromptu trip isn't a bust.

Instead of heading to class like I should, I head towards Lexington. I can't keep putting it off.

The drive gives me time to figure out how I am going to break it off with him. There is no easy way for it to happen.

I need to let Matt know where I am going so he doesn't freak out when I don't show up for lunch.

Grabbing my phone, I find Matt's contact, then hit the call button.

"My lady," he answers.

I laugh. "Let me guess, English class?"

"Yup. What's up?"

"Um, well, I'm just calling to tell you to not freak out when I don't show up for lunch today."

"Uh oh, what are you getting yourself into?"

"I'm heading to Lexington," I say as a way of explanation.

"Ah, so you're finally breaking the guy's heart. Make sure you let him down easy."

There is no easy way of breaking his heart. No matter how I say it, Brad is going to be hurt.

"I'll do my best. I will be back this afternoon."

"Good luck."

Once I hang up with Matt, I go back to preparing myself. *You have to do this.*

Finding his fraternity wasn't too hard, but I realize that maybe I should have called first instead of dropping in on him. It looks as if they are having a party. Cars are lined up down the street, filling up both sides. I park as close as I can to the frat house.

Exhaling, I climb out of the car and walk the quarter of mile to the house.

The yard is packed full of people. My eyes scan the crowd for Brad, but I come up empty. I spot a guy who is wearing a blue t-shirt with Brad's fraternity symbol on it standing by the entrance to the house. I bet he has some idea where Brad is.

I push through the rest of the crowd, finally making it to the steps.

The guy appraises me as I walk up to him.

"Hi, I'm looking for Brad. Can you tell me where he is?"

The guy stares at me for a moment. "And you are?"

"Alexis, his girlfriend."

He pulls out his phone and dials a number. "Dude, you have a special visitor on the porch." He hangs up, then says, "He'll be right down. I'm Jake by the way."

"Nice to meet you, Jake."

Jake looks out of place here with all his tattoos. I thought only preppy people joined fraternities and sororities?

"Alexis?"

I turn and smile at Brad. "Hey." I give him a small wave.

Once the shock wears off, he walks up and bear hugs me. "Wow, what a surprise. I'm so happy to see you!"

When he pulls away, he surprises me by kissing me.

"I see you've met, Jake?"

I nod. "Yep."

Draping an arm over my shoulders, Brad leads me inside the frat house. The house is as I expected it to look. Sports memorabilia hangs on the walls, covering just about every inch. Surprisingly, the house doesn't look as dirty as I figured it would. Their TV is huge, looks like a seventy inch, if not larger.

Jake yells to the three guys who are standing in the kitchen when we walk in. "Hey guys! Get your asses over here and meet Brad's chick that he can't stop jabbering about!"

Brad shakes his head as I laugh.

They practically run over to us. One of them even jumps the couches that are in his way.

Brad points to each of them and calls off their names. "Alexis, this is Chad, Nate, and James."

Chad looks as preppy as they come. Nate dresses more like a rock star like Jake. James is tricky, I can't figure him out. He dresses casual, like t-shirt and jeans casual.

"Nice to meet you all."

Chad grabs my hand and lifts it to his mouth. "The pleasure is all mine."

Nate pushes him out of the way. "You're prettier in person." He looks up at Brad. "You've got my approval."

James is the last to walk up to me. "What are you doing with, Brad? You should be with me?" He winks, then says to Brad. "I'm just messing with you, man. You've got a hell of a catch."

Brad nuzzles my neck. "I know I do, James. I'm the luckiest guy in the world."

I turn my head to whisper in Brad's ear. "Can we talk?"

He was about to answer me when someone yells, "It's party time!"

Brad looks to me. "Can we talk later?"

Not really. I'd rather get this over with.

Brad is suddenly dragged away from me before I can reply. This is not going how I planned it.

I let Brad go do his thing with promise that we will be talking soon.

Jake throws his arm around my shoulder, leading me further inside the house. "Don't worry, you will get to see him soon enough." Jake pours me a drink then hands me the cup. "Might as well enjoy yourself."

I take a huge swallow of the drink. The beer is nasty, but I continue to drink it regardless.

A couple hours pass without any sign of Brad. I've been hanging around Jake for the sake of some company. Jake seems like a pretty cool guy. I've gotten to know him a little while I wait for Brad to find me. I'm a little leery of parties since the night Ethan came to rescue me. I do not want to wind up in a situation like that again.

I finally find Brad after waiting another hour with Jake.

"Hey, babe. Sorry about that."

I wave him off. "It's okay."

I am about to ask him if we can talk when Jake speaks up. "Hey, Alexis, you ever played beer pong?"

"Once."

Jake hands me a paddle. "Good, I need a partner and your boyfriend sucks at this game."

I arch my brow at Brad. "Really? Then I guess I need to show him how it's played."

A round of cheers erupt around the table as Jake and I step up. Chad and Nate end up being our opponents.

Nate and I are chosen to determine which team goes first. We begin our stare-down or "Eyes" as the rules call it. I keep my eyes locked on Nate's as we both take our shot. Cheers from my end of the table erupt when mine sinks in the cup and Nate's ball hits the edge and bounces off the table.

Jake high fives me. "I knew it was a good idea to pick you!"

Jake takes the first shot and it falls in perfectly. Chad groans and drinks the beer, tossing the cup aside.

Jake lets me take the next shot, which I make.

Our streak ends when Jake misses the next shot.

Chad and Nate are grinning like fools now.

"This is for you, Alexis," Nate says as he takes the shot, landing it in the cup right in front of me.

Sighing, I pick up the cup and drink.

Unfortunately for us, they make the next four shots. I end up drinking three cups total.

With only five cups left compared to their eight, I knew we would have to have a long streak here.

I pull Jake back to plan. "Can I just shoot this time?"

Jake looks at me like I'm crazy, but agrees. He steps to the side so I can do my thing.

Tilting my head, to each side, I loosen the muscles in my neck.

Nate and Chad take one look at me and laugh, but I ignore them.

Turning around so my back is to them, I toss the ball behind me, sinking it in the middle cup.

I waste no time putting my next trick shot in motion. I turn to the side and throw the ball behind my back, watching it land in the cup in front.

I toss the next one effortlessly, hitting the nearest cup.

The crowd around us is loud, yet it doesn't affect my next three shots.

Brad kisses my cheek. "You're amazing!"

"Holy shit!" Jake exclaims when he notices our five cups to their, now, three cups. "Are you sure you've only done this once?"

My answer is to wink at Jake.

"Well played, Alexis, well played!"

Nate is up first and sinks the shot. I toss back the cup, letting the liquid slide down my throat.

The alcohol is flowing through my veins, spreading throughout my body.

Chad throws next. I see the ball heading for the cup closest to me. Right before it lands in the cup, I swipe my hand across, batting it away.

Brad grabs me from behind and swings me around.

Jake is jumping around, high-fiving people around us.

When he settles down, I look at Jake for permission to shoot.

I laugh when he bows before me.

My next shot is an under the leg throw.

They are down to one final cup.

I put up a fade away and Nate tries to block the shot. He swings his hand too soon.

When I make the last shot, Brad scoops me up in his arms, slamming his mouth to mine.

And I kiss him back.

chapter twenty-six

Alexis

I wake up to warmth and an arm around me. *Please, tell me I didn't…*

But I knew I had. My head is pounding and mouth feels like cotton, yet, it doesn't erase the panic.

"I've been waiting so long for this moment," Brad *murmurs in between kissing my neck. "I love you, Alexis."*

I slept with Brad. Oh no! This wasn't supposed to happen!

I slip out from under his arm and start gathering my clothes which are thrown in the floor.

What was I thinking?

I quietly put my clothes on and slip out of his bedroom without waking him.

He's going to be mad when he realizes what I've done, but I can't face him after this. I can't act like everything's okay when it isn't.

The whole point of me coming here was to end our relationship, not to get drunk and have sex. I royally screwed up and made things worse.

My mind is racing as I tiptoe down the stairs. What will I say to him when he calls?

I'm sorry, sleeping with you was a mistake?

"Leaving so soon?"

I halt in my tracks and whip around to see Jake relaxing on the couch. His look is questioning, and I hope he doesn't see right through my actions.

"I, um, I have to go," I stammer, still reeling from waking up in bed with Brad.

"You know, Brad really loves you. You are all he talks about since we met him. Please, don't hurt him."

I swallow the lump in my throat. In the end, Brad will be the one hurt.

I don't know what to say, so I give him a nod and turn around and leave.

The sun is peeking over the horizon as I make my way to my car.

Once I'm in my car, I take a few slow deep breaths, trying to stay calm. Freaking out will not help solve this new problem I created.

Maybe Matt will know what to do.

I start my car and drive away from the frat house before I dial his number.

"You better have a good reason for calling me this early," Matt grumbles when he answers.

"I slept with Brad," I blurt out.

Silence greets me. I think I have successfully succeeded in rendering Matt speechless.

"So, let me get this straight. You drive to Lexington to break up with him, but instead you sleep with him? I'm not understanding the logic here."

"It all happened so fast. One minute I was playing beer pong with Jake and we won, then Brad was kissing me. And then, I am waking up in his bed this morning. Oh, god, Matt. What am I going to do?"

The panic is stirring again.

"First I want to congratulate you on your win. Have you talked to, Brad?"

"Eh, no."

Matt scoffs. "And why not?"

"Well… He is still sleeping."

I hear Matt sigh. "Alexis, please, tell me you didn't…"

"I panicked, Matt!"

My phone beeps and I cringe because I know it's Brad calling.

"Oh my god, he's calling me! What do I say to him?"

Where is a paper bag when you need one?

"Calm down. Just tell him the truth."

Matt is right, but I don't know if I can do it. "I can't hurt him, Matt."

My phone beeps again.

"You need to talk to him. It's going to crush him, but he deserves the truth."

"Okay," I murmur sadly.

"Talk to him, Alexis. Be careful driving home. Text me when you get here."

"I will. Bye, Matt."

I hang up with Matt, however, I still can't find it in me to hear Brad's voice.

Placing my phone on silent, I turn up the music and focus on getting back to Bowling Green.

When I turn into the parking lot of my apartment complex, I still have not come up with a solution on how I will end things with Brad.

As promised, I text Matt letting him know I made it home safely.

As much as I want to fall on my bed and sleep, I need some girl time.

I text Kaylee to make sure she is free before I hop in the shower.

As I am sticking my key in the lock, I notice a brown envelope sticking in my door.

Tentatively, I open it and pull out the contents. My blood runs cold and I shudder as I look at the pictures of Brad and me.

Unlocking my door, I slip inside, making sure I lock it back.

The pictures were of us from last night. But, they aren't of us laughing or talking. We are having sex.

Okay, this is just plain scary.

As I am stuffing the pictures back in the envelope, a note falls out.

I pick it up and read it. *"Did you have fun on your little trip? I guess whore is fitting for you."*

I crumple the note in my fist and let it drop to the floor. Whoever is behind this will not win.

Kaylee replies just as I am about to hop in the shower. She tells me she is free. I tap out a reply, letting her know I will be by shortly.

The shower feels refreshing, but I don't take time to enjoy it.

In ten minutes, I am fully clothed with my hair brushed.

Let's hope the rest of my day is better than this morning.

"So how have you been?" Kaylee asks as we relax on the couch with the twins in between us. Jackson and Jasmine are growing so fast. I need to come see them more often.

"Been better," I answer with a hint of sadness in my voice. "I have been meaning to break up with Brad, but something always prevents me from actually ending our relationship. Yesterday, I drove to Lexington so we could talk. Well, there was a party going on and I never got a chance to talk to him."

Kaylee arches a brow. "And?"

Clenching my eyes shut, I blurt it out like I did to Matt. "We slept together."

I hear Kaylee gasp.

Slowly, I open my eyes and look at my best friend. "I didn't mean for it to happen. We both had been drinking, then one thing led to another. To make things worse, I left early this morning and I have been ignoring his calls."

Kaylee sits quietly, processing the information I have given her.

I pick up Jackson and cradle him in my arms, trying to keep myself busy.

"Are you planning on talking to him at all?"

I'd rather not, yet eventually I will have to. I can't avoid him forever.

"I will, but it's a matter of when."

I kiss Jackson on his head and lay him back down on the couch so I can hold Jasmine.

"I don't think you should wait, Alexis. The longer you put it off, the worse it will be."

"I know, okay!" I snap. Feeling bad, I apologize. "I'm sorry, Kaylee. I shouldn't have snapped at you. This situation with Brad and then the pictures-"

"Pictures?"

Ah, crap. Me and my big mouth.

I wave her off. "It's nothing. Drop it."

"I'll call my brother," she threatens.

I cringe at the thought of Ethan seeing the pictures. "Kaylee, please, leave it alone."

"No. When everything was happening with Riley, it hurt you because you didn't realize it sooner. You wanted to help me with my problems and I want to do the same with you."

I sigh, knowing she is right. If the tables were turned, I'd be as persistent as she is. "Fine. Someone left an envelope of pictures of Brad and me from last night in my door along with a note."

"What did the note say?"

"It said, " "*Did you have fun on your little trip? I guess whore is fitting for you.*""

Kaylee looks at me sympathetically. "I'm sorry, Alexis. Do you have any idea who could be behind it?"

My eyes burn with tears. This is all starting to become scary. First, my tires, then the break in, and now the pictures.

"I don't have a clue."

"Alexis, someone is clearly stalking you."

"I'll be fine, okay."

Kaylee shoots off the couch, a furious look on her face. "You *have* to go to the police with this! They will not stop!"

At her words, the tears spill over. I freeze and whip my head up to the entryway when I hear footsteps.

To my horror, Adam *and* Ethan walk into the living room. They stop and glance at us with confused looks.

I kiss Jasmine's head like I did Jackson's before laying her down next to her brother.

"Kaylee, is everything, okay?" Adam asks warily.

"Everything is fine," I answer for her.

Kaylee huffs. "No! How can you say that?"

Grabbing my keys and my phone, I head for the door.

"Alexis, you're like my sister, and I love you. I can see this has you rattled. I would be spooked too if-"

I whirl around. "Enough! For the last time, Kaylee, drop it!"

Spinning on my heels, I brush past the stunned guys and run out the door.

When difficult situations come about in my life, I like to deal with them on my own. I know I got onto Kaylee for not telling me what Riley was doing to her, but this is different.

Right now, I just need a pint of ice cream and Matt.

chapter twenty-seven

Brad

I wake up to find Alexis gone. The spot next to me is cold, telling me she has been gone for a while. I groan when I sit up, my head pounding. I thought that when I woke up, she would still be lying next to me. I would have smiled to myself as I admired her.

I pick up my phone and call her. She doesn't answer, so I keep trying. I finally give up and find my clothes. I had just buttoned my jeans when Jake comes barging in my room.

"You have a visitor my friend. Two girls in twenty-four hours." He makes a tisk sound while giving me a wide smile.

Confused at who would be here to visit me, I throw my shirt on and follow Jake out of my room. "Do you know who she is?"

"No, never seen her before. She's pretty, though." He winks and slaps my back.

Before we round the corner, I stop. "Have you seen Alexis this morning?"

His smile fades. "Yeah, she left at the crack of dawn."

SHELBY REEVES

I hang my head, not understanding what went wrong between us.

"Don't sweat it, all right." Jake tries to cheer me up, but what am I supposed to think when my girlfriend runs out on me and doesn't tell me that she is leaving after our first time together?

I nod stiffly then, walk into the main room to see a girl with bleach blonde hair looking around, holding a large envelope. I have never seen this girl in my life.

"Can I help you?"

She whirls around and I can tell she has been crying. "Hi, I know you don't know me, but I really need to talk to you about something important." She thrusts her hand out, and I shake it.

"And this pertains to me how?"

She looks over my shoulder at Jake who gets the hint. "Fine, I'll leave."

Knowing Jake, he will be listening around the corner.

"Would you like to sit?" I ask her.

"Sure."

We move over to the couches and sit. "You never did answer my question."

"Right, my name is, Kate, Ethan's girlfriend." She looks down at the brown envelope in her hands. "I hate that I'm here, but I really think you need to know what has been going on."

I honestly didn't know Ethan had a girlfriend, but if she is here, it could only mean one thing.

Kate sniffles as she hands me the envelope. I almost don't want to open because I know what's inside. Can I bear to see her with him? Giving in, I open the flap and pull out the contents.

"I had suspicions that he was cheating on me with her, but I needed proof, so I followed them," she cries.

Alexis might as well just have stabbed my heart with a stake. Deep down, I knew something was going on between them, I just chose to ignore it. I trusted her with my whole heart.

I feel bad for Kate. We are the ones who are hurt by them.

180

Kate is full on bawling now. What am I supposed to say to her? I set the pictures aside and wrap my arm around her. She falls easily against me.

I wordlessly hold her until she calms down. I, however, will not calm down. Alexis and I need to talk.

"Can I keep those?" I gesture to the pictures.

She nods, sniffling. "Do you have tissues?"

"I'll go find something." I walk into the kitchen and grab a couple paper towels and bring them back to her. "Here."

She takes them and blows her nose. "I guess I better get going."

I walk her to the door. "Thanks, for telling me."

She nods once then leaves.

As suspected, Jake walks out from around the corner.

"Not now, Jake."

I slam the front door behind me and make my way to my truck.

Pulling out my phone, I send Alexis a text.

Me: **We need to talk. I'm on my way now.**

I am about to turn out of the driveway when I realized I forgot the pictures. I run back in and quickly grab them.

The whole two and a half hour drive, I ask myself why over and over. Why did I trust her when she told me nothing was happening between the two of them? Why did I not see it?

I love her for crying out loud. After last night, I thought we were finally getting somewhere.

When I arrive at her apartment, I take a deep breath and grab the photos. I'm ready for answers. If Ethan is here, there will be nothing stopping me from punching him.

I knock on her door and wait. When she opens the door, neither of us say anything. I step inside and glance around the room. "Is he here?" I don't try to hide the bitterness in my voice.

"Is who here?"

I spin around to face her. "Don't act stupid, Alexis. I know you have been seeing Ethan behind my back."

She doesn't deny it. Instead, her head drops to the floor. "You weren't supposed to find out this way," she murmurs.

A bitter laugh escapes me. "Oh really? How was I supposed to find out since it is obvious you weren't going to tell me."

"I was going to tell you last night."

"Before or after you slept with me?"

"Brad…"

I'm trying to rein in my anger, but the more I think of them together, the angrier I become. "Save it! You broke my heart, Alexis! I loved you so much." I pause, trying to compose myself. "All I want to know is why? Why him? Why couldn't you be honest with me? I deserved at least that much."

"I didn't want to hurt you."

"Yeah, well, that didn't work out so well, did it?"

Her gaze drops to the floor. "I'm sorry for hurting you like this."

I shake my head, disgusted. "Whatever, have a nice life." I throw the envelope down on the couch and head for the door. Pausing, I turn to look at her one last time. "You know, if you were honest with me this wouldn't hurt so bad. I didn't think you were the type of person who would do this to someone."

I close the door behind me like I do on my heart. If loving someone hurts this much, then, I don't want any part of it. Maybe I should have called her more, visited her more. Lord knows I'm not perfect, but she should have talked to me about what was wrong. I feel like I just wasted the last ten months of my life.

Bottom line, love sucks.

chapter twenty-eight

Alexis

I slump down onto the couch after Brad slams the front door. It shouldn't sting, right? I needed to break up with Brad since I'm not in love with him. I didn't want it to happen like it did, but what *did* I think was going to happen? Did I really think Brad and I could be friends and go our separate ways? I should have been upfront with him and told him everything.

I text Matt, asking him if he can come over and bring ice cream. At the rate I'm going, I will be eating ice cream more frequently.

He responds immediately saying he is on his way. While I wait on him to arrive, I curl up in a ball on the couch and try to block out the voices that keep repeating, "I told you so."

When I hear a rap on my front door, I get up and open the door to let Matt in. He takes on look at me and his face falls. "What happened?"

I take my ice cream from him and plop back down on the couch. "Brad just left," I say as a way of explanation.

"Ah, so, what did the poor guy say?"

I sigh and take a bit of my favorite ice cream. "Well, he found out I had been staying at Ethan's. He is really hurt over it, which I can't blame him."

I eye the envelope he left, wondering what's in it and why he left it. I'm itching to open it, but if what's in it is anything like the last envelope I received, then no thanks.

Matt sighs. "I feel bad for the guy, I really do, but it had to happen. You and Brad weren't meant for each other. Now, the way it happened…"

"I know, okay?" I twirl my ice cream with my spoon. "Now, I need to figure out what I'm going to tell, Ethan. I kind of ran out on him."

Matt arches a brow. "Oh? Do tell."

I crack a smile. "I woke up from a dream which started with Ethan kissing my neck. Long story short, he morphed into Brad who starting saying stuff like, "How could you do this to me," stuff like that. Normally, I would wake Ethan up or if he had to work, he'd wake me up when he came in. But this time, I didn't wake him, I just got ready and left. At the last minute, I decided to head to Lexington. You know the rest, other than I haven't seen or talked to him since yesterday morning."

"Oh dear," Matt says. "I know I don't really like him all that much, but this isn't good."

I set down my ice cream to massage my temples. How am I going to break it to Ethan? Do I even need to since Brad and I are done?

"I'll figure it out. Although, now, I do need a date for Kaylee's wedding next month. You game?"

Matt smiles. "I'd be honored."

Matt and I make plans to attend the wedding together while we finish our ice cream.

Soon, Matt is leaving and I'm left with nothing to do until practice tonight. My mind keeps wandering back to the envelope. Giving in, I sit down on the couch and open the flap. I close my eyes and breathe deeply before grabbing what I know is pictures. The material feels the same as the other photos.

I pull them out and glance through them. This time, they are of Ethan and me. There is one of us sleeping in his bed with his arm wrapped around me. The next one is of us drinking coffee and laughing. The third one is of us gazing into each other's eyes. It was after I got off the phone with Matt and I had told Ethan the real reason why I didn't want to go back to my apartment.

I jump when someone knocks on my door. Quickly, I stuff the photos back in the envelope and rush to open the door.

My breath hitches at the sight of Ethan standing before me. "May I come in?"

"Sure." I step back and let him walk through.

When he doesn't make himself at home or step closer to me, I know he is upset.

He stands with his back to me at first, then he slowly turns around. When his gaze meets mine, it's hard. "You left."

Swallowing hard, I start to explain before he cuts me off. "I went to Lexington-"

"How is Brad by the way? Did you two have *fun*?" His tone is angry, making me realize he already knows *everything*.

"Ethan, I can explain!"

He shakes his head, moving closer to the front door. "What is there to explain, Lex? You *slept* with him!" He pauses for a brief moment. This time when he speaks, his tone is softer. "This past week with you being at my place has been indescribable. I loved having you there when I came home from work and waking up to you lying next to me, wrapped in my arms."

I loved every moment, too.

"And I loved our morning chats over breakfast and coffee before you left for class."

"I did, too, Ethan," I murmur.

He places his hand on the knob. "I'm sure you did, but I can't continue this when you are back forth between us. You tell me to get my shit together, yet yours is still scattered. I finally got mine figured out, now you need to."

With that, he walks out the door. He never let me explain. My heart is breaking worse than it ever has.

Ethan

When I woke up to find Lex already gone, I didn't know what to think. Now, I feel hurt, betrayed, and angry. When I found the envelope outside my door, the last thing I thought I would see were pictures of her and Brad together. I couldn't bear to look at the pictures so I ripped them up and threw the pieces in the garbage. Now, I need to erase it from my memory.

My night at work is already starting off shitty. I'm not concentrating on anything but, Lex. I finally 'get my shit together' as she said, only to rethink my decision.

"What the fuck is wrong with you, man?" Farris asks, shaking me out of my depressing thoughts.

Not wanting to talk about it, I reply in a clipped tone. "Nothing."

Farris shakes his head. "What happened between you two now?"

I don't answer him. Of course, he would know it's about Lex.

When realizes I'm not going to answer, Farris sighs. "Harper, this is the saddest I've ever seen you so it must be something huge. If you don't want to talk about it, then fine, but know I'm here to listen to you whine about how much you miss her."

I crack a smile, except it isn't wide. "Thanks, Farris."

The moment I arrive home from work and walk through my front door, my heart starts racing like it did when I *knew* she was here. After a week, I had gotten used to waking up beside her or walking in my room and seeing her sleeping peacefully.

You never know what someone means to you until they are not in your life anymore. I feel like I lost all of her.

I pick out some clothes and head to the shower. It's kind of hard to forget someone when they consume your soul. It would be easier to pretend she didn't exist to me if her stuff wasn't still scattered around my apartment. Lex and I were practically a couple this past week, only we didn't kiss nor did I touch her like I want too.

Racing back to her apartment and apologizing to her crosses my mind, but then, I remember the photographs and my heart breaks all over again.

I have the urge to box her stuff up, yet I can't bring myself to do it. I was ready to give her every piece of me because somewhere along the line, I fell in love with her. It stunned me at first, but I shook it off and embraced my feelings for her. Now, look where it's gotten me.

I fall asleep with the haunting thought of not being able to tell Lex how I feel.

chapter twenty-nine

Alexis

One month later...

Wake up, think about Ethan, go to class, think about Ethan, work on homework, think about Ethan, practice, think about Ethan, and then repeat. Oh, and helping Kaylee put the finishing touches on her wedding. This is practically my daily routine with the exception of weekends when we have games. I've been keeping myself as busy as possible so I wouldn't have time to think about my broken heart. *Yeah, that worked out real well didn't it.*

Kaylee's wedding is in two days. I will be seeing Ethan's handsome face tomorrow at rehearsal, and again on Saturday *all* day.

My 'stalker' as Kaylee calls them, has been kind of quiet lately. In the last month, the only note I have received came the next morning after Brad broke up with me. It read, *Getting your heart broken sucks doesn't it?*

There is a rap of knuckles on my door. I can only assume it is Matt since he has been my only visitor here lately. Alice has been keeping to herself lately. I wonder if she is okay? I make a mental note to go see her when I come back from the beach this weekend.

I open the door for him and let him in. He takes one look at me and says, "Girl, you look like death."

"Thanks for the compliment," I grumble as I shut the door.

"You ready for our road trip?" Matt asks cheerily.

I grab my suitcase which weighs a ton and follow Matt to his car.

Once we are the road, Matt says, "I can't tell if you need sleep or shots of tequila."

Even in my state of exhaustion, I laugh out loud. "I think I need both."

Matt chuckles. "The tequila I can help with. Who needs sleep?"

This road trip will definitely be an adventure, one I will remember for sure. If I know, Matt, he will do everything he can think of to cheer me up.

Kaylee and Adam are having a small intimate beach wedding with only family. I'm so happy she found Adam and that he stuck by her side through the hell she was going through.

Not only will I have to face Ethan, Brad will be here, too. Oh, and I am walking with him since he is the best man and I am the maid of honor. Yeah...this wedding will be *so* much fun. I was originally supposed to ride with Brad to Virginia Beach, but a lot has changed since then.

I manage to sleep for a bit since I haven't been sleeping well here lately.

It's late when we arrive at the hotel so we call it a night, with promise from Matt that we will have a night of fun tomorrow.

Morning comes too soon for my liking. Matt almost gets slapped when he shakes the bed so hard I thought an earthquake was happening.

I glare at him. "Was that necessary?"

Matt laughs and yanks the covers off of me. "Get your ass up. We have a beach to go to."

Huffing, I roll out of bed and grab my clothes for a shower. I'm determined to make today a good day despite having to see my ex and the guy who broke my heart tonight.

Matt bangs on the door twenty minutes later. "Alexis! Let's go! We are wasting precious beach time!"

"Keep your panties on!" I shout back.

We spend hours at the beach, tanning, searching for seashells and even swimming in the ocean. By the time we walk back to our room, I am exhausted. To my dismay, I have no time for a nap since we have to get ready for rehearsal and then dinner.

This time, it's me fussing at Matt to hurry up. He reluctantly gets ready and soon we are out the door for what will be an interesting night.

As we walk back down to the beach where the ceremony will be held, Matt says, "Tonight is going to be *so* much fun!"

I groan. "Tonight will be horrible." I can already feel it.

"Maybe it won't be that bad?" Matt offers, trying to cheer me up.

I give him a sideways glance. "Really?"

He holds his hands up defensively. "Hey, I'm trying to help."

I spot Brad first. He stands with his back to me, wearing jeans and a plaid button up shirt.

"Catch up with you?" I ask Matt. I need to apologize to Brad.

Matt nods and walks ahead of me. I slow to a stop, standing shoulder to shoulder with Brad.

Brad glances at me out of the corner of his eye but doesn't say anything.

"Can we talk for a second?"

"Sure," he replies.

We walk away from everyone towards the edge of the water. I slip off my sandals and hold them while we walk along the water.

"I'm sorry for hurting you the way I did. I didn't deserve you from the beginning, but I wanted to give us a shot. You were right when you said I should have been honest with you," I murmur.

I hear him sigh. "I was so in love with you, Alexis. Not a day goes by that I still don't think of you. I knew you liked, Ethan, and maybe I was in denial, but I wanted us to work. The heart wants what the heart wants, I guess," he says the last part with bitterness.

I stop and turn to him. "Can we at least be friends? You really are a great guy, Brad, and someday you will make the right girl happy."

"It's going to take time, Alexis, because I'm still hurting, but we can try for friends." Brad pulls me in for a long hug. When he pulls away, I reach up and kiss his cheek.

We walk back to curious eyes from everyone.

"Where have you two been? We can't start without the maid of honor and the best man!" Kaylee asks, drawing even more attention to us.

Brad clears his throat. "We were just talking. We're here now so let's get started."

Brad and I line up and I place my hand in the groove of his elbow. As we walk up towards the makeshift altar, I can feel someone's gaze burning into my back. I know without a doubt it's Ethan's. Brad and I part and I take my spot diagonal from the preacher.

Ethan is next. He is carrying Jackson and Jasmine down the aisle. I catch his eye, but he quickly looks away. He hands them off to Jack and Anna and walks back to walk his sister down the aisle. I try to catch his gaze again, but he either looked at Kaylee or kept his eyes forward.

The preacher goes through the spill of what he will say during the ceremony, yet I'm not paying the least bit of attention. It seems like Ethan is done with me. I don't dare try to talk to him for fear he will shoot me down.

Relieved that we are through, I quickly walk away, not wanting anyone to see the hurt and the unshed tears.

I hear someone run up behind me. I expect it's Matt, but to my surprise, it's Brad.

"Hey, are you alright?"

I want to lie and say things are fine, but I don't. "No, but it's not something you want to hear me cry about." Why would my ex-boyfriend want to hear me cry about the same guy I practically cheated on him with?

Brad drapes his arm around my shoulders and side hugs me. "Look, it doesn't take much to see that you and Ethan aren't together. I realize he is the reason for my broken heart, but like I told you earlier, I still care about you and seeing you cry still tugs my heart strings."

Brad guides me to the nearest patio that overlooks the ocean. He pulls out a chair for me and I sit down.

"So, if you don't mind me asking, what happened between you two?" Brad asks once he is seated.

"Not long after you left, he showed up. Somehow he found out we slept together and he didn't like it. Ethan and I were never officially together, we just hung out. Sometimes we saw each other by accident. We kissed a few times over the last few months and he regretted it." I pause to gather my thoughts. "I love him, Brad. Maybe I shouldn't be admitting this to you since you are already hurting because of me, but I'm being honest with you. He was always it for me. I haven't figured out how or why, but I just know."

Brad nods and reaches across to place his hand on top of mine. "As much as it sucks to hear the truth, I'm glad you told me."

For the first time tonight, I smile. "I take back what I said about you. You aren't great, you're amazing."

Brad laughs. "Tell me something I don't know."

My smile is wide as I shake my head at him. "Let's go eat, I'm starving."

We stand and walk together to the restaurant a few blocks down from our hotel. Brad and I are the last to arrive and we get the same stares as earlier. They all know we broke up so their minds are running with questions. There are only two seats left which are next to each other. I take one closest to Matt, leaving Brad to sit next to, Ethan.

Brad leans over and whispers in my ear. "How dare you make me sit next to the guy who wants to slit my throat?"

Laughter erupts from me, attracting more attention. I pat Brad's shoulder, silently wishing him the best.

Kaylee gives me a pointed look. She and I will be talking later.

I am in the middle of sipping on my water when Matt leans over and whispers, "Don't tell me you humped him again."

I choke on the water I was in the process of swallowing. "Matt," I hiss.

"What? It is a valid question."

"Shut up, Matt," I reply through clenched teeth.

"So is that a yes or a no?"

"No, I did not have sex with Brad!" I whisper harshly. When everyone at the table starts laughing or choking on their drinks, I realize I was louder than I thought.

I bury my head in my hands, utterly embarrassed.

"Thanks for already kicking me while I am down. You could have at least sounded disappointed about it," Brad says, amused.

No doubt my face is fifty shades of red.

"At least you answered the burning question in their minds," Matt reasons.

I swear I'm going to kill Matt if he doesn't stop talking!

I fist the knife lying next to Brad, planning to stab Matt if he says another word.

Brad pries the knife out of my hand then looks over to Matt. "You should thank me for saving your life."

Matt waves Brad off. "I'm not worried, she won't hurt me, thanks, though."

"Don't test me," I grumble.

I knew this dinner would suck. Is it bedtime yet?

chapter thirty

Alexis

Kaylee's wedding was beautiful. Simple, but beautiful. They didn't need a big wedding anyway.

Growing up, I always dreamed of what my wedding would be like. I had every single detail planned out how I wanted it. Now, after Kaylee's wedding, I think I'd rather have a small, intimate ceremony rather than a grand one.

Kaylee and Adam have just finished their first dance as husband and wife so now Kaylee is dancing with, Jack, Adam's dad, while Adam is dancing with, Anna, his mother.

This part must be hard for Kaylee without her father being here. I'm so proud of her, though. Even after everything she has been through, she is still going strong.

The twins and I are sitting at one of the tables while they dance. These two are just the cutest things ever. Jasmine has little curls that I love to play with. Her eyes are just as soft as Kaylee's. And Ethan's. Adam says that's his favorite part about her. Other than their eyes, Jackson and Jasmine look nothing like Kaylee. They are the spitting image of their father. Well, their sperm donor, as I like to call him. Jasmine and Jackson are not biologically Adam's. Kaylee's psycho ex-boyfriend raped and abused her. So when she found out she was pregnant, Adam, didn't think twice about wanting to be there for her and the babies. Riley, the piece of shit ex, is where is pathetic ass should be, in jail.

I still feel a little bit guilty that I didn't see what he was doing to her. How could I have not seen the signs?

When I see Adam and Kaylee together I get a little bit jealous. I want what they have. I want a love that people can spot a mile away. A love that shines so bright between us that people can feel it and see how happy we are. I want that with Ethan. When I first met Ethan, I knew right then he was the one I wanted. I don't know how to explain it, but just one look at Ethan and I knew that I didn't want anybody else…at least until Brad popped in the picture leaving me so confused for a while.

"Can I have this dance?" a voice whispers in my ear. Speak of the devil and he comes running.

"Sure." I kept my voice tight so he doesn't think I am overly thrilled. On the inside, I am jumping up and down and doing cartwheels. Anna has finished her dance with Adam so she sits down at the table so she can keep an eye on the twins. I let Ethan lead me out to the makeshift dance floor in the middle of the conference room.

I was worried there would be a fight between Brad and Ethan since it's clear they don't like each other. To my surprise, they've kept their distance from one another and they both are being civil for the sake of the wedding.

Ethan murmurs low in my ear, "You look beautiful as always, Lex." I blush and look away. My parents used to call me that and I hated it, but when Ethan says it, my heart skips a beat.

Aerosmith's, *"I Don't Want to Miss a Thing,"* starts flowing through the speakers. "This song's for you, beautiful."

His arms wrap around my waist, holding me close to him. The stubble on his jaw brushes my cheek. Unconsciously, I lean into him, letting him lead. Our bodies sway in sync with the music leisurely. Ethan has ignored me since we arrived so what's changed?

This is what I hope for, long for. I want him, need him. I wonder what goes on in his head. Why is he trying so hard to stay away when it's obvious he wants me? Of course, it didn't help when I screwed things up by sleeping with Brad.

When Ethan is like this, so sweet, so intimate, I'm putty in his hands. But like every song, every book, every moment, it always comes to an end and he walks away like nothing happened. This time is no different. Sometimes I wonder why my heart is still so hung up on him.

So like always, I regain my composure and pretend that my heart isn't breaking into a million pieces. How can he play me a beautiful song like that and walk away like nothing happened?

"You okay, Alexis?" I look up at Brad and nod, lying about how I really feel. "Want to take a walk with me?" I look at Brad's outstretched hand, then his face.

Glancing over Brad's shoulder, I spot Ethan with a scowl on his face. Talk about whiplash.

Returning my gaze back to Brad, who is waiting for an answer, I reply, "I'd love to." I smile and place my hand in his. *Take that Ethan.* Let him think what he wants about us.

Brad and I walk through the hotel with no destination. We are quiet for the most part until Brad decides to speak. "Want me to go punch him?"

I laugh softly. "You wouldn't do it and you know it. You aren't that guy, Brad. Now, Matt, on the other hand, would."

He chuckles. "You're right, but he still deserves it."

My smile fades. "Why are you being nice to me?"

"I know I said I needed time, and I still do, but I'm trying here. Like you, I want us to be friends."

I wrap my arms around his middle, closing in for a friendly hug. "Told you I didn't deserve you."

Brad chuckles and pulls away. "Let's head back. We wouldn't want anyone to think we were having sex now would we?"

I scoff and shove him playfully. Now that things between Brad and I are better, maybe Ethan and I can work things out.

Ethan

I'm an asshole, a huge one. I just keep leading her on, only to hurt her every time, just like Matt pointed out. I want her so bad, but I'm afraid that she is too good for me. Not to mention our age difference and the fact that in a couple short weeks from now, I will be on the other side of the country for nine freakin' months. How am I going to make it? Being away from her now is hard enough as it is.

My stupidity is really showing since I'm practically pushing her into Brad's arms. Judging by what my eyes are seeing, I'd say I just lost her for good this time. My chest constricts every gut-wrenching second they spend another moment together. The urge to go down there and knock his teeth in is strong, but my feet stay planted like they should. I don't need another reason for her to hate me. I'm the reason this is happening anyway. I don't know what is worse, watching it or knowing that I opened the door for Brad? I'm going to go with the latter.

Why am I still standing here torturing myself?

Forcing my body to turn away, I do what I always do best; I walk away from the only girl who means something to me.

I need a drink, stat. As I walk back into the conference room, I spot my sister embraced in her new husband's arms. I try to block the surge of jealousy that rips through my heart. When I see how blissfully happy my sister is, it makes me want to be that happy. The one person I could see being that way with I pushed away. Sucks doesn't it?

After all that my sister has been through, she deserves this and more. Adam is a great guy. If it wasn't for him or Lex...this is supposed to be a happy day so why am I so down about everything? Oh, right now I remember, I have myself to blame for that.

A couple beers in and I'm still feeling the pain in my chest. It hasn't lessened like I hoped it would. Deciding to call it a night, I say my goodbyes to everyone except Lex and him, giving extra attention to my niece and nephew.

Needing something stronger, I head to the liquor store across the street. Stopping at the door, I glance at the neon lights a block away. I know I shouldn't, but what else do I have to lose? Changing my mind, I make my way closer to another thing I'm going to regret. Against my better judgment, I walk in and head straight for the bar.

The loud banging on the door didn't help the pounding that's currently going on in my head. I wonder who the hell it can be?

"Hang on," I growl as I get up and throw some shorts on when I realize I was naked. I wish I knew what went on last night. I don't remember coming home or anything after walking to the bar. Naked and hung over...yeah, I'm pretty sure I just figured it out, although, I don't see a girl anywhere. She must've left already. Fine by me.

I open the door to find a fist flying at my face with a pissed off Matt on the other end. "What the hell!" I snarl at him. "What was that for?"

"I should beat the shit out of you and get it over with. Lord knows you deserve it, but I'm not going to add to the hurt that you've caused her already. What you caused last night iced the cake." Last night? What did I do? Do I even want to know? "Do you even remember what you did?" I shake my head and he laughs humorlessly. "That doesn't surprise me at all. Allow me to refresh your memory so you can feel guilty about hurting her."

Shit…I already don't like where this is going. "We ran into you and some girl in the hallway and you said some things." He let out an aggravated sigh. "I'm not going to say it word for word, but basically you called Alexis a whore and a tease and then to top it all off you proceeded to tell her how you just played her because you never wanted her."

I said all of that? I just twisted the knife further into my own heart.

I should have listened to that little voice that told me going to the bar was a bad idea. Those things I said were just hurtful lies that a drunk, bitter version of me said because he was pissed off and jealous.

If there was any chance left for me to be able to turn things around, no matter how little of a chance it was, I ruined it. I just ruined any hope of having a future with her.

After picking up a lone shirt on the floor and grabbing my room key, I proceeded to walk out the door. Matt steps in front of me, stopping me in my tracks. "What do you think you're doing?" he asks, as he crossed his arms across his chest like he is a badass.

"I need to talk to her. I need to apologize." I try to sidestep him, but he is quicker. Damn him.

"Like hell you are. What makes you think she even wants to even see you, let alone talk? What makes you think *I* will let you?"

"I need her to hear me out. She needs to listen to what I have to say. Whether or not she forgives me is up to her, but I'm not about to walk away and not apologize. She deserves that much at least." I can tell he is fighting an inner battle with himself about whether he should let me or not. It doesn't matter because I'm going to do it anyway. If she doesn't listen it will hurt, but I tried at least.

Finally, he caves and I follow him up to the hotel room she is in.

Hesitantly, I knock on the door that stands between us. I hold my breath as the door swings open, reveals her in a pair of yoga pants and tank. Her hair is messily pulled back into a bun that rests on top of her head. Her eyes are red and puffy from crying. *The knife just keeps twisting.*

She goes to close the door in my face, but I stick my hand out and stop it. "Go away, Ethan." The pain that is evident in her voice cuts me deep, slices me open.

I need to get this out quickly while I have the chance. "Lex, I'm sorry, I'm so sorry. I was so drunk and pissed off. I didn't mean any of it." I held my breath waiting for a response. Matt leans against the wall next to me. My guess is he is making sure I won't do anything stupid. Ha, well I've already done that.

The door opens a little wider only to reveal a pissed off version of Lex. "Didn't mean it? Isn't that what everyone says when they apologize?! Well, guess what I don't believe you and I sure as hell don't forgive you! What made you so mad that you had to go out, get drunk, and come back and talk to me like you did?" She spat.

"I was pissed because I saw you with Brad again!" I roar. "I was jealous and hurt because I thought you'd gone back to him, which meant I'd lost you."

"I don't understand you, Ethan! You say you can't be with me and you make it your mission to stay away from me, but yet you get jealous because you saw me with Brad? And you were right; you have lost me for good. Goodbye, Ethan." She slams the door in my face while I stand there frozen, breaking from her words. I made her hate me. I pushed her away. The one girl who had the power to turn my world upside down just slammed the door in my face all because I broke her heart.

Pressing my palms against the wood, I lean in and press my forehead to the door. I can hear her gut-wrenching sobs through the door. "I'm so sorry, Lex. Hopefully one day before it's too late you will forgive me."

Squeezing my eyes shut, I rub my hands over my face in regret. Suppressing the urge to punch the door, I turn abruptly and start to walk away when Brad walks up.

He looks to the door, then to me. "You know, I told her *months* ago I loved her and she has yet to tell me in return. In the beginning, I thought I spooked her because saying 'I love you' is a big deal. When I found out she had been staying with you, I finally realized why she hadn't told me she loved me. She couldn't love me when she has feelings for someone else. As much as it hurt, I let her go because I knew she would never be the one for me."

Lex has feelings for me, yet, I don't know if I can return those feelings like she wants me too. "Well Brad, it looks like I lost her for good now. She doesn't forgive me, and I don't blame her. You deserve her more than I do. You can give her things I can't." It hurts something fierce to tell him that, but what choice do I have? It's not going to change anything.

Matt steps forward. "You're right, *you* don't deserve her. So, why don't you go and leave her alone, while I try and mend her broken heart."

Brad grunts. "As much as I would like to try having a relationship with her for a third time, I won't do it. She doesn't love me, she loves you." He steps forward and places his hand on my shoulder. "If you really care for her, show her. Girls like her don't come around often so you need to take advantage of what is in front of you before you lose her forever."

With that, he walks away.

Matt places the key in the door, and after one last look at me, he shakes his head in disgust and walks in to comfort Lex.

chapter thirty-one

Alexis

I haven't been out of bed since I slammed the door in Ethan's face and on my heart. Matt has been lying with me, holding me, telling me everything will be okay and that I didn't need him.

Pulling myself together for Matt's sake, I climb out of bed and hop in the shower. We leave to school in two days, so I want to make the best of the time we have left. Lying in the hotel bed crying isn't that thrilling and will get me nowhere. I need to suck it up and move on, get over him.

When I emerge thirty minutes later, Matt is sitting on the edge of the bed fully dressed. He is wearing light wash jeans with a Braves t-shirt. His matching Braves hat is turned backwards on his head with his dark brown hair sticking out from under the cap.

He stands meets me halfway. He reaches out and tucks a lone strand of hair behind my ear and I sigh. "I'm sorry you're hurting," he says softly.

"Don't apologize for his actions. What's done is done, he can't take it back." I shrug as he wraps his arms around me. I stand in his embrace for a moment before pulling away. "Ready to go?" I ask, displaying a small smile.

Grabbing my purse on the way, we walked out of the hotel room. Hopefully, I won't run into Ethan.

Matt opens the door of his car for me and waits for me to climb in before shutting it and jogging around and climbing in the driver's seat. "Where did you want to go?" He is waiting on me to decide before backing out of his spot in the parking lot.

I ponder for a moment where we could go, but I only came up with one thing. My lips curl into a smile that reaches my ears.

"No," he says out of the blue like he can tell what I'm thinking.

"No?" I repeat like I wasn't sure what he said.

"Exactly, no. I know what you're about to say and I'm not about to lose my man card." I laugh out loud at his serious demeanor.

"Come on, Matt! It's therapy! And to be fair, you lost your man card already," I argue.

"Therapy my ass! Torture is what shopping is!" he bellows seriously. "And you're right, I did. I just added it for dramatic effect."

Sticking my bottom lip out, I give him my best pouting face. "Please," I say, batting my eyelashes. "It will be fun!"

"Ha! I call bullshit! That's what all girls say before they subject you to hours of pure agonizing torture!"

Amused, my brow lifts curiously. "What kind of shopping trips have you been on?" I tease him.

"The ones where a girl talks you into going, saying it will only take an hour or two because she is only getting a couple things when in reality she meant six hours and fifty shopping bags full. The ones where the guys are the pack mules who get stuck carrying all fifty fully loaded bags to each store while he answers the same question over and over again. The question where she asks if this looks okay and you say yes every time even when it doesn't because she will get pissed and slap you." I try not to laugh, but I can't help it. I laugh so hard my stomach starts hurting and tears are forming in my eyes. "I just told you about a traumatic experience I went through and you feel the need to laugh at me? Seriously, could you wound me anymore?" That made me laugh even harder.

Matt huffs, turning forward. "Could pick something manlier like go-karts or mini golf… something other than shopping? I mean I'm still a guy."

Come to think of it, that does sound fun. I haven't done either of those, ever. "Okay, how about we compromise?" Matt looks at me curiously or shocked, not sure which one. "We can go ride go-karts and play mini golf…" He sighs in relief. "…if we go shopping before we head back to the hotel." He groans and I laugh.

"Since I think you're beautiful and I love you, why not?" He smiles, flashing his pearly whites while backing out of the parking lot. My breath catches at the word beautiful. For some odd and seemingly wrong reason, Ethan's face pops in my mind. Here I was trying to go at least one day without things reminding me of him and I can't even do that.

It turns out that doing more "manly" things is kind of fun. Matt still kicks my ass and laughs his ass off at me during miniature golf. Go-karts are even better. He leaves me in the dust the first couple of rounds since I am trying to get my bearings under control. It's good that Matt isn't a sore loser when it comes to these things since I won the last two races.

Now for my favorite part of the evening: shopping. I had half a mind to be all dramatic and take my sweet time adding another traumatic shopping experience to Brad's list because let's face it; he hit the nail on the head. He described my shopping trips like he has seen it firsthand. I decided against it because Brad has been super sweet and I'm drained after our day together.

Every shirt, every pair of jeans, every piece of lingerie I tried on I wondered if Ethan would like it. Yes, he hurt me. Yes, I'm still mad at him, but that doesn't change how I feel about him. Maybe I will let him stew a little bit more before I talk to him.

As soon as we make it back to the hotel, I plop on the bed in exhaustion. The moment my head hits the pillow I drift off to sleep. Vaguely, I remember being covered with a blanket.

Vacation is over which means, it's time to head back to reality. School is all I have to keep me occupied for now since Kaylee is on her honeymoon. I'll likely see Ethan more now and I'm not sure how I feel about that. On one hand, it will hurt because when I see him it will remind me of how he hurt me, but, on the other hand, I miss him. How crazy does that make me after what he did?

When I sit up in bed Matt, is pacing the floor nervously. "Matt? Is everything okay?"

He thrusts his hands through his hair and blows out a long breath. "No. I don't know. My grandmother had to be taken to the hospital. They don't know what's wrong," he talks so fast I almost didn't understand him.

"Then what are you still doing here? Matt, you should be on your way home already!"

"I didn't want to just leave you here," he says apologetically. What he is trying to say is that he didn't want to leave me in case Ethan decided to make an ass of himself again.

"Don't worry about me. Your grandmother needs you. I will catch a ride with Anna and Jack."

"Are you sure?"

"Yes, now go!" I all but shove him out the door.

"Let me know when you make it home." He grabs his bag and bolts out the door.

"Be careful!" I holler as he leaves the room.

Once he is gone, I change into some comfortable jeans and t-shirt for the ride home. I throw my hair up into a messy bun not caring at all what it looks like.

I am in the middle of packing my stuff up when there is a soft knock on the door. I crack open the door to find Ethan standing with his hands in his pockets staring down at the floor.

His head jerks up from the sound of the door opening. "What are you doing here Ethan?"

He scratches the back of his neck like he is nervous. "I, uh, just wanted to make sure you are okay and I, um, wanted to apologize again for the things that I said."

"Apology accepted, now goodbye." I go to close the door, but he stops me.

"Wait-" He shifts his weight from one leg to the other. "Can I come in?" he asks hopefully.

"Actually no, I'm in the middle of packing so I can catch a ride with Anna and Jack."

"Where's, Matt? I thought you'd be riding with him?" Ethan asks in surprise.

"I was, but he had a family emergency."

His eyes brightened with hope. "Why don't you ride with me?"

"No." As soon as the words slip from my tongue, the light in his eyes dim.

"It's not like you have another choice since Anna and Jack already left." *Ugh! Of course, they have.*

I groan and laid my head against the door. "Let me get my stuff then we can go."

"I'll get them," Ethan says as he pushes past me and grabs my bags.

"I'm perfectly capable of carrying my bags myself," I huff.

"Chivalry isn't dead, Lex."

I take one last look around the room, making sure I didn't forget anything before following Ethan out. Ethan and I stand side by side, neither of us saying a word as we wait for an empty elevator. I peek out of the corner of my eye at the man who can make me so impossibly mad and hurt, then turn around and make me smile right after. Ethan is looking down at me with a burning intensity that makes my stomach swirl in desire.

When the elevator dings, announcing its arrival, I almost jump out of my skin.

This is going to be a very long car ride home.

chapter thirty-two

Ethan

Riding in an elevator with Lex is giving me thoughts that I don't need act on. The way she is dressed, the way her hair is pulled back haphazardly into a bun, makes me want to push her against the wall and show her how beautiful she is. Alexis always looks beautiful, but when she dresses casual, she looks even more beautiful. Especially with the way a few strands of her hair fall in front of her face...

Damn, screw holding back. I crush her against the wall of the elevator, taking her mouth with a savage intensity. Her hands fist my shirt tugging me closer like she couldn't get enough of me, and hell if that didn't make me want her more. My tongue trails the seam of her luscious lips. She parts them eagerly, allowing me to thrust my tongue in her mouth.

When the elevator comes to a stop, I don't jump away from her like some teenager getting caught making out. I stayed planted firmly against her, gazing into her olive-colored eyes.

I would've stayed in that position all day, too, if it weren't for someone ruining our moment. "Are you kidding me? I've been gone half an hour and you're already with him after everything he has done to you?"

"M-Matt, I thought you had an emergency?" Lex stutters, completely caught off guard.

"It turned out to a false alarm so I came back to get you and low and behold guess who I find you with. I figured you would have learned by now that all Ethan will do if hurt you, Alexis. Don't come crying to me when he breaks your heart again. Our ice cream binges are over as long as you continue to let him make you cry." Matt shakes his head and walks away.

I look back down at Alexis, still in my arms, and sigh as I lean my head against hers. She looks on the verge of tears and that makes me feel like an ass since I'm the one whose resolve broke and kissed her when I swore I wouldn't. Now, I broke her heart again. "Come on, let's go get some breakfast," I murmur, kissing her nose. I'm determined not to let a single tear fall from her eyes. For once, I'm determined to make her smile today.

Keeping one arm around her, I grab her bag, throw it over my shoulder, and walk her out of the elevator.

Lex is relatively quiet as we leave the hotel lobby. Grasping her elbow gently, I lead her over to my car, which seemed to take me forever to rebuild. Now, she's a beauty, a dream car, and she's all mine.

I open the trunk and start loading Lex's suitcases. When I'm done, I look over to find her gaping at my car.

"Whose car is this?" she asks in a dead serious tone.

"It's mine," I answer as I walk over to open the car door for her. She looks at me like she is in utter disbelief. "This is your car?"

"Yep. It's she a beauty?" I ask as I hold the door open for her.

Lex looks between me and the open car door like she is stunned that I am holding the door open for her. What? Doesn't she think I know how to be a gentleman?

"I do have manners, Lex," I say pointedly when she doesn't seem to snap out of her trance or whatever she is in.

She shakes her head, snapping out of it. "Funny, you haven't been using them," she quips and slides in the seat.

I lean down, inching my mouth closer to her ear. Her breath hitches from my close proximity. "I know I have been an ass to you, and I'm sorry. I plan on trying to redeem myself today."

Withdrawing, I shut the door.

I crank the car, loving the sound of the engine purring.

Looking over at Lex, I ask, "When do your classes resume?"

"Tomorrow."

Crap, I think to myself. With only a few weeks left before I leave, I want to show her that I'm not fully an ass. I might be kicking myself in the end since I'm sure it will only spike my feelings towards her.

I need this time with her. I can't explain why I do. Maybe it's because I don't want her to hate me. When-if- I return home, I want her to run to her and catch her as she leaps into my arms, welcoming me home. I dream about that moment, fantasize about my head swooping down to capture her lips.

A slap on my arm has me snapping out of my thoughts. I glance at Lex out of the corner of my eye, my brow raised in questioning.

"I asked why you wanted to know about my classes."

Dropping the car in gear, I pull out of parking lot, heading in the direction of Kentucky. Maybe we can make a couple stops on the way home to sightsee. I don't have to be at work until Thursday night, which is three days away.

Clearing my throat, I reply, "Because, I wanted to take you somewhere."

Shifting in her seat so she is somewhat facing me, she regards me curiously. "I don't understand you. First you tell me you have to stay away from me, and now you actually want to spend time with me? I don't get it. You are so confusing, Ethan. You can't just decide to one day want to be in someone's life. It's not fair to me."

Wow, I didn't expect her to say all of that, although, I deserve it. I reach for her hand, surprised when she lets me clutch it in mine. My thumb caresses the back of her hand, feeling her soft skin.

"I'm sorry for hurting your feelings. I like being around you, even though I screw it up. Can we just forget about the past for now and just enjoy the next two days?"

"I haven't agreed to the two-day excursion yet. What if I have a major test tomorrow?"

"Do you?"

"No, but that's not the point."

My heart sinks a little, assuming the worst. From her tone, she doesn't sound like she wants to go anywhere with me. "Please, Lex," I plead, squeezing her hand gently.

She suddenly jerks her hand out from under mine, and I miss the warmth of her touch. "Tell me why, Ethan. Why now after all this time do you actually want to be around me? Is it because we are far away from home?"

"No," I reply quickly. Sighing, I try to conjure up the right words. "When I said we can't be together, I wasn't lying. I don't want to discuss it right now, though. Just trust me when I say I'm not doing this to mess with you. I like being around you, spending time with you. I don't mean to intentionally hurt you, Lex, I swear."

She swallows hard. I'm sure she is wondering what I'm meaning by all of this.

"If I go on this overnight trip with you, you better not go back to treating me like you have been."

Trust me, I don't mean to. I reach over for her hand again, and surprisingly, she lets me hold it in mine. "Lex, I want a fresh start with you, okay? I may screw up from time to time, but I promise you, it won't be intentional."

"Fresh start," she murmurs, making my heart soar in relief.

I bring her hand up to my lips, placing a light kiss to her delicate skin. I fight a smile when I hear her breath hitch.

"Will you tell me where we are going?" she asks, sounding a little breathless.

I love that I have such an effect on her.

I grin, knowing she will have a blast. "Six Flags," I say coolly.

She gasps and starts squealing. "No way! Are we really?"

I laugh at her reaction. "Yep, the closest one is in Georgia. So I figure we make it there by tonight and then have all day tomorrow to spend at the parks and drive home on Tuesday."

"How did you know Six Flags is where I have been wanting to go?"

I shrug nonchalantly. "I pay attention to little things."

"Oh," she replies quietly. "How long will our drive be?"

"We have about nine hours to our destination in Georgia and only about five hours home."

"That isn't as bad as I was expecting it to be." I think she was going to say more until her cell phone rings.

She pulls her phone out of her purse and when she sighs, I pretty much knew who was calling.

Lex looks at me with questioning eyes. "Should I answer it?"

My answer would be "No," but I can't tell her that. "It's up to you, Lex."

She looks back at her phone, indecisive, about what to do.

Lex sighs and answers Matt's call. I try to not eavesdrop on her conversation with him, but I'm curious to know.

"You really hurt my feelings, Matt... I know, okay?...I will see you when I get back...Bye."

Should I ask her about the conversation or not? Clearing my throat, I ask, "What did he want?"

"He was just calling to apologize for the way he acted earlier. Matt couldn't believe I am with you after what you did last night. Even after I said I didn't forgive you, I still wound up with you."

She reaches for my hand and links our fingers. She let go when she had to dig for her phone. "I'm still upset at you for hurting me,

Ethan. I don't know what it is about you, but it takes a lot for me to cry, yet when you break my heart I cry like a freaking baby."

Shit, this is only hurting me, but she's right. I always hurt her for some stupid reason. My track record for making her cry would earn a darn gold medal.

I lift her hand and brush my lips against her knuckles. "I'm sorry, Lex. I know you need more than that, and I'm working on it. I don't expect you to forgive me right away, it's going to take time, but one day, you will because I'm going to make up for it as long as I need to, starting today."

Lex surprises me by leaning over and kissing my cheek. Feeling her lips on my skin, is something I have dreamed about. I suppress my groan, my hand tightening around the wheel. My skin is on fire where her lips were.

"As long as you don't make me cry anything, but happy tears, we will be good."

"Okay, I'm going to have to remember that."

chapter thirty-three

Alexis

This impromptu trip with Ethan is starting off really well. The whole ride to Georgia, we talked, about anything and everything. Maybe it's just paranoia, but I am still waiting for the rug to get ripped out from under me. It is starting to seem too good to be true.

We check into our hotel and head out for a bite to eat before settling in for the night. As luck would have it, or fate, however, you want to look at it, there are only one-bed rooms left. Ethan smirked when the receptionist told us. I became a mixture of emotions. On one hand, I want to lay next to him, hopefully, wrapped in his embrace. On the other hand, if he is not looking at a relationship with me, then I need some space before I fall completely in love with him.

I'm in the bathroom freshening up for dinner when I light knock on the door.

"You can come in," I tell, Ethan.

He pokes his head inside and asks, "Are you about ready?"

I quickly finish styling my hair as I answer him. "Just about."

Ethan nods once and steps fully inside. Gradually, he leans against the wall behind me.

When I glance through the mirror at him, I notice he has a rather odd expression on his face. It's almost like he wants to ask me something, but is afraid to.

He looks up and catches my gaze through the glass. "I've been wanting to ask you…" He pauses, making me slightly nervous. "…are you, uh, planning on getting back with Brad?"

I sigh and drop my head, my heart leaping in my throat. "No, Ethan. We are only friends."

The next moment happens so fast I don't have time to blink. Ethan spins me around and crushes his mouth to mine. The kiss is mind-blowing, oxygen stealing, good. His mouth attacks mine over and over like he can't get enough of me, and damn, it is such a turn on.

My hands grip his shoulders as he effortlessly lifts me up onto the bathroom counter. My legs wrap around his waist, locking him in place.

Ethan rains hot, open mouthed kisses down my jawline to my exposed neck. My hands make their way up to his hair, my fingers gripping the strands tightly.

His name comes out as a breathless moan. "Ethan."

He draws back slightly, only allowing an inch of space between us. "Do you know how incredibly sexy you are? Do you know how bad I want you?"

One hand cups his cheek. "I'm yours."

His lips find mine again. "I want to do this right, Alexis, which means I'm going to take you out to dinner. As much as I want to keep this going, I want to do right by you. Lord knows I have hurt you so many times, so now, I need to make up for those."

For once I want him to throw caution to the wind, but I respect his decision.

"Okay," I murmur.

Ethan sets me back on my feet and kisses me profoundly. "Let's go before I change my mind."

I giggle and follow him out, grabbing my clutch on the way out the door.

The next day flies by and before I realize it, we are on our way home to Bowling Green. I feel Ethan and I are growing closer now that we have spent some much needed time with each other. My fear is this closeness will all disappear the moment we arrive home.

I can't shake the feeling that something is about to tear us apart. When Ethan smiles at me, the feeling diminishes.

Reality is a bitch. My 'stalker' problems resurface, reminding me nothing is going to change. The last two days have been blissful, but all the smiles and laughs fade away when I see Kate leaning up against her car.

Ethan curses under his breath. "I wish she would leave me the fuck alone."

Kate shoots daggers at me while Ethan climbs out of the car. Her face instantly brightens as she watches him walk up to her.

I climb out of the car and lean against it. I can only hope this drama doesn't tear us apart.

"I can't believe you, Ethan! How could you be with her when you are still with me?!" she screeches when she notices me.

My body locks up at her words. Is he with her?

Ethan curses again. "I ended things with you weeks ago!"

She folds her arms across her chest and cocks her hip to one side. "And yet, you still came over after you supposedly dumped me."

Unsure of whether I should stay or leave, I stand quietly, listening intently as they argue.

Finally hearing enough of the same thing, I step between them, facing the chick who clearly isn't 'understanding' their relationship, or whatever, is over.

"Listen here, *Kate*. It's painfully obvious he wants nothing to do with you so take your skinny ass on and leave him alone. Pretending to not get the picture makes you look more stupid than you already are."

I hate girls who act like Kate is. They think they can have any man they set their eyes on. And when the guy wants nothing to do with them, they throw a hissy fit, thinking he will give in. It pisses me off.

Kate's face is so red, I'm beginning to think her head is going to explode.

She takes a step forward, not backing down in the slightest. Her eyes narrow into slits as she stares me down. "You have a lot of nerve talking to me like that. Once he is done playing with you, he will come back to me like he always does. You mark my words. I will *never* be out of his life."

Kate marches away, her heels clicking against the concrete. As she drives away, I turn to Ethan. Before I can get a word out, Ethan's mouth is on mine. Rough and possessive, his mouth continues to connect with mine. One hand is in my hair and the other is locked around my waist, holding me flush against him.

I hold on tight, clinging to this moment like I will never get another. With each kiss, I fall further in love with this man.

"That was so hot," he murmurs breathlessly in between kisses.

A giggle bursts from my throat. "Well, there is more where that came from."

He scoops me up in his arms and carries me up the flight of stairs to his apartment. "I would hope there is more. It would be a shame to stop now," he says with desire filled eyes. He kisses my nose then kicks the door shut.

My jumbled up brain is just now catching on to what he is meaning. Is he finally going to give us a chance?

He frames my face in his hands and dips his head once more. All the stress which has been building over the last few weeks melts away his tongue slips past my lips.

My hands are pulling his shirt, tugging him closer. I *need* him as close as two people can get. He removes his hands from my face, dropping them to my waist.

As his hands slide up, so does my shirt.

Oh my goodness, we are really about to do this! Finally!

My happiness is short lived when we hear a knock on the door.

Ethan's head drops to my shoulder. "What now?" he grumbles, then pulls away. "This better be fucking good."

I definitely agree with him. Ethan and I are finally going to take our relationship further and now we are being interrupted. Why is it that something always prevents us from being together?

Ethan opens the door and the woman I have yet to meet steps in. His mother.

"Mom, what a surprise." Ethan leans down to hug her and kiss her cheek. I frantically start straightening my shirt and run my fingers through my hair to make sure I look presentable.

"Well, you haven't called or stopped by so I decided I would come see you." She turns and her eyes connect with mine. A smile forms as she steps forward to greet me. "And who is this? She sure is pretty, Ethan."

My cheeks heat from her compliment.

His mother takes me by surprise when she hugs me. "Hi, I'm Julie. It's so nice to meet you!"

I beam at her. "It's nice to meet you, too. I'm Alexis."

"Kaylee's friend?"

I nod. "Yep, that's me."

Julie is wonderful, as I knew she would be. I didn't expect to meet her at all since she wasn't able to make it to Kaylee's wedding.

After talking with his mom for a while, I think Ethan is starting to feel a little left out since she is mostly talking to me. I casually send him an apologetic look for stealing all of his mother's attention. He would laugh it off like it's nothing.

Noticing the time, I stand. "It was great meeting you, Julie, but I need to go home. I have things I need to do before classes tomorrow." Ethan and I will have to wait I guess.

As I am hugging her, I see Ethan stand up out of the corner of my eye.

"I'll be right back, Mom," he tells Julie. I wasn't expecting him to walk me out, but these days I never know what will happen between us.

Ethan places his hand on the small of my back as we walk down the stairs.

"I had a lot of fun this weekend. Thank you for taking me to Six Flags," I say to break the silence.

We stop and I turn to him as we reach my car. Kaylee and Adam brought it here for me.

He gazes at me for a long moment, his hand reaching out to tuck my hair behind my ear.

"Are you sure you can't stay?" he murmurs, lowering his mouth to mine.

In my head, I am weighing my options. Homework and laundry are on my to-do list tonight, which I have to do. Although, I really want to stay with him again. The week I stayed with him comes to mind, reminding me how much I miss being spending so much time with him. Our quick getaway was wonderful and Ethan was a complete gentleman, a side of him I haven't seen very often.

My eyes flick up to meet his. His expression is hopeful, pleading. Sighing, I know I will be giving into him. "Let me get some homework and laundry done and I will come back."

He flashes a wide smile. "I'll be waiting." My breath hitches in anticipation of the kiss I know will be coming. The moment he lowers his head to mine, I throw my arms around his neck, meeting him halfway.

As I anticipated, the kiss sweeps me off my feet. My knees suddenly become weak as his lips fuse with mine.

"See you soon, Lex," he whispers, his soft lips brushing mine.

I didn't want to walk away from him, but I knew I had things which needed to be done. Saying the hell with it would have been nice, too, but I can't do that every time Ethan gives me butterflies and ask me to stay with him. The flunking out of college conversation would go over real well with my parents.

Ethan fogs up my head, making me unable to think clearly. Maybe tonight will put us where we need to be in our weird relationship.

chapter thirty-four

Ethan

It's going on ten o'clock and I haven't heard from, Lex. Did she change her mind? I dial her number and get no answer. I text her and get no reply.

Mom left a couple hours ago and I have been pacing my apartment waiting on Lex. I haven't seen her in like eight hours, and it's killing me.

Deciding I am not going to wait any longer, I swipe my keys off the counter and leave my apartment. I'm so nervous I'm starting to sweat. What if I lose her the moment I realize how much I can't live without her? An ache forms in my chest just thinking about losing her. I'm finally pulling my head out of my ass and taking a chance. I hope it's not too late.

When I arrive at her apartment, I notice the lights are still on and her car is parked in its normal spot. Racing up the stairs, I try to calm my nerves. Alexis has opened my eyes to a whole new meaning of the word 'living'. She has taught me to take life one day at a time. Being in the military, you learn how precious life is quick. I should have never put off my feelings for her even though I was scared of what the future would hold. That's the thing, no one knows what's in store for them do the road. We will all have good and bad days along with some terrible days. It's life, and now I am fixing to start living mine, the way I should've been, with Alexis.

My knuckles rap against the door and I exhale as I wait impatiently for her to open the door.

I am about to knock again when the door slowly opens, revealing a disheveled Alexis, holding a bottle of Pepto in one hand.

Her eyes widen a fraction and she immediately starts apologizing. "Oh my god, I'm so sorry. I started feeling bad and I decided to nap to see if I would feel better when I woke up."

I step inside and close the door behind us.

"Lex, it's okay. You could have called me, though," I say as I usher her to the couch, urging her to lie back down. I wish she would have just stayed with me.

She lies down and I cover her up with the blanket, which is lying on the back of the couch.

"Will you stay with me?" she murmurs softly. She really didn't need to ask, I had already planned to. Taking the Pepto from her, I place on the coffee table behind me.

I brush her hair back with my hand. "Of course." I take off my shoes then gently scoop her up in my arms, carrying her to her bedroom.

I lay her down then crawl in beside her. My arm automatically goes around her and she curls into my side, her head resting on my chest. I sigh, feeling content, and press my lips to her forehead.

"Night, Lex."

"Night," she whispers back.

Tonight didn't go as planned, but that's okay because as long as I am with, Lex, I'm happy. It's taken me some time to realize how much she means to me, and I'm kicking myself for it, but now the future's looking brighter for me, for us.

Throughout the night, I am awakened by the sound of Lex getting sick. Each time I would get up and take care of her and carry her back to bed. I also made her drink some water to keep her hydrated.

This time when I woke up, the spot beside me was empty and the apartment was quiet. Noticing the light coming from the bathroom, I throw the covers back and run to the bathroom to find Lex sprawled out on her back on the tile.

I crouch down and shake her gently. "Lex," I call out. She stirs, but doesn't wake. I pick her up off the floor and lay her back in her bed. Glancing at the clock on the wooden nightstand, I realize it's almost six o'clock. She will definitely not be going to classes today.

Mom couldn't go to Kaylee's wedding because she was sick with the stomach virus. If I had to guess, Lex took it from, Mom, who I guess thought she wasn't contagious anymore. Hell, Lex had more contact with my mother than I did today.

After Alexis left, Mom still couldn't stop going on about her. Mom also pretty much told me how stupid I was and she even slapped me up side my head. If I hadn't of already realized how much I loved her, mom's slap would've done the trick.

Peering down at Lex, I drink her in, my heart swelling with so many emotions. How I managed to keep denying myself from what I truly wanted, I don't know, but from here on out, I'm not letting her go. She's mine, forever and always.

The way her lips are parted slightly, to the sound of her soft snores, how could I not want to be with this beautiful woman who, time after time, dealt with my insults and me pushing her away for so long? I am a fool for hurting her. As I told Lex, I will be making it up to her, by reminding her each and every day how much I love her and need her in my life.

These upcoming nine months will be an ultimate test of our relationship, yet I know without a shadow of a doubt, Lex will still be waiting, ever so patiently, on my return.

Wrapping my arms tighter around her, I pull her closer, careful not to churn her stomach or wake her. Her face still looks as pale as it did when she opened the door last night. The night has been a long one, but I won't leave her side. She needs me to care for her, to make sure she is staying hydrated, to hold her.

I am so in love with, Alexis Collins. When I finally tell the guys, they will tell me it's about time, and they're right, along with everyone else who will say the same.

It's going on nine and she is still sleeping. I had Adam swing by and pick up some ginger ale and crackers for her. I don't want to leave her side in case she needs me.

"Thanks, man. I owe you," I tell him when he arrives with the stuff I asked for.

"Not a problem. I hope she gets to feeling better soon." He turns for the door but stops and pauses. "It's finally happening, isn't it?" he asks with a grin.

"Yes," I answer proudly. "I have finally pulled my head out of my ass and seen what I was missing out on." I roll my eyes as I say the words.

His smile grows. "I'm happy you finally did it. Now, don't screw it up," he says with a laugh.

I chuckle along with him. "I don't intend to."

When Adam is gone, I walk back to check on Lex. She is still asleep so I try waking her again.

She groans, slowly opening her eyes.

"Lex, babe, you need to eat or drink something."

"No, not hungry," she mumbles.

Her eyes start to flutter closed, but I am quick to keep them open. "No, no. Just a couple crackers and few sips, Lex, that's all I am asking."

She caves and holds her hand out. I open the package and hand her a cracker first. She munches on it for a few minutes and holds her hand out for another. When is done munching on crackers, I pour her a glass of ginger ale and help her sit up before I hand it to her.

"Better?" I ask as she takes small sips.

She nods her head. "A little."

Emptying my hands, I lie down beside her, cradling her in my arms once more.

Lex has been wrapped in my arms all morning long and it feels surreal and indescribable. I kiss Lex on her cheek, leaving a note on my pillow letting her know I am running to my apartment to grab some clothes.

When I arrive, my mood immediately dissipates the second I see Kate. Dear lord, when will she realize I don't want to have anything to do with her?

I try to act like she isn't there as I walk quickly to the stairwell.

"Ethan!"

I shake my head and continue on, ignoring her.

"Ethan Harper! I know you can hear me!" The clicking of her heels behind me have me cringing.

"Leave, Kate."

I manage to make it inside and slam the door before she can follow me inside. Locking the door, I head to my room and throw some clothes into a bag as quickly as I can. Getting back to Lex is my number one priority right now. Kate can fuck off.

Kate is still outside my door when I step out. Ignoring her completely doesn't take away the fact she is still screeching my name and spouting off nonsense behind me, but I'm not answering her, not this time.

I make it to my truck and jump in, effectively locking the doors before she has a chance to keep me here longer than I want to be.

Cranking my truck, I drop it in reverse and slowly back out. Kate started backing away once she realized I wasn't stopping.

The idea of changing complexes comes to mind. I wouldn't mind living closer to Lex, especially if Kate doesn't know where I moved to.

My phone rings on my way back to Lex. "Harper," I answer in greeting.

"Harper, how have you been?" my Sergeant, Winstead, asks.

"Good. You?"

"Excellent, though, I'm afraid I have some rather bad news. They want us to leave Monday at 0800."

Shit. This day just keeps getting better. "Yes sir. I'll be there."

"Sorry, Harper. Have a good day. See you Monday."

I hang up and curse my luck. I still had a few more weeks, which I planned to spend with Lex.

How am I going to tell, Lex? This will crush her. It seems like the universe is trying to keep us apart.

chapter thirty-five

Alexis

Having Ethan take care of me these past couple of days has only intensified my feelings for him. I'm beginning to believe I have completely fallen in love with him. I miss him when he is not around, I'm constantly wondering what he is doing when he is not around, and I find myself smiling as I think about him.

Something is bothering him, though. Since he came back from his errand, he seems distant. And this has been going on since yesterday afternoon. He hardly utters a word and I am beginning to think he has grown tired of taking care of me.

This morning when I woke, the first thing I did was take a nice long shower to wash away the sickness and the grime. I felt instantly better.

I also made breakfast for the two of us, hoping it will knock him out of his funk, but it didn't work.

I still feel a little weak, but being up and about has helped me gain a little strength back.

Ethan is stretched out on my couch, watching TV. I wish I knew why he looks so sad.

Deciding I want to see if I can get him to tell me, I stride over to him, grab the remote and turn off the TV.

He looks up at me with a confused look but doesn't say anything.

"Ethan, what is wrong with you? You act like someone kicked your puppy."

He sighs heavily then wraps his arm around my waist, pulling me down on top of him. Laying my head on his broad chest, I wait patiently for him to tell me what is eating him.

When he finally does tell me, it's not even close to what I suspected.

"They want us to leave sooner than planned," he finally says.

My whole body stiffens. Drawing back, I cup his cheek. "How soon?"

His piercing stare holds mine for the briefest moment. "Monday."

"Wha—wh—can they do that?" I barely form a sentence as I am too choked up to respond.

He nods. "I'm sorry, Lex."

"I only have you for two more days?" I ask in utter disbelief.

Ethan holds me tight as I face plant into his chest, crying.

"I don't know want you to leave," I sob.

He doesn't say anything, he just holds me while I cry.

That night, we both go to bed still upset. He continues to hold me gently in his arms while my heart aches for us both. As Ethan sleeps, I vow to make these last two days I have for nine long months the best.

But when morning comes, he is gone. There is no note left to explain his disappearance. All my calls go straight to his voicemail.

He never calls me or comes back to my apartment.

If I couldn't hear his voice when I get his voicemail, it'd be like he never existed to me. A figment of my imagination. A dream.

But this can't be a dream. The feelings are far too real and pain of him leaving without so much of a goodbye feels like a dagger to my heart.

Watching Lex break down in my arms was too much for me to handle. So, I did the best thing for her, leave. I knew all along this would happen, that I'd shatter her heart. Lex doesn't deserve me or a man who is gone nine months at a time not knowing if he will return home.

Breaking the news to my mother had been just as hard. It was even harder when I told her *everything*. When she asked about Lex, I couldn't answer her. This is the hardest thing I've ever had to do. *This is for the best.* I keep telling myself this over and over, yet my words hold no conviction to them.

Mom gives me a pleading look and I know she is about to have one of her motherly talks. "Honey, pushing her away will only keep you both from happiness. I love you, son, but you have been a downright idiot when it comes to her. You love her, and she loves you, what more can you ask for?"

I do love her, which is why I left. "She deserves more than the life I can give her, mom."

I flinch when mom pops me up side my head. "Excuses! Are you willing to let go of the best thing that has ever happened to you, a girl who is willing to wait for you? Alexis knew this day was coming and she still wanted to be with you. Doesn't that tell you something, son?"

I've thought about it, poured over the thought of her actually sticking by me through my military career. I can see it, it's right there, yet I'm afraid it will get too hard for her. Does Lex really know what is in store for if she joins me on this journey?

"You need to go back and apologize to her. Make it right before you leave."

I hug Mom tightly, hearing her sob on my shoulder like Lex did is not easy. But, I chose this career and I don't regret my rash decision seven years ago. It's molded me into who I am as a man.

I tell mom I love her and kiss her cheek before climbing in my car and heading home.

The debate I have with myself on the hour long drive home is whether or not I should head on over to Lex's apartment and apologize like my mother told me to do.

Should I give her some space? Time? Unfortunately, time is not my friend right now.

I still haven't made a decision by the time I reach my apartment. Right now, I'm just wasting time in which I could be spending with her.

Needing to get out of the place which reminds me of the girl who consumes me, I head over to my sister's for a while to spend time with her and her little family.

I want what my little sister has, a family. And Lex is the only woman I want to share that life with.

Even as I realize it, I'm still heading in the opposite direction.

chapter thirty-six

Alexis

Tomorrow is the dreaded day. Ethan leaves for Iraq and he will be gone for nine months. I haven't seen him since the night he broke the news to me. I haven't called or texted him since the next morning and he hadn't tried to contact me either. I don't want him to leave with this wedge between us. Longing for the open road, I climb in my car and start my drive to my destination. I'm going to see Julie hoping she can give me some insight on her son. I know they talk and visit often and I know how close they are so I'm sure he has said something to her.

The drive felt long, but I needed the time to come up with a solid plan and a backup if the first one goes wary. I realized I should have probably called as I turn in her gravel driveway.

Taking a long deep breath, I rap my knuckles on the wooden door. Obviously, she is surprised to see me, but she quickly masks it.

"Hello, dear. This is a nice surprise," she says pulling me in for a hug.

"I hope this is not a bad time, but I kind of wanted to talk to you if that's okay."

She opens the door wider and waves me inside. "Of course, dear. Come on in and make yourself at home."

"How are you feeling? Better?"

"Yes, much better!" Thank goodness the stomach virus or whatever I had is gone.

I walk inside and gingerly sit on the couch. I knot my hands together to hide my nerves.

She sits down next to me on the couch, her body turned slightly in my direction. "Is this about my idiot son who keeps putting that frown on your face?"

I nod slowly. "Yeah. I wish I knew why he keeps ripping my heart to shreds," I murmur sadly.

"He and I had a talk last night about you and I must say, even though he is my son, he has no sense when it comes to you. He's told me everything, even what happened a few weeks ago. I'll have you know I smacked him upside his head and called him an idiot."

I smile at the image of her actually doing just that.

"Alexis, sweetie, he's afraid. Ethan is big on promises and he hates letting people down so the reason he keeps pushing you away is because he is afraid of making you promises and not being able to fulfill them if he...doesn't return home." Her voice starts cracking so I hug her.

Tears threaten and I fight to urge to cry. Thinking about not being able to see Ethan again creates an ache deep in my chest.

She pulls away and wipes her eyes. "If something happens to him, I don't know what I'd do, but he needs to pull his head out of his butt and realize he is close to losing you."

"Even though he has broken my heart several times, I still love him, Julie."

"Go to him and try to talk some sense into that thick skull of his," she urges.

We say our goodbyes and I run to my car. I drive at least ten miles over the speed limit the whole way home, praying I don't get pulled over.

I make it to Ethan's in forty-five minutes and run up the stairs to his floor. I knock on the door and wait. I cringe at the thought of Kate being here.

The door swings open and Ethan is standing in front of me shirtless. "What are you doing here, Lex.?"

"I love you," I blurt out. He sucks in a harsh breath. "I can't stand the thought of you leaving without telling you how I feel."

I wait for him to say something, but when he doesn't I continue. "I know you're scared, Ethan, and I am too, but please don't shut me out. I know why you won't let me in and I have to say that is the dumbest excuse I've ever heard in my life."

"Lex," he breathes, sounding pained.

I close the short distance between us and wrap my arms around his middle. He tenses but doesn't push me away. "Don't turn me away, not anymore. Let me in, Ethan."

"I don't want to let you down if something happens," he murmurs.

I remove my head from his chest and cup his face in my hands. "Listen to me, you are going to come home to me, you got that? Regardless, I'll still cherish the time we had together. I'd rather have some time with you than none at all."

His arms fly around me, flattening me against him. "I'm sorry for everything, Lex. I didn't intend to hurt you, I swear."

I hoist myself up, wrapping my legs around his waist. I capture his lips with mine and he wastes no time returning the kiss. I'm so wrapped up in kissing him, I barely register us moving.

I feel the softness of the sheets beneath my skin. He breaks away, placing feathering hot, open mouth kisses along my cheek, across my jawline, and down to the sensitive spot behind my ear. I gasp, arching my back.

He pauses and starts to draw back. I tighten my hold around his neck, keeping him from moving. "No running, remember?" I remind him.

He drops his head, resting his forehead against mine. His blue eyes penetrate mine, a mix of sadness and lust lingering. "I want to do this right, Lex."

I silence him with a soft kiss. "Give me everything, Ethan. Don't hold back," I whisper, my lips grazing his with every word that rolls off my tongue.

As confirmation, he cradles my head, angling my mouth up to his as he meets my demand. Our kisses become greedier, hungrier, as time passes. I run my hands up his hips, slipping them under his shirt. His shirt rides up as I run my fingers up his taut muscles along his abdomen. When his shirt reaches his shoulders, I jerk it off of him, breaking his assault on my mouth.

Leaning forward, I kiss along the rigid lines on his stomach, my tongue darting out, lightly tracing the lines of his muscles. He mutters under his breath, obviously enjoying my teasing. My hands grasp the button on his jeans and tug gently, unbuttoning them. My hands drag his jeans down his legs slowly, then he steps out of them.

He nudges me back gently and removes my shoes first before yanking off my leggings, my underwear going with them in the floor.

Ethan's mouth trails up my leg, stopping mid-thigh, then switching to the other leg, doing the same. I groan loudly when his mouth leaves my skin, his warmth leaving me.

"Patience, Lex," he breaths, then his mouth is on me again, a place no one's mouth has been before.

My hands grasp the sheets as my belly tightens.

"Ethan," I moan his name as his tongue flicks me. I squirm, my body rising off the bed.

"Keep still," he orders, placing his hand on my stomach to hold me in place.

I do my best, but the sensations pulsing through my core prevent me from keeping still.

He abruptly pulls away and I whimper in protest.

Ethan wraps one arm under me and moves me farther up the mattress. His hands glide my shirt up just a tad. His kisses his way up my abdomen as he inches my shirt upward. My shirt flies across the room, my bra following it. I am completed exposed to him now.

His eyes rake me from head to toe, lust turning to desire. "I know you think I'm pretty, but can we please get a move on?"

He shakes his head as he lowers it to my neck. "Not pretty, Lex. Breathtaking, irresistible, and a goddess," he says in between kissing my neck and along my collarbone. "I've wanted you for so long," he rasps as his mouth finds my breast.

"Ethan, please."

"Not yet, baby."

A mix between a groan and a whimper leaves my lips.

"You get so far under my skin, Lex. I don't know how you do it, but I don't want you to quit. I'm not sure when I fell in love with you. It could have been the first time I laid eyes on you, it could have been on the way home Kaylee's wedding, or it could have been one of the many moments when you smiled at me. I am a sucker for your smiles, Lex."

I gasp loudly when he thrusts into me without warning, my nails digging into his shoulder. His hands slide under me, cupping my butt, arching me into him.

"You feel like Heaven, baby."

I match him thrust for thrust, feeling the familiar tightening return with a vengeance. My teeth nip at his collarbone as he continues to thrust in and out of me.

Ethan grabs both my hands, pinning them above my head. He dips his head low, capturing my bottom lip between his teeth. I cry out, trying to break the hold he has on my wrists. I want to fist his hair between my fingers.

"Come apart for me, Lex."

And damn do I come apart. His name falls off my lips in a scream of pleasure.

A moment later he moans softly, then relaxes.

Ethan drops his head, resting it on my chest as we both catch our breath. He releases his hold on my wrists and my hands automatically go to his face. One hand toys with his hair while the other one rests on his cheek. We lay like this for a while, both of us deep in thought. My mind is racing, trying to comprehend how I ended up in this moment.

This would have happened sooner if he hadn't of kept keeping me at a distance. Sex with Ethan is far better than I have fantasized.

I kiss his hair, wondering where we go from here. Will he say he regrets it? My heart cracks thinking of that scenario. He finally let me in, gave me a part of him, but I want the rest of him. He already has my heart in the palm of his hand, now I just need his.

He lifts his head off my chest and kisses me soundly. He gazes at me, twirling a strand of my hair around his finger.

"Lex, I'm sorry."

I still at his words. I squeeze my eyes shut, hoping to block out the painful words I don't want to hear him say.

"Baby, open your eyes and look at me." I compile to his command, trying my hardest to not let a tear slip out. "Hey, hey, I would never regret this. That's not what I was going to say."

I didn't realize I had been holding my breath until I went to speak. "It's not?"

"No, baby. I was apologizing because I forgot the condom. I'm clean of course."

All then tension leaves my body. "Oh, I'm on the pill so we're good."

Silence blankets the room again. Ethan rolls us on our sides and wraps me in his arms.

"What do we do now, Ethan?"

He kisses my forehead, letting his lips linger against my sweat coated skin. "Now, we spend every moment we have left together until the morning."

Sadness creeps in, but I force it down. I'll deal with it after he is gone.

"That sounds perfect."

chapter thirty-seven

Ethan

I'm trying to wrap my head around what just happened. Lex, is in my arms, her head against my chest. I just made love to the first girl I have ever loved, and it was indescribable. I'm at a loss for words. Every cell in my brain is all jumbled up right now.

I pull her as close as possible to me. "I'm going to miss you so much, baby," I murmur in her hair.

Her eyes flutter close, a pained look crosses her features. "Can we not talk about that right now? It hurts to think about it and I want these last few hours to be a happy memory for us."

I'm not going to argue with that. With having already said my goodbyes to everyone earlier, it will just be me and her. "Are you hungry?"

"Starved."

"Well let's get cleaned up and I'll order us something."

We shuffle to the bathroom and I start the water for a bath. Lex is standing in front of the mirror fiddling with her hair. I walk up behind her, resting my hands on her hips.

"I don't know why you are wasting your time on your hair, it's just going to get messed up again later," I smirk at her through the glass.

She flushes, her face turning pink. "Well, at least I'll look presentable until then."

I turn her around so I can look into her soft brown eyes. "You're beautiful no matter what, baby."

She tilts her head up for a kiss and I happily oblige.

I climb into the tub and shut off the water. Lex rests between my legs, her back against my chest. I wrap my arms around her and just hold her.

"Don't forget that you can stay here anytime you like," I tell her.

"Ethan, I don't need it since you won't be here. I have my own."

"It's a 'just in case' deal so you will have it if you ever need it, okay? You can come and go as you please. My apartment is yours."

"Okay," her voice sounds so small, so sad.

I need to take both of our minds off me leaving. I turn her so I can capture her plush lips.

"When did you realize you were in love with me?" I ask her.

"Um, I'm like you. I don't think it was one particular moment. It just hit me like a ton of bricks. Even though you broke my heart constantly, I still wanted you."

"And I'm going to spend the rest of my life loving you, baby, making sure you never doubt my love for you again."

I let my hands drift over her smooth skin, loving the way she feels beneath my hands. Her head falls back onto my shoulder and I hear soft little whimpers escape her lips.

I twist her in my lap, her legs parallel with mine. She sinks down on me and my head falls back against the tile. Her hands brace my shoulders and mine fall to her hips. It isn't long before we cry out each other's name for the second time.

She lays against me, her head on my shoulder until the water turns cold.

"So much for getting clean," she says.

"Yeah, we kind of got sidetracked."

"I'm not complaining."

We quickly wash off and get out before the water gets any colder. We towel dry off and I give her one of my clean shirts to wear.

I groan at the beautiful sight before me. I wrap my arms around her from behind, resting my chin on her shoulder. "I love seeing you in just my shirts."

"I love wearing them."

I kiss her cheek. "What do you want to eat, Lex?"

"Pizza sounds amazing."

"Pizza it is, then."

After placing our order, we curl up on the couch and pick a movie off of Netflix. Tonight could not be more perfect.

"What are you thinking about up there?" she asks me.

"How I'm an idiot."

She laughs softly. "Your mom said the same thing."

"She's right. Don't tell her I said that, though," I add quickly.

"I'm just glad you finally came to your senses," she teases.

The pizza arrived so I reluctantly had to remove my arms from her and get up.

Lex starts dozing off toward the end of the second movie so I scoop her up in my arms and carry her into the bedroom. I lay her down gently and crawl in next to her. We are both lying on our sides, facing each other. In the middle of us our hands are entwined.

She is trying so hard to stay awake. "Sleep, baby."

"No, I don't want to spend the last few hours with you asleep. Talk to me, keep me awake."

"Stubborn girl," I say with a laugh.

"You love me and my stubbornness."

"That I do, but do you want to know what I love most about you?"

"Hmm, what's that?"

"Your beauty. You're beautiful inside and out, Lex."

A sleepy smile creeps across her face. "I know what we can do."

I arch my brow at her. "I bet it's not the same thing I'm thinking."

Her phone rings grabbing our attention, but neither of us makes any move to go answer it.

"If it's important they will call back. Now, back to your idea."

"Well, I kind of need your phone for it."

Intrigued, I roll over and grab my phone off the nightstand behind me. She has a sneaky smile on her face when I hand it to her.

She curls her finger at me. "Scoot closer to me."

I do as she says, wondering what she is up to.

She instructs me to lay like I was to begin with. Out of the corner of my eye I see her hold my phone above us and snap the picture. She brings it back down and we look at it.

"I had to capture this moment," she says softly.

I watch as she sends it to herself and sets it as the background picture on my phone.

We spend the next hour taking tons of selfies. Some were funny, some were pretty normal, but most of all they were us.

"This was a good idea, baby," I say as I scroll back through all of them.

"I know. I'm awesome like that,"

"Well, I wouldn't go as far as saying that." I grunt when she elbows me in my stomach.

"So what do you want to do now?" she ask as a yawn escapes her.

I look at the time on my phone. "Well, it's going on one in the morning. I have to leave here by seven in the morning to report to the armory."

"This is going to be a long nine months."

"I know, but the months will fly by and I will be back before you know it."

"You will be gone the amount of time a woman is pregnant," she jokes.

I turn her so I can look her right in her beautiful eyes. "Lex, when I come back, I want to marry you and I want us to start a family."

Her eyes widen in shock. "You're serious?"

"Hell yeah. You are my future and besides, I don't want to wait any longer." I really wanted to try now, but I'm going to push my luck.

"What will I do about school, Ethan?"

"You can still go, baby."

"Well, I guess it's a good thing I'm leaving the squad. I had already planned on taking fifteen credit hours this next semester anyway."

"Why would you take so many classes and leave the squad? You love cheering."

"I wanted to get ahead in my classes so when you came home I could either take a semester off or just take a couple classes so I'd have more time to spend with you."

"Baby, I want you to do what you love. Don't quit for me."

She grins widely. "Well, if we follow through with your plans then I won't be able to cheer."

I smile back at her, happy that she wants the same things I do. "Give me a second. I got something I need to show you."

I crawl out of bed and walk over to my ACU's which are draped across my bag. I grab what I am going to show her out of the front pocket.

"Close your eyes, Lex."

She eyes me suspiciously but does it anyway. I place the small photo in the palm of her hand.

"Open your eyes."

Her breath hitches when her eyes see the photo in her hand. I had my favorite picture of her printed in the wallet size so I can carry it in the pocket close to my heart while I was away. The picture is of her on Kaylee's wedding day.

"I was going to carry you with me regardless, Alexis. I didn't want to be without you."

"Is it selfish for me to not want you to go?" Lex asks me with tear filled eyes.

"No, it's not. It's going to be so hard to leave you here, baby. There won't be a day that passes that I won't think of you." I lower my mouth to hers, hoping to reassure her.

"You'll write me, won't you?"

"Of course, and sometimes I'll even Skype with you, just so I can see your beautiful face."

"You better because I'll need to see for myself that you're okay."

I hate this for her. This is exactly why I didn't want to pursue her, but I admit, I was wrong. I'm glad we are together now, spending time in each other's arms. I needed this, needed her.

"As long as I know that you're here waiting for me, I'll be more than okay."

Over the next hour, Lex and I just lay wrapped in each other's arms until finally around two-thirty in the morning, she gives it up.

I wait until she is sound asleep before climbing out of bed. I had written her a letter the night before and I had planned on either leaving it in her mailbox or letting Adam or Kaylee give it to her, but things have done a one-eighty since then.

I pick up my notebook and pen and write her a new letter.

When I am done, I fold the letter up and place it on top of her purse for to see after I leave. I set my alarm on my phone just in case I doze off with her in my arms. The letter was hard to write, but I wrote from the heart.

My alarm blares at six a.m. sharp and I force myself to unwrap my arms from around Lex.

When I go to get up, her arms tighten around my waist, preventing me from going anywhere.

"No, don't go," she murmurs, sounding half asleep.

I sigh and roll over to face her. "Remember those promises I had you make? Well, now I need you to keep them."

"I'll try," she whispers. I press a kiss to her forehead, holding it there for a long beat.

She hesitantly lets me go and I leave the comfort of having her arms around me to get dressed.

Lex is in the kitchen making coffee, still dressed in only my t-shirt. I walk up behind her and wrap my arms around her, my chin resting on her shoulder.

She leans back in my embrace and sighs heavily. "This is going to be a very long nine months."

"I'll be back before you know it, baby." At least, I hope these next several months fly by.

"Since I'm not going to be cheering anymore I think I might get a job. I'm not sure, though, it's just a thought."

My lips brush her cheek. "Why don't you see how your classes go first, just to make sure you don't get overloaded."

"I am, I just feel like I need to keep busy, but at the same time I need to be available so I won't miss any of your calls."

Lex twists in my arms and wraps her arms around my neck. She buries her face in the crook of my neck and clings to me tightly. A moment later, I hear her sniffle so I mold her body to mine, hating the fact that I will soon have to let her go and not see her or be able to hold her in my arms for a while.

chapter thirty-eight

Alexis

I promised myself I wouldn't cry until after he left, but who am I kidding? This is hard to come to terms with. Letting your boyfriend of twelve hours, who you have been in love with for months, leave you to go fight for your country.

Ethan's arms are crushing me to his body while I give in to the tears. I let them stream down my cheek and onto his shoulder. I didn't know how the people in this position felt until this moment. Watching your son, daughter, significant other leave, not knowing if you will ever see them again is indescribable. The ache in your heart spreads throughout your chest, weighing heavily.

I need to keep it together because I promised him I'd be strong for him and his family.

"Lex, baby, I hate to say this, but I have to report to the armory."

With one last squeeze, I drop my arms. He wipes the wetness away from cheeks and kisses each one before descending to my lips.

"Be safe," I murmur. I will be clinging to all of our memories from last night and this morning until I get to be in his arms again.

"Always."

He kisses me long and hard, another memory I will cling to while he is gone.

"I love you, Lex."

I jump in his arms for one last hug. "I love you, too." I kiss his cheek, then his full lips before letting him walk out the door, the pain growing with every step he takes in the opposite direction.

I watch him until climbs in his truck and drives away. When he is out of sight, I close the door and fall against it. Choking on a sob, I slide down until my butt hits the floor. I hug my knees to my chest and drop my head to my knees. This time, I don't hold back, I let out all the pain that is weighing on my chest. I thought I hurt when he kept breaking my heart by turning me away, but this is far worse than anything I have ever felt in my entire life.

I don't move or stop crying until my butt has gone numb so I wipe my face with my shirt sleeve and stand. I drag my emotionally wrought self to the shower so I can clean up and get ready to go talk to my coach about my resignation. Ethan is right, I love cheering, but as heavy as my schedule was this past semester, there would be no way I would be free to answer his call. I'd miss it every time and I can't have that.

There is a tentative knock on the door so I walk over to it and check the peephole. I hadn't been expecting anyone so when I see my best friend standing on the other side I throw the door open and launch myself at her. We both burst into tears, crying over Ethan's departure.

We finally pull away from one another and walk into the apartment.

Kaylee relaxes on the couch next to me. "Ethan called me, said you were here."

"Yeah, we spent yesterday evening and all night together. It feels like a dream. If I wasn't at his apartment I would have thought I had imagined the whole thing. Good thing I can still feel him touching my skin with his fingers and his mouth.

"Okay, spill. I don't need you to go into detail since he is my brother because that is gross, but I would like to know what happened yesterday."

So I tell my best friend how I was sick and all the events leading to his sudden disappearance. I also told her how I went and visited his mother for advice since I was feeling lost about Ethan leaving the next day and I didn't want to leave things like they had been. I told her how we talked and she opened up to me about Ethan's fears. Then, I get into the confrontation and bits and pieces of our night together. I even pull out my phone to show her all the pictures we took. I had Ethan send them to me so I could have them to look at when I needed to see him.

"Who knew my brother could be so in love. I mean, I know he can be a dork, but in love?"

I smile, but it doesn't reach my eyes. "He is a sweetheart. I just wish we could have resolved the rift between us sooner."

"We all tried to tell him, Alexis, but he is stubborn and he didn't listen."

I know Ethan is stubborn, but I also know he was afraid of pursuing me when he would just be leaving. I get it, I really do, but you only get one life. You can't worry about all the 'what ifs' or the consequences. Last night, Ethan gave in to his fears allowing me to show him just how beautiful our relationship can be.

"None of that matters now. We are together so now I am just waiting on him to return home to me."

My chest may feel hollow, void of my heart, but I know that Ethan is carrying it safely with him, and it gives me confidence in believing he will return to me safe and unharmed.

My phone vibrates in my lap and my heart leaps wondering if it is Ethan. The hope fades when I see it's not the person who makes my heart race and my face light up.

I scrunch my nose up, trying to figure out if I know the number flashing on my screen. I answer it anyway.

"Hello?"

Silence is all I hear…at first, then breathing.

"Hello?" I call again, but still the only thing I hear is breathing.

I hang up and check my call log. Whoever it is called me last night, too. It was the call we ignored. Weird.

"Who was it?" Kaylee asks, noticing my expression.

"Not sure." Chills erupt across my skin causing me to shiver. It is probably just some kid or immature adult playing tricks.

Nerves knot my stomach as I pull into my usual parking space at the school's gymnasium. I have all of my uniforms and anything else I suspect she will want to be returned after I resign. I need to call Matt and Alice and let them know. I will miss them, but I'm ready to start a new chapter in my life with Ethan. I know they will miss me fiercely, but they will understand. I will make it a promise to see them often.

I knock timidly on Coach Hamilton's door and wait until she calls for me to come in.

She looks up from the papers on her desk in surprise. "Alexis, what a surprise. What can I do for you?"

I sit in the plush chair across from her and take a deep breath. "I'm leaving the squad," I blurt out.

She pulls her glasses off her face, laying them on her desk. "Alexis, you are one of my best girls. May I ask why?"

"My boyfriend left today for Iraq and between my classes and cheering I'm hardly at home and I don't want to miss any of his calls."

It feels so good to call Ethan my boyfriend.

"Oh dear, I'm sorry Alexis. I didn't know you had been seeing anyone."

"We've known each other for about a year, but we've just recently made it official." I barely get the words out. Talking about Ethan and his departure is still too raw.

She gets up from her desk chair and takes the seat next to me. "I know this is going to be tough for you dear. My husband was in the Army back in the day. He joined right out of high school. We had been dating on and off for a year before he was sent to Fort Benning, Georgia to live on base. We weren't married at the time so I couldn't go with him. I remember thinking my world was gone. The sun didn't rise or set for the longest until I finally got a letter from him. We wrote letters back and forth for about a year then he left to go fight in a war. I remember the day he came back vividly. I was outside helping mom in the garden when a cab pulled up to the house. I was like a statue for a long minute until mom finally jostled me out of it and I ran and jumped in his arms. After that, we were married and I went with him wherever he had orders to go."

"This may be a stupid question, but does the void fade away or will it always be there?"

"Some days will be better than others, Alexis, but just continue to pray for him daily and just keep on with life. Everything will work out my dear."

I thank her and we hug as we say our goodbyes. Hearing her story didn't help alleviate the weight on my chest, but it gives me hope that things will work out for the better.

I text Matt and Alice and ask them if they want to meet me for lunch. They both reply instantly and we decide to meet at Lost River Pizza.

I am the first to arrive so I go ahead and get us a seat, by the window and slide in, waiting for them to arrive.

Alice is the first to arrive a few minutes later. I wave her over and she hugs me when she reaches me. We make small talk until Matt strolls in, a look of concern etched on his face. I swear Matt knows when something is wrong with me. It's like he has this sixth sense.

"Hello, my favorite girls," Matt croons, giving each of us a hug. He holds me longer. "Are you okay?" he asks quietly in my ear.

"Yes and no."

He pulls away and he takes a seat beside me.

Matt waits expectantly for me to elaborate on my cryptic answer to his question.

"So, um, I talked to Mrs. Hamilton today. I am no longer a part of the squad."

Alice gasps. "Wait-what?"

"Please tell me you're joking," Matt says, looking less than thrilled at my decision.

"No, I'm serious. Ethan and I are toge-"

Matt cuts me off. "For the love of God, please, don't tell me you are with that asshole." When I don't answer he shakes his head, his lips setting a firm line of disapproval.

I know Matt can't stand Ethan, but he needs to understand that Ethan is it for me.

"Why, Alexis? Did you forget how many times we binged out on ice cream and crappy romantic movies because of him? How about how many times on those same nights, I listened to you cry yourself to sleep over that douche?"

"We talked and he apologized, Matt. Can't you be happy for me?"

"Just because he apologized doesn't mean you have to forgive him, I don't. But that doesn't explain why you are not cheering anymore."

"Matt calm down," Alice interrupts. "Alexis has got a good head on her shoulders. Just listen and hear her out."

I mouth 'thank you' to her and she just smiles.

"Fine," he grits out.

I breathe in and out slowly, hoping I can get through this without tearing up. "Ethan left this morning to go overseas and he will be gone nine long months. I wanted to take extra classes while he is gone so I can take a semester off or take only a couple classes when he is back. I don't want to miss a call from him at any time and you know with our cheer schedule I would probably miss everyone."

"Did he tell you to do this?"

"What? No! He even questioned why I was quitting."

Alice gives me a sympathetic smile. "Well, I am here for you girl if you need me."

"Thank you."

"Alexis, I'm not happy with your decision, but as long as you are happy, I will be too. Just know that if he makes you cry anything other than happy tears, I won't hesitate to put him in his place."

My body sags in relief. I'm glad Matt is trying for me. I know him and Ethan have a lot of beef between them because he kept hurting me, but I hope eventually they will be getting along.

Matt side hugs me before getting up and ordering us a pizza. We sit, talk, and cut up for a while. Other than Kaylee, Julie, and my parents, I will need these two to help me through this deployment.

I just want Ethan back home safe and sound.

chapter thirty-nine

Alexis

Back at the apartment, I try to keep myself busy. Ethan keeps his house spotless so I have nothing to clean. I strip the bed and throw our tangled, messy sheets in the washer. While those are washing, I fix myself something to eat and relax on the couch. I clutch his pillow to my chest, trying to find something to watch on T.V. Nothing interests me so I search Netflix for something that catches my attention. It hasn't been one day yet and time is already dragging. Giving up, I switch off the T.V and head back into Ethan's bedroom.

I decide I want to go see Jasmine and Jackson so I bend down to grab my purse and freeze. Laying on top of it is a white envelope with my name on it. It's obvious by the handwriting Ethan left it for me.

I had been in such a rush earlier to meet Matt and Alice I just grabbed my phone and keys. My phone case has a flap that opens up where you can store your debit card in.

My hand trembles as I pick it up. I stare at it for a long moment, debating whether or not I want to open it right now.

Decision made, I tear open the envelope and pull out the letter.

My beautiful Lex,

Sitting here watching you sleep, makes me dread leaving you in a few hours. God, it will be so hard to be away from you. It will take every ounce of strength in me to get unwrap my arms from you and go. I don't want to be without you in my life ever again. Last night was the best night of my life. That along with seeing you smile, hearing you laugh and being able to gaze into your gorgeous eyes. Every memory I have of you will keep me going. It will keep me pushing forward.

I'm sorry for all the hurt I caused you in the past. I was stupid and I think I knew deep down that one day we would be together. I just wish I would have made it happen a lot sooner.

Remember all the promises you made me, Lex? I need you to keep them. I know this is hard for you, believe me. But always be happy, Lex. Do things that make you happy. Be around people who make you happy. Do not let anyone tell you that you are anything less than beautiful. You're breathtaking, Lex, and I'm so lucky that you want to be with me.

Now this is the hardest promise, but the most important one. I need you to be strong for me while I am gone, okay? I know you can do it, beautiful. My faith is in you. Stay strong, and hold on because no matter where I am, I'll always come home to you.

I love you, Lex, and I can't wait to see your beautiful face again.

I love you,

Ethan

A drop lands on the letter and I realize I'm crying. I bend down to pick up the envelope I had dropped and notice something inside. I hold the letter tightly and bring it to my chest.

Ethan's words echo in my brain. *I know you can do it, beautiful.*

I wipe the tears away, determined not to break my promise to him.

After stashing the note in my purse, I walk into the bathroom to freshen up before I head to Adam and Kaylee's. I know if they see me crying, they will hug me and I'll lose it.

When I arrive, I turn the knob and walk in like I always do. I hear the laughter and the squeals of my favorite twins.

Kaylee is in the kitchen washing dishes, Adam nowhere in sight.

"Hey!" Kaylee exclaims when she notices me. She rinses off her hands and dries them with a towel before pulling me in for a hug.

"How are you?" I ask her.

Her expression softens. "I'm doing okay. I have these two to keep my mind occupied. How about you?"

"I have a lot to tell you!"

She arches a brow. "Oh really? Adam went to help his dad with something real quick. He should be back shortly, then we can talk."

The twins and I play while Kaylee is finishing up in the kitchen. They both holler they are hungry after a few minutes so I help Kaylee round up the kiddos and place them in their highchairs.

We are in the middle of feeding them when Adam walks in.

He kisses Kaylee first then the twins on top of their heads.

"Hey babe, Alexis and I need to have a girl talk for a few minutes."

Adam never looks up from playing with the twins when he answers her. "Sure, sweetheart. Go on, I'll finish up here."

Kaylee and I decide to take a walk through their neighborhood. It's a quiet and peaceful neighborhood. A far cry from my apartment complex. Maybe one day Ethan and I can have this. *'Lex, when I come back, I want to marry you and I want us to start a family."*

"So best friend, what other juicy stuff do you have to tell me?"

Mainly, I just wanted to walk and clear my head, but Ethan did tell me that when he came home he wanted to start a family."

She screeches and starts jumping up and down. "What? What did you tell him?"

"At first I was speechless, but I want a family with him eventually so I told him my plans of loading up on classes."

We turn around and start our trek back. "I'm happy for you two, I really am. You're officially going to be my sister!"

"You don't think it's too soon, though?"

"No, you two have been in love with each other for months and I honestly believe you two are perfect for each other."

My jaw drops. Did everyone see it and not us?

"Oh come on! One look at you two and you knew! Even though there was so much tension between you both, you just always gazed at each other like no one else was around. Brad even knew, I just think he refused to believe it. I mean, I hate that he got his heart broke, but you did the right thing by breaking up with him. You were always happier around Ethan than you were with Brad."

"I hated hurting Brad because he was an amazing guy, but I just wasn't attracted to him like I was Ethan. I hope it doesn't hurt his friendship with Adam."

She waves me off. "Girl no, they still talk all the time despite him being two hours away. I think Adam mentioned something about him meeting some girl."

"That's good, I'm happy for him."

I genuinely am. Brad deserves to find his happily ever after. He is a sweet guy. Any girl would be lucky to have him and his charming personality.

I start wondering what I am going to do tonight. I don't want to go home to my empty, quiet apartment. Staying at Ethan's tonight will only result in me thinking about him and probably crying myself to sleep because I miss him so much already.

"Hey, Kaylee? Do you and Adam want to have a date night?" Keeping the babies will keep me occupied for tonight. They will be a handful for sure, but I got this.

"You know I'm always up for that, but what made you ask?"

"I know you guys don't get to go out much and I just want to keep them tonight." That much is true. I love watching Jackson and Jasmine.

She gives me a knowing smile. "Sure, let me just run it by Adam."

Adam is all for it. I offer to keep them all night for them, but they decline my offer, wanting them home with them at night. I understand, I'm just thankful I can give them a few hours of alone time.

An hour later, they are saying goodbye to their babies.

"Don't forget, they usually eat around seven-thirty and we start putting them asleep by nine. Jasmine sleeps with her pink flower blanket and Jackson just likes you to cuddle him," Adam informs me.

Kaylee starts talking about things I already know. "You know where all the diapers and wipes are-"

"Guys, chill, I got this. Go on and enjoy your night together. I promise if I have any problems I will call you," I say as I shoo them out the door.

"Okay, but call us if you need us for anything. I mean it, Alexis."

"How many times do I need to tell you, I got this! Now go! Shoo!"

After another round of hugs and kisses for the twins they finally leave. Jackson, Jasmine, and I get right to playing. I start building blocks with Jasmine while Jackson plays with his cars.

Throughout the night, I cuddle them and read them stories.

Two hours in, Kaylee calls to check in. After assuring her they are fine, I hung up.

At seven-thirty I feed them and then bathe them. Once I have them both dressed and ready for bed, I pick out a couple books and we pile in the recliner. Jackson is on my left, Jasmine on my right side. Both of them are lying against me.

I get through the one book after dinner, and halfway through the second one before they fall asleep on me. I recline back, feeling content with them in my arms. I know I should probably lay them down in their cribs, but I'm enjoying this precious moment with them. I kiss the top of their heads and then my eyes drift close.

chapter forty

Alexis

Eight months to go

I'm growing more anxious as I wait and wait to hear from him. On top of my worry, I'm getting sick again. I had the stomach bug a few days before Ethan left, and I had only been over it a little over twenty-four hours before I went and saw Julie and spent that amazing night with Ethan. I'm pretty sure I have to stomach virus now and it's kicking my butt. If it keeps up, I am going to the doctor to see what the crap is wrong with me. I've already missed a full day of classes and I don't need to miss anymore or I will be so behind.

I'm lying in bed, curled under the covers, feeling like I am about to throw up again. I don't have a fever so that's a plus. God, I hate feeling nauseous. It's one of the worst feelings in the world. I feel so tired and weak from lack of sleep and not being able to keep anything down.

I finally give up and send a 911 text to Matt. Maybe he will see it and get here soon.

As I hoped, it was only thirty minutes later when I hear Matt walking in my apartment. "Alexis!" he calls from the living room.

Using all my strength, I yell, "In here," as loud as possible.

Matt runs into my room, straight to my side. "Oh, girl, are you sick again?" he murmurs, giving me a sympathetic look.

I just nod slowly.

"Have you eaten or drank anything?"

"Can't keep the food down. Have water," I mumble weakly, hoping he can understand me.

"I think you need to go to the doctor."

I don't want to go, but maybe they have something that will help me feel better.

Matt helps me sit up and change into clean clothes. He grabs the empty bucket I have in the floor beside my bed in case I need it. I don't want to be throwing up in his car, or mine.

When I am completely standing, I start feeling a little lightheaded. I stumble slightly against Matt, who tightens his arm around my waist.

I lean on him, letting him carry me out to the car.

The car ride has me keeping my head in the bucket. The motion of the car just makes the nausea worse.

"It's a good thing I don't have a weak stomach," Matt grumbles as he takes the bucket from me and tosses it in the garbage can nearest us.

He comes back and helps me out of the car since I don't have enough strength to do it on my own.

Matt kisses my temple. "Let's go get you some drugs to knock this mess out of you."

If I had the strength, I would laugh at his comment.

Matt signs me in and we wait, and wait, until finally a nurse calls me back. At first, I didn't think I was going to be seen today. I had almost fallen asleep on Matt's shoulder since we had to wait so long.

Once in the exam room, the doctor asks me a series of questions. "When did all of this start?" "What are my symptoms?" "Could I be pregnant?"

That question made me pause. I don't think so, but I am figuring up when I should have had my period, and I realize, I am late.

"I'm late," I murmur aloud. I feel Matt squeeze my hand comfortingly.

"When was the date of your last menstrual cycle?" the doctor asks.

I start thinking again. I had one a couple weeks before Ethan left, and I don't remember having one since then. Holy crap! I've been so busy worrying about Ethan and my classes that I didn't notice I didn't have my period this month.

"I'm roughly two weeks late."

"Well then, let's get a urine sample first.".."

Matt walks me to the bathroom, closing the door behind me. Using the rail, I sit down on the toilet, hoping I will be able to pee.

What if I am pregnant? Ethan said when he got back he wanted to marry me and start a family, but what if he isn't ready right now? I mean, technically, we have only been dating for a month. What about school?

Taking a deep breath, I finish and wash my hands. I breathe in deeply, exhaling slowly as I walk out of the bathroom.

Matt holds my hand in the room as we wait for the doctor to come back and deliver the news. What will Mom and Dad say if I am? I don't figure they will disown me, but I don't want them to be disappointed in me. My education is important to them.

There is a light knock on my door, then it opens as the doctor walks in, with no answer written on her face.

Then, she smiles. "Congratulations, you're pregnant."

I don't whether to cry or be happy. I will admit, I'm a little scared.

I will need to talk to Kaylee.

The doctor tells me I need to make an appointment to determine how far along I am, among other things. I make a note to do it after I talk to Kaylee. The doctor also points out that if I don't start eating and drinking, I will wind up in the hospital for dehydration. Yeah, I definitely don't need that to happen.

Matt is quiet and I don't like it. He hasn't said a word to me since the doctor wondered if I could be pregnant.

"What are you thinking, Matt?" I ask tentatively.

Matt sighs, telling me he is not happy. "What do you want me to say, Alexis?"

"I want you to say something. I don't like it when you're quiet, it means you're mad."

"I'm happy for you, I really am, it's just I wish he wasn't a dick to you."

"Ethan is not mean to me. Yes, he broke my heart a few times, but we have resolved things and he has apologized."

"Don't get me wrong, Alexis, I hope things will be great between the two of you. I hope the best for you. I want nothing else than to see you happy, so as long as he makes you happy, I will be happy."

I give him a tight smile. "Thank you, Matt."

He winks at me, telling me his bad mood is vanishing. "Anytime friend. Now, have you thought about how you are going to tell your parents? What about him and his mom?"

"I don't know. I'm scared to tell Mom and Dad because I don't know how they will react. Ethan wants to start a family when he comes back; I just hope he doesn't think this is too soon. As far as his mom, it could go either way with her."

"If you need me to go with you, I will in a heartbeat. I got your back," Matt replies encouragingly.

"You are awesome, you know that?"

He simply shrugs. "It's a gift that many people do not have so I cherish it."

I laugh out loud. "Oh wow. You have some ego issues."

Matt drives me back to my apartment and stays with me for a while. He even sanitized my bedroom and bathroom after my puke fest so they smell a lot better now. I owe him big time.

He even goes as far as driving to the grocery store to grab me some Pepto, soup, Gatorade, and anything else he thinks I will need.

While he is gone, I realize I haven't had my phone with me so I jerk back the covers and snatch my phone.

Please tell me, I haven't missed a call!

My heart plummets in my chest when I notice I have two missed calls. Checking my call log, I visibly relax when I don't see Ethan's name. It's just the crazy person who has been calling my phone a lot.

Dimming the screen, I lay back down, pulling the covers up to my chest. Sometimes I hate when it's so quiet because I start thinking, and it puts me in a bad mood.

My phone vibrates in my hand, its Ethan calling. I answer my phone quickly.

"Ethan!"

"Hey, Lex. How's my beautiful girlfriend?"

It's so good to hear his voice. "Better now," I murmur softly.

"What's the matter, Lex? You sound sad."

I kind of wanted to wait to tell him so I can surprise him, but the worry of not knowing how he will react is not good for me or the baby. "Well, I got some news today. It was rather shocking to say the least."

"What kind of news, Lex? Is it bad?"

"No, it's not. It's kind of scary, though. I-"

"Just spit it out, baby."

"Okay." I take a deep breath in and let it out. "I'm pregnant, Ethan. Honestly, I thought I had the stomach virus or something. I kept throwing up so much and I couldn't keep anything down at all. I finally sent an emergency text to Matt who to me to the doctor and the doctor suggested I take a test and it came back positive."

Silence is not a good thing right now. He is quiet on the other line and I'm starting to freak out and think the worst.

"Ethan?" I whisper tentatively, scared of what he could say.

"You're pregnant?"

"Yes," I murmur. "I know this might be too soon, but we can make this work. I love you and yes, having a baby is a scary thought, but I love you and-"

"Lex, you're taking it all wrong. I'm so happy right now, baby. Like, I'm speechless. It is totally unexpected, but man I'm excited."

"You are?"

"Yes, baby, I am. But I have to go. I will be writing you soon. I love you, Lex."

I wish he didn't have to go so soon. "I will be waiting to hear from you. Be safe, Ethan. I love you, too."

I hang up, feeling both relieved and sad. Deep down, I knew Ethan would be happy since this is what he wants, a family.

I hope I hear from him again soon. Hearing his voice keeps me going, keeps me positive. We are one month down in this deployment, a month closer to being home. A month closer to being able to hug him hard and kiss him endlessly. I can't wait for the day I get to lay my eyes on him again.

chapter forty-one

Alexis

Seven months to go

It's been almost two months, two long agonizing months without Ethan. I miss him more and more each day that passes. I have a calendar on my bedroom wall in my apartment. Using a red pen, I mark off a day at a time as it comes to a close. It reminds me I am one day closer to seeing my man again.

I've been staying at Ethan's more often than not. I snuggle his pillow every night I am there.

I am still getting those weird phone calls. Once a week, they will call and after the first two I received from them, I just ignore them and send them to voice mail, which they never leave. I don't know who it is, but I wish they would quit. It's getting on my everlasting nerve. They have even called in the middle of the night a couple times. I'm beginning to think I will have to change my number.

I see Matt and Alice pretty regularly around campus. We meet up once a week, sometimes twice, depending on our schedules, to hang out. Matt is still a little grumpy about Ethan and me, especially now that I am pregnant but I think he is warming up a little more now.

My classes are going great. Since I'm putting all of my focus into them, I'm acing all five classes. I'm still debating whether I should apply for a part-time job somewhere. I heard people mentioning the library possibly having an opening.

As I'm walking to my English class I feel my phone vibrate in my hand. I rarely put it down anymore since I'm so afraid of missing a call from Ethan.

My heart picks up speed as I stop and check to see who is calling. I almost burst into tears when I see his name flash on my screen.

"Ethan," I cry into the phone in greeting.

"Hey, beautiful," he croons.

The second his voice filters through the phone, I lose it.

"Lex, don't cry baby, I'm fine," he says soothingly.

I find the nearest bench and sit, wiping my eyes. "It's just been so long since I've heard your voice…"

"I know, baby. I miss you so much. How are your classes going?"

"So far I'm keeping up. I've been spending all my time studying so it is paying off."

"That's good, Lex. I'm so proud of you."

"Matt is getting better with the idea of you and me more so now that he is going to be an uncle."

Ethan sighs, making me wish I hadn't of told him. "Honestly, he has every right to not be happy with me, but I'm going to prove to him that I care about you. I love you, Alexis, and nothing is going to keep me apart from you. How is my baby girl doing?"

I laugh softly. "Oh, so you believe it's a girl? Well, she's doing good. Keeping me nauseated, but other than that, I'm good."

And emotional too. Man, I swear I cry at the drop of a hat now.

"Yep, it's a girl, I just know it. Take care of yourself, Lex. I wish I was there. I hate I'm going to miss everything."

The sadness creeps in again, but I force myself not to cry.

I hate him being so far away. I understand this is what he signed up for, and what I signed up for when told him how I felt, but it's so hard.

"Me too, Ethan. I'll take care of our baby. You just need to come home to us."

"Soon, baby, I promise. I love you."

"Love you too."

I hate hanging up with him, knowing this might be the last time I get to hear his voice.

Checking the time, I notice I am five minutes late for class. I guess I still better go, although I probably won't be paying much attention at all.

With a sigh, I stand up from the bench and walk briskly to English, sending up a prayer for my man and the rest of the troops overseas, fighting for our country.

The cold air is bitter, making my nose run. I hate this weather! I rush to open the door to the building my class is in when I bump into someone.

"Sorry, I-" I stop mid-sentence when I look up to see who I ran into. All the color drains from my face.

"Hey there, Alexis. Long time no see, where have you been hiding?" Josh, the guy from the party who Ethan saved me from, asks in a voice that creeps me out.

"I've been busy. I need to get to class, though, I'm already late," I mutter, brushing past him. His face looks like it's healed from the damage Ethan created with his fists.

"I'll be seeing you around, Alexis. Hopefully, at another party. The last one ended too soon," he replies with a wink that makes me shiver from fear.

I don't dare reply to his creepy remark. I hope this is the only encounter I have with him or otherwise, I will not be walking alone anymore. After that, I don't think I want to anyway.

I turn and jog up the stairs, which turned out to be a bad idea since it has me running to the nearest bathroom. *Baby girl, you are already keeping me on my toes.*

I finally make it to class, fifteen minutes late, but at least I'm here. The class is long and boring. I stick with the masses when class ends, afraid to walk alone. Josh has spooked me. I think it must be my hormones again because it takes a lot to spook me.

I make it to my next class safely, and on time, with no run in with Josh.

I wish I could rewind and start this day over. Maybe tomorrow will be better, I hope. The only highlight of my crappy day was hearing from, Ethan. I pray I don't go so long without hearing from him again.

Lunch time has finally arrived and I am starving. All this eating for two has me eating more and more. I try to watch what I eat so I won't look like a giant whale during the last trimester.

I messaged Matt during class to tell him to meet me outside the building I'm in after class. He said he would and asked why like I figured he would. I just replied and said I would explain at lunch.

Matt pulls me aside just as I am about to walk in the cafeteria. "I don't mind walking with you, Alexis, but something's going on and I want to know."

"Before my first class, I ran into Josh and he acted creepy. He said things like he couldn't wait to see me at another party because the last one ended too soon. It just spooked me."

Matt curses under his breath. "From now on, I'm walking with you, okay."

"Okay," I respond quietly.

Matt side hugs me right before he opens the door to the cafeteria for me. The smell of food hits me as soon as I step in the cool building, making my stomach growl loudly.

Matt laughs next to me. "Let's go feed that hungry baby!" he jokes and walks with me to stand in line.

Matt, Alice, and I spend the next hour talking about our classes and about my pregnancy. Alice brought up, Ethan, which made Matt turn grumpy.

I am telling Alice about the call I got from him earlier. When I get to the part about Matt not being happy with our relationship, Matt then chooses to speak up.

"He shouldn't want to prove to me that he cares about you. The only person he should prove it to, is you, Alexis. As long as he treats you right, proving to you that he loves you, I will see it for myself."

"Well, you will see when he comes home that he truly loves me, Matt."

Matt grunts, displeased. "He better, or I will beat his ass."

I sigh, knowing Matt has my best interest at heart. "Thank you, but this time, I don't think you will have to worry about him breaking my heart again."

"I guess we'll see won't we?"

"Yep, because it's going take a lot for him to get me to like him again."

I know it shouldn't matter if my friends like who I'm dating or not as I love him, but it would mean a lot to me if Matt and Ethan could get along with each other.

chapter forty-two

Alexis

Six and a half months to go

My dearest Lex,

It's hard being here and not there with you. Especially now, when you told me the best news I could ever hear. I can't wait to get home to you and our baby. Remember when I asked you to be strong? Well, now I need for you to be strong for our little miracle, too. I hope it's a beautiful baby girl and that she looks just like you. I hate that I am going to miss pretty much all of your doctor's appointments. Write to me about them, Lex, I want to know what you see, what you hear. I want to know everything about our baby, and you of course. You both are the light of my life, my everything. I love our baby so much already, Lex. It's killing me not being able to be there with you while you go through this. I won't get to watch you grow with our child, I won't be there to argue with you about what the theme will be for our baby's nursery, and I won't get to be there to feel our baby kick and move around. If you make it full term, I will get to experience it for only a few days. I hope and pray I make it back in time for the birth. I definitely do not want to miss watching our son or daughter come into this world and I don't want to miss being by your side and holding your hand through it all. I want to be right beside you, telling you how proud I am of you as I kiss your forehead. I miss you so much, Lex, and I can't wait for you to be in my arms again.

I love you, Alexis Blair Collins, until the end of time.

Forever yours,

Ethan

Telling my parents went better than expected. Mom started crying and my dad laughed like I was playing some sort of joke on him. No lie, he thought I was messing with them. His face, when he realized I was serious, was priceless. The joke was on me when they started asking me if Brad knew. It took a few seconds, but it eventually clicked as to why they would think that. So then, I had to explain the last few months to bring them up to speed.

"I want to meet him," Dad blurts out, trying to sound stern. My father doesn't have a mean bone in his body.

"Well, you will have to wait about six and a half months since he is overseas right now." A deeper ache than the one currently ripping through my heart settles in. I miss him so much. I'm impatiently waiting to hear his voice again.

My phone is constantly right beside me or clutched tightly in my hand. The fear of missing his call has me afraid to just leave it lying around.

Mom winks in my direction, her approval, I assume.

"Is he good to you?" Dad asks in a voice which makes him sound all big and bad.

I can't help but smile. "He is. I love him, Dad."

"Then that's all I can ask for. I still would like to meet him, though."

I make a promise to dad about getting to meet Ethan when he comes home.

Since then, Mom has been telling *everyone*. The whole town probably knows by now. I'm getting closer to finding out if we will be having a little princess or a lil man. A few more weeks and I will know.

His mother was more thrilled than my parents. She started bawling and hugging me until it was hard for me to draw in a breath.

The annoying caller is back. Getting calls six times a day makes me want to throw my phone out of my window while I am driving down the road. With no way of getting a hold of Ethan today, unless he calls, then I am not changing my number for any reason. Even though I'm very tempted to. I've tried blocking them, but then they would start calling from a different number.

Matt is coming over in a little while to hang out. Alice said she couldn't make it. She seems to be pulling away from Matt and me. Maybe Matt or I can talk to her and see what's up.

Later when Matt arrives with mouthwatering food, he brings up Alice too. Thankfully, I'm not the only one who notices her withdrawing.

His expression is soft, full of worry. "I don't what's going on with her and I want to help, but I am afraid it will upset her and I will push her away for good. What should we do, Lex?"

"We will never know unless we ask. Not trying will leave worrying and regret for not being there for her."

He nods, agreeing with me. "She told me she was behind on her assignments. You know Alice as good as I do. She's always ahead. *If she is behind like she says she is then something either has happened or is happening.*"

He's right. Alice is a genius so she wouldn't let herself intentionally slip behind.

"I'm really worried about her, Alexis. I hope she is okay."

I look at him sympathetically. "I'm sure she is, Matt. We will talk to her," I assure him.

The next day, Matt and I head to campus housing to talk to Alice. Matt seems to be more nervous than me.

I timidly knock on her door then wait for her to answer. Matt is growing antsy standing next to me.

The door opens slowly before us. Alice looks a wreck with her wild hair, dark circles, and her red, blotchy eyes.

Matt and I barge in without asking and begin asking her what's wrong.

"I'm fine, I swear," she insists, but from what we are seeing, she isn't.

"Then why have you been crying and why have you been so distant lately?"

Her gaze drops to the floor as she nervously tucks some hair behind her ear. "I'm sort of seeing someone, I guess."

My jaw along with Matt's hit the floor.

"Okay, who is this dick and why is he making you cry?" Leave it to Matt to say the first threatening sentence.

"Why couldn't you just tell us?" I ask in a nicer way than he did.

She falls back on the couch, sighing. "He attends college two hours away, but we have been meeting as much as we can. I was embarrassed to tell you guys. I met him Facebook for goodness sakes. Yes, it was dangerous and reckless, but I love spending time with him." Alice sits up and rings her hands together. Matt and I listen intently to her. "I haven't told you about him because he is the type of guy you wouldn't picture me with. Heck, I couldn't see myself him either."

I sit down next to her, sort of understanding why she was afraid of telling us. "We wouldn't judge you at all, Alice. Will you please tell us why you are crying though?"

Matt is on the other side of her, holding one of her hands. He leans forward slightly, waiting for her to talk.

"He texted me earlier and said we couldn't see each other anymore. No explanation. Nothing. And he never responded when I asked him why." A sob leaves her throat when she finishes. Matt and I comfort her by wrapping our arms around her.

"You don't need the idiot, Alice. He isn't worthy of your time," Matt assures her, his tone bitter.

"Matt's right. Forget about him."

"I wish I could," she murmurs softly. I know exactly how it feels to not let go of someone she truly cares about.

I was open about my feelings to Ethan from the start. It may have taken him some time to sort out his feelings, but my heart had been his.

"You scared us, friend! All of this over a stupid male," Matt scoffs.

"Matt," I hiss. "You're not helping!"

His eyes switch to Alice, softening as he gazes at her. "Sorry," he mutters an apology. "I was afraid something terrible was going on."

She looks between us. "I should have told you guys. I'm sorry for making you worry."

As I side hug her, I say, "What are friends for?"

chapter forty-three

Alexis

Four months to go

Ethan should be here with me at the doctor, yet instead, he is thousands of miles away from me. Not a day goes that I don't wonder if he is okay and wondering how he is doing. This appointment is a special one. Today, I find out if Ethan is getting his little princess. He should be holding my hand, telling me how excited he is. I won't get to see the joy on his face when the nurse reveals the sex of our baby. Too many milestones have already been missed, and now he is fixing to miss another.

As much as I wanted too, I didn't ask anyone to come with me. It didn't feel right since Ethan couldn't be here.

"Are you ready to know or would you like it to be a surprise?"

Swallowing past the lump in my throat, I murmur, "I want to know."

A few beats later and she tells me what Ethan has said from the beginning. "It's a girl."

I managed to hold in my tears until I make it to my car. Tears of joy and love flow from my eyes. Ethan needs to call soon, so I can tell him the wonderful news. Ethan and I would be ecstatic even if the baby is a boy, but there is something about a man wanting a daddy's girl.

Keeping it a secret will be tough since I want to shout it from the rooftops, but Ethan will be the first person I tell.

It was a week later before I got to hear his voice. As suspected, he is thrilled.

"Are we really having a girl, Lex? Oh baby, I'm so happy." Hearing him go on and on about our baby has my bursting at the seams. "What are we going to name her?" Ethan asks.

"I've been thinking about Kinslee Nicole. What do you think?"

He is silent for a minute. My heart beating fast as I wait for him to say something. "It's perfect, baby. I love you and Kinslee so much, Lex."

"Four months," I whisper into the phone.

"Four months," he echoes.

Five months ago, I hugged him tight, wanting to beg him not to leave even though I knew he couldn't stay. It's been a long five months, but we are over halfway through this deployment. It hasn't been easy. There have been times I would withdraw from the world and just lie in his bed, wearing his hoodie, and clutch his pillow tightly.

In about one hundred-twenty days, I will be wrapping my arms around him, welcoming him home. Even though I will be miserable, I want Kinslee to wait and make her appearance when her daddy is home.

"I love you until the end of time, Alexis Collins." God, I love hearing him telling me he loves me.

"And I love you until the end of time, Ethan Harper."

I hang up and hug my belly. I look to my nightstand where my favorite picture of us sits, but it's gone. I search behind, underneath, and anywhere else trying to find it, but the picture, frame and all, is gone.

I don't remember moving it since I set it there last month.

About twenty minutes later, a knock on my front door startles me. Hesitantly, I peek through the peephole to see a delivery man holding flowers.

"Can I help you?"

"A delivery for Alexis Collins."

"That's me," I tell him.

He hands me the vase filled with at least two dozen roses. "These are for you. Have a nice day."

Stunned, I close the door and walk into the kitchen to set them on the table. Who would send me flowers?

Pulling out the card, I read it.

Thank for blessing me with the most precious gift I could ever have besides your love; a child. I love her so much already and I can't wait to meet her. I love and miss you more than you know, baby.

Always and forever,

Ethan

A new round of tears stream down my cheeks. I wish I could call him back and thank him and tell him I love him again. Hearing his voice is what keeps me going. Knowing we are closer to him being here with and our daughter helps somewhat soothe the ache in my chest.

I miss her perfect white smile, hearing her laugh, and most of all, I miss her luscious body molded against mine. It's hard being away from her, but in no time, I will be on a plane heading home to my girl.

My heart warms in my chest as I gaze at the pictures Lex sent me. My daughter. Wow, I can't believe I'm going to be a dad. I won't get to hear my daughter's heartbeat or watch Lex's belly swell as she continues to grow. It all fucking sucks. Knowing I will have both of them waiting for has me pushing forward.

I pick up the next picture and smile as I take in my beautiful girl and her ever growing belly.

Grabbing a blank sheet of paper, I begin to write.

My dearest Lex,

Seeing you grow with our child makes me the happiest man alive. I can't wait until Kinslee arrives. I can picture her now, hair as dark as yours, my eyes, your cheeks, and my smile. She will look more like you and act like me. I'm going to have to buy another gun to scare off all the boys that will flock around her. Oh, I've decided she can't date until she is thirty years old. No if's, and's, or but's about it.

Keep continuing to be strong, baby. I will be home before you know it.

I love you, Alexis Collins. Give Kinslee my love. Tell her every day for me.

Forever yours,

Ethan

Alexis

Weird things have been happening the last few days. More things have come up missing. His hoodie I have been sleeping with is gone, more pictures of us have mysteriously disappeared, and my ultrasound pictures have been misplaced. I wish I could say it was my pregnancy brain, but I highly doubt it is.

Especially now that I see all the key marks on my car. Not only that, but my tires have been slashed. Again. I take pictures of the evidence in case I need it for later.

Now, I am getting scared. Whoever this person is, is starting to go to different lengths.

Something white on the windshield catches my eye. Another note. Should I even read them anymore? I don't understand who is doing all of this and why.

Against my better judgement, I open the note that was tucked between my wiper blade and the glass.

He's mine.

Two words. Two short words are all that is written and yet they hold a powerful meaning. A threat.

Crumpling up the paper in my hand, I pull out my phone and make a call to Adam.

As usual, Adam is my lifesaver. This time, I am definitely calling the police. This person is going too far.

Adam arrives and begins inspecting the damage. Shaking his head, he looks up at me. "Please tell me you will report this. Enough is enough, Alexis."

Emotion clogs my throat, leaving me unable to speak.

Adam rounds my car and side hugs me. "It's going to be okay. Let the police handle it, okay?"

I just nod and stare at the mess which is my car.

Moments later, the police arrive and I give them my statement. They also take their own pictures and search for any clues.

They wind up having Adam take my car in so they can check for fingerprints.

Before he drove off, he instructed me to go see Kaylee and the twins. He claims he needs to talk to me. I can only assume he wants to know if anything else is happening.

I had to make a trip back up the stairs to get Ethan's keys for his car. As I slide in the driver's seat, I am overwhelmed by it all. The deployment, the notes, the calls, the attacks on my car, and becoming a mother.

My arms hug my belly as I let it all out. When I feel like I am calm enough, I drop the car into reverse and drive to Adam and Kaylee's.

Adam pulls in shortly after I do. He leads me in the house and asks me if I want anything. I ask for some water. I don't think I can stomach anything else.

"Alexis, hey!" Kaylee jumps up and wraps her arms around me. "Wow, look at you!" She steps back and admires my belly. Then she proceeds to start talking to Kinslee. I know what she is doing. Adam has called her I'm sure, which is why she is pretending I'm not upset. I know she can tell I have been crying. If she didn't know, she would be asking me a million questions.

"Where are the twins?" It's so quiet in the house.

"Taking their nap," she explains. Ah, that explains it.

Adam comes back in with my water and I take small sips. I can feel him and Kaylee watching me.

Adam clears his throat and begins his questioning. "Have other things happened other your tires being slashed and your car being keyed?"

Lying wouldn't work since I know they will be able to see right through me. I'm terrified now that something bigger will happen. Protecting my daughter comes first and in order to do that, I have to let someone other than myself take care of things.

My eyes shift between them. "Promise me you won't say a word to Ethan about what is happening. The last thing I need is for him to become worried and mess up his military career." I wait for their word before I begin filling them in on all that's been going on.

When I am done, sorrow, pity fill their eyes.

"You're welcome to stay with us for a while if you want," Kaylee offers and Adam agrees.

Not wanting to let my stalker feel like he has won, I decline their offer. I wouldn't want to impose anyway. They have their own lives to worry about, their own children to protect. There is no way I am bringing them into my mess.

"What are you going to do? You don't need to stay at either apartment."

Adam is right. I just hate that this person is running me out of my home. If I wasn't pregnant, I would stick it out, fight back, but with Kinslee growing inside me, I need to protect her at all costs.

"I guess I will move back in with mom and dad," I mutter, not happy that I am. My lease is about up for my apartment anyway and I have been staying at Ethan's more often than not.

I love my independence, buy my freedom is dissipating slowly away from me.

Mom and Dad will know what to do. Besides, it's the safest place for me for the time being.

chapter forty-four

Alexis

Two months to go

By the next week, I had successfully moved back in with my parents. Everything has been removed from my apartment and all of my things from Ethan's have been removed as well. If my stalker has been watching he's probably smiling to himself, proud that he has effectively removed me from my home. Dad has amped up the security at the house and both him and mom have talked me into withdrawing from all my classes.

I hate it because I feel like I am locked inside the house. They are too scared to let me go anywhere alone and it's driving me crazy.

Matt and Alice have been by to keep me company and were sad to know they wouldn't see me around campus.

They both got to feel Kinslee move around in my stomach, which made their night.

I'm restless at night now. All of a sudden, I can't sleep at all. I'm exhausted all the time and I'm not eating as much as I have been, which is worrying my mother.

This whole situation is taking a toll on me and I'm not sure how much more I am able to take.

My mother has been religiously planning my shower since I moved in two months ago. I'm not in the mood to have a party. Hell, I'm not in the mood to do anything anymore. All I do is lie in bed and talk to Kinslee. The highlight of last night was getting a call from Ethan. It was hard, but I managed to stay calm and not burst into tears. I wanted to tell him everything, yet I knew I couldn't. Hopefully, Adam and Kaylee have kept their promise.

He wanted to talk to Kinslee so I placed the phone on speaker and held the phone next to my belly so she can hear him. Next thing I knew, she was moving. She was kicking fiercely and it felt like she was doing somersaults in the womb. Needless to say, she loves listening to Ethan's voice.

I've started reading to her to pass the time. Apparently, it's good for the baby.

Mom actually let me out of the house yesterday to go shop for the nursery. I was genuinely surprised. I was so giddy to actually get to do something besides sit on my butt all day. By the time we got back home, I was regretting staying out that long.

Dad started putting the crib together last night so I would be able to put things where I want them, for now at least.

Other than the endless calls, nothing has happened since I moved back home. It should make me feel better, but yet it only frightens me more since I know they are waiting, planning.

The detective finally called, but unfortunately, he didn't have any good news. They didn't find a single fingerprint on my car other than mine. Pretty much, the case closed since there is no leads and nothing that has us any closer to finding out who damaged my car.

My phone vibrates in my lap so I pick it up and unlock the screen to see who messaged me. It is the same number who has been calling me non-stop.

Once you have the baby, he will leave you. He will look at you differently.

It's utter bullshit, I know it is.

He's going to resent you for trapping him.

Trapping him? I would never do that to Ethan!

He'll miss his freedom, his old life.

Having enough, I block the number.

A couple minutes later, another message pops up from a different unknown number.

I'm not going anywhere.

That message sends unwanted chills up my spine.

I want to power off my phone so I don't have to deal with this person right now, but I can't. What if Ethan calls while my phone is off? I don't suspect he will call for another two to three weeks, but with my luck he will. Then, I'd be heartbroken I didn't get to talk to him.

My shower went well. People I haven't seen before and people I haven't seen in a long time came with gifts for Kinslee. I smiled, pretending to be happy, but without Ethan here, it wasn't enjoyable.

The days seem to be dragging the closer it gets to Ethan's homecoming. In less than sixty days, I will be hugging my man.

"Yo, preggo! Hope you're hungry because I brought food!" Matt yells as he bursts in my room.

Smiling for the first time in weeks, I sit up in my bed and switch off the TV.

"Starved!" My stomach growls from the mouthwatering smell.

"Wow, Alexis! You're huge and still beautiful!"

I know he meant it as a compliment, but I still grimace at the thought of gaining all this weight.

"Alice not come?" I ask to take the attention off me and my weight gain.

Matt shakes his head, his facial features hardening. "She's back with the douche again. The story I was fed was an ex-girlfriend sent the text and he didn't know it."

My brows draw together in confusion. "Why did she have his phone?"

"Exactly, it's all a lie and she believed the bullshit he fed her."

"Matt," I say between mouthfuls of food. "Alice is smart and innocent. She is taking a chance on this guy. Who knows if he is the one for her or not, but you have to let her make her own mistakes. What if she had listened to you and he was actually telling the truth? She would be wondering what if for the rest of her life."

Matt huffs. "I get what you're saying, but we know nothing about this guy, Alexis. For all we know, he could be a serial killer!"

I roll my eyes dramatically.

"Look, she met him on Facebook and she did say he was someone no one would picture her with. Two red flags right there."

"Why don't you see if she will invite him to have lunch with us? Will that make you feel better?" I suggest.

He perks up. "Great idea." He pulls out his phone and starts typing furiously. "They are down for meeting us tomorrow," he says a minute later.

A night out of the house with friends sounds amazing. I've been cooped up in this house too long.

chapter forty-five

Alexis

Dressing up now days take longer than normal. My big belly gets in the way. Matt is rushing me as he is in a hurry to leave.

"We have plenty of time, Matt. Chill," I chasten for like the tenth time in the last thirty minutes.

Once I brush my hair, I apply my make-up and brush my teeth. Taking one last glance at myself in the mirror, I grab my phone and wallet off the bed.

Satisfied we are finally leaving, Matt mutters, "Finally," under his breath.

The evening air is warm and I am grateful the summer months are here. As Matt and I pass my car, I spot another note on my windshield. I snatch it and place it in my pocket, planning to read it later.

Matt pulls into the restaurant and texts Alice, letting her know we arrived.

After a minute, he says, "She's here. Let's go meet this douche."

I grab his arm before he can open the door. "Be nice. Give him a chance."

"Fine," he grumbles as he throws open the car door.

Matt guides me into the restaurant to where Alice and her mystery man are sitting, waiting for us.

We round the corner to our table and I freeze when I see him.

"Jake?"

He looks away from Alice when he hears his name called. "Alexis? Well hell, what a coincidence," he laughs as he stands to greet me.

"I can't believe you're her mystery man!"

"Look at you, all preggo and stuff. How much longer?"

Smiling, I reply, "I'm thirty weeks."

When I turn to introduce Matt to Jake, he and Alice are staring at us with equally confused looks.

"Jake is Brad's best friend," I explain. Matt and Alice nod in understanding. They know of Brad from what little I have told them, but haven't met him.

Jake suddenly becomes very nervous. He starts constantly checking his phone.

A moment later, it's abundantly clear why. Brad's here. Brad's eyes drift over me and grow hard.

"Oh shit," I hear Matt mutter under his breath.

Brad walks right up to me and tells me we need to talk. I let him lead me to a quiet corner of the restaurant.

He clears his throat. "First of all, I want to say you look beautiful, Alexis." He pauses and rakes a hand through his hair. "I just need to know." His eyes drop to my swollen belly. "Is the baby mine?"

Taken aback, I place a hand on my chest. "No, Brad this is not your baby. If it was I would have already had her by now. How could you think that I would keep her from you? I would never keep a child from her father no matter what our relationship is."

Regret immediately swarms him. "I'm sorry. I had to be sure. You were with Ethan behind my back so excuse me if I have doubts."

What is wrong with him? "Ethan and I didn't have sex while you and I were dating. The first time we did was the night before he was deployed which was months after you and I broke up."

"You still cheated, Alexis," he replies in a clipped tone.

Tears form in my eyes from being so frustrated. "Don't you think I know that? What has gotten into you?"

"Nothing," he says sternly and walks away.

I head to the bathroom, taking a much needed moment to compose myself. It angers me to know Brad thinks so lowly of me. Did he not count the months? It's plainly obvious the baby isn't his.

As I am heading back to the table, my phone vibrates.

Poor Brad. How does it feel that he doubts you?

Judging by the text, I'd say this is a setup. But who is behind it?

Taking one last deep breath, I continue to our table.

The air at the table is filled with tension. No one looks happy.

Matt and Jake are glaring at Brad, who still looks pissed. When I take my seat, everyone's eyes shift to me.

Jake gives me a nod, silently asking if I am okay. Alice is gazing at me sympathetically. Matt drapes one arm over my shoulders and squeezes me.

"Are you okay?" he whispers in my ear.

My throat clogs of emotion so I only nod.

"Don't let it get to you, Lex."

How can I not? Brad knows better, or rather he should. What's worse is he listened to someone he doesn't know. He reacted before he thought it through.

Tonight was going well until Brad wanted to talk and now all I want to leave and curl up in my bed.

Since I didn't want to ruin everyone else's night, I stayed. Matt tried to cheer me up, but it was no use. Brad didn't join the conversation much either. He mostly stayed silent, tensed.

Jake adores Alice, it's evident on his face. He constantly looks over at her and smiles. His smile is definitely real and you can tell he is smitten with her. I'm happy for Alice. Maybe she and Jake will work out and stay together. Alice was right when she said he isn't her type, but as long as they are happy and treat one another right, then that's all a friend can ask for.

After two hours of eating and listening to everyone else talk, it's finally time to go.

"I actually like him," Matt says after we say goodbye and walk outside.

"Yeah, Jake is pretty cool," I agree.

Just as we reach Matt's car, I hear a familiar voice. "Well, well. Isn't it the baby mama!"

Smiling, I turn to see Farris. "Hey, Farris. Long time, no see." I walk into his open arms for a hug.

He pulls back and places his hands on my belly. "Ethan called me a little over a month ago and told me I was having a niece?" His eyes shine with excitement. "I about fell out when he told me he was gonna be a dad. No lie, I thought he was messing with me."

Matt clears his throat, reminding me he is standing next to me.

"Oh, sorry. This is Matt, my best friend."

They shake hands and mutter hellos.

Farris' eyes grow soft. "So how are you dealing with him being gone?"

The void in my chest grows like it does each time I think of him. "I'm dealing. Hearing his voice is what keeps me going."

Farris nods in understanding. "I miss him too. The guy I'm working with now is an idiot, worthless. I need my partner in crime back," he chuckles.

I laugh along with him. "Don't worry, your partner in crime will be back soon."

"Well, it was good seeing you, Alexis. Let me give you my number in case you need it."

He rattles off his number and I give him mine.

"It was good seeing you. If you ever need me just call or shoot me a text, okay?"

"Will do," I say as I hug him once more.

"Nice meeting you," he says to Matt as he walks away.

As soon as Matt and I are in his car and he is backing out, he turns to me with a wide smile. "How come you know all of these hot guys? Why can't you hook your brother up?" he teases.

"One day, Matt. I'll find you the perfect guy, I swear."

"And I can't wait for that day."

chapter forty-six

Alexis

One month to go

This past month has been the longest month of my life. It has slowly dragged by. The closer I am to having him home, the more the days seem to drag. I'm getting anxious as time grows closer.

Braxton-hicks contractions have started as my due date looms. Sleep eludes me at night and I'm growing so uncomfortable that it's becoming almost unbearable.

Feeling somewhat better today, I decide to visit Julie. This will be the first time I have driven my car since someone decided to vandalize it. They key marks are still visible and seeing them makes me cringe.

My stalker has been relatively quiet for the most part, although I'm sure I will hear from them soon.

The drive consists of me being lost in my thoughts. Hoping to hear from Ethan, Kinslee coming soon, and my stalker issue keeps my mind occupied. Knowing I should probably tell Farris before it gets even more out of hand, I send him a quick text as soon as I pull in Julie's drive, asking him if he can meet up with me one day this week.

As I am walking up the steps, the front door swings open and Julie appears with a huge smile. "Oh dear, it's good to see you!" she gushes as she bear hugs me. She talks about how excited she is about being a grandma as we head inside.

"Sit, sit," she urges me. "Tell me everything that has been going on with you."

I opt out of telling her about the unknown psycho. Instead, I tell her about my doctor appointments and how I moved back in with my parents, leaving out the main reason why.

In the midst of me telling her about my living arrangements, a knock sounds on the door.

Julie mutters something about how she isn't expecting anyone as she makes her way to the front door.

An unsettling feeling knots in my stomach. I've had this feeling way too much lately with my stalker coming around in spurts.

Did they follow me all the way out here?

I whip my head around when I hear a gut wrenching sob come from Julie. When I see the two men standing at the door, my heart stops. My worst nightmare has just become my reality.

On shaky legs, I stand, but my legs are unable to move any further.

"My baby," Julie wails and I feel my heart being ripped from my chest.

Why is this happening? My mind screams.

The tears are flowing like a river down my face. The sergeants are offering their condolences, but I block them out. Nothing they say will change the fact that I just lost my Ethan, the man who I love with every beat of my heart is gone.

Julie turns to me and hugs me tight, both of us sobbing uncontrollably.

I thought I felt pain each time Ethan would break my heart. This type of pain will never cease. This kind of pain is a thousand times worse than what I thought I felt.

Julie and I have been clinging to each other for hours now, crying. Not only am I mourning for myself, I'm also mourning for Kinslee, our daughter. She would have been his pride and joy. Hell, she isn't here yet and he is already wrapped around her finger.

How can I go on without him? Living without being able to hear his voice or see his handsome face or watch him smile will be hard. I hope I can be strong for Kinslee.

Blindly, I search for my phone. "I need to call Farris," I murmur.

Julie lets me go and I fumble my phone. It takes me five times to click on Farris's name in my contacts since my hands are shaking horribly.

"Hey, preggo!" he greets in his usual happy tone. Too bad I am about to ruin his day.

"Farris," I choke out on a sob. "He's…" I couldn't say the word. "Gone" implies he's not coming back and I don't want to believe he is dead.

"No," he whispers. Farris doesn't want to believe it either.

We sit on the phone for a while, not saying anything. I hear Farris sniffle several times which makes me only cry harder.

Finally, Farris speaks. "Where are you?"

"At his mom's."

"I'll be there soon."

Farris arrives an hour later and lets Julie and me cry on his shoulder. He is sitting on the couch between us, quietly staring off into space.

I'm grateful Farris is here. This is just as hard for him as it is us. Ethan was more than a friend to him, he was more like a brother.

Sitting here, staring at the crack in the window in front of me resembles my own heart, only my heart has hundreds of cracks.

"Let's get you home," Farris says out of the blue.

Numb, I can only nod.

Everything is a blur after we leave. My life seems to have halted in its tracks, forcing me to face my new reality.

Lying on Ethan's side of the bed only makes me cry harder, yet I'm unable to force myself to move. His scent is all around me and I consume it. Clutching his pillow to my chest, I stare off into oblivion.

Faintly, I hear Farris asking me if I need anything. What I want is what he can't give me. He can't bring Ethan back. No one can. So I shake my head a couple times.

I hear the bedroom door creak closed and the emptiness drags me further down.

chapter forty-seven

Alexis

Ten days without him

It's been ten days since my world was flipped upside down. Two weeks ago, I went to visit Julie and my life forever changed that day.

Farris has not left my side since and I am grateful for him. He makes me eat even when I tell him I'm not hungry. He makes me get up and move around even though I'd rather lie in Ethan's bed and wallow in my tears. Farris is keeping me alive right now. Kaylee and Adam have called and even dropped by a few times. We don't say much to one another, just sit and listen to Adam and Farris talk in hushed murmurs.

Matt and Alice stop by occasionally to check on me. Matt stays the night some nights.

Why did he have to die? Better yet, how am I supposed to live my life without him? We were just starting our life together and now, he has been ripped away from me, taking my heart with him.

Julie has also visited me. Neither one of us talked much either. She brought me one of his old shirts, a photo album, and some gifts for Kinslee he was going to surprise me with when he came home. The last gift she handed me was enclosed in a small, black velvet box. My throat clogs as I clutch it in my hand, holding it up to my chest. I hold it over where my heart used to be.

"Alexis, honey, I know losing him is the hardest thing I'm sure you've gone through, but I need you to fight through this tragedy for my granddaughter. Ethan wouldn't want you upset and crying over him. Remember he is always with you and Kinslee." She pauses and places a hand on my belly. "He loved her with all his heart, just like he did you. Every time I talked to him, you could hear the excitement in his voice. I have no doubt in my mind he would have been an excellent father. Promise me, Alexis, you will live your life, not a shell of yourself like you have been."

She wants me to move on without him? The only way I can enjoy my life is with Ethan here with me. So I lie and promise her something I'm not sure I will accomplish.

The box in my hand grabs my attention. I had known Ethan was going to ask me to be his wife one day. We had talked about it before he left. But this soon? Nothing would make me happier than to become Mrs. Harper.

Thrusting the box at Julie, I beg her to take it. I couldn't bear to open it. Maybe someday I will have the strength.

Wake up. Force myself out of bed. Try to eat. Attempt to do normal things. Go to bed. Repeat.

This has been my routine since Julie came to see me. It's harder than most people believe. The question is, why would I want to move on? Ethan was my forever. No one will be able to take his place. If I move on and leave him in the past, he won't be a part of my future and I refuse to accept him not being by my side.

"Hey, just making sure you're awake," Farris murmurs as he sticks his head in Ethan's room.

I struggle to sit up, my belly hindering me. Farris moves to help me. I have another doctor appointment today. I'm fixing to cross thirty-eight weeks in this pregnancy and I should be happy about it, yet I can't bring myself to be excited.

"You're making progress, preggo. I'm proud of you." Farris' praise does little to make me smile. Nothing can make me smile anymore. "I need to run a couple errands. Meet you there?"

I nod and mutter some words, not caring if they make any sense. Nothing makes sense in my life anymore.

He nods once and flashes me a small smile as he walks out.

My phone vibrates on the nightstand. I have unread messages I couldn't bring myself to read. Condolences and people apologizing only make my nightmare more real.

Sighing, I figure I need to at least let them know I am alive. Scrolling through the threads, one by one, I reply in only a few words. The last thread makes me pause. I'd forgotten about my stalker until now.

How does it feel to have your heart ripped out? Welcome to my world.

I'm changing my number. Today.

I dress quickly, throwing on a sundress and sandals. After brushing my hair and teeth, I'm ready to go.

The number change didn't take as long as I expected. When it was completely switched, I messaged only the people I am close to, explaining who I was and that my number had changed. Again, I leave out why.

It hits me that Farris and I never got to talk. Deciding I will talk to him after my appointment, I slide in my car and head to the doctor.

I send a quick text to Farris letting him know I am on my way.

Pulling out onto the highway, the unsettling feeling creeps up my spine. Feeling scared, I glance around quickly but see nothing. Shaking off the weird vibe, I focus on the road in front of me.

A few miles down the road and the feeling still hasn't left me. Suddenly, a truck rams into my bumper from behind. Startled, I grip the steering wheel tighter and press on the gas.

Before the truck can hit me again, I swerve into an open space between two cars and slow down.

I manage to get a better look at the truck and it's not one I recognize. It has to be my stalker. The windows are tinted so dark, I can't see inside the vehicle.

With my turnoff up ahead, I slow down some more. Wrong decision. The truck slams on his brakes and rams into back left finder as I was fixing to move into the turn lane. My car spins and I scream.

Ethan holding Kinslee flashes before my eyes. Then I am with them, his arm wrapped around me.

The impact, the sting, the sound of metal crunching, and the shattering of glass brings me back to the present.

As the blackness takes me, I feel a presence next to me.

"Thought you could take him from me and get away with it? Well, you thought wrong, bitch."

A sharp sting pierces my left side as everything goes back.

chapter forty-eight

Alexis

Thirteen days without him

I hear voices, but they sound distant, faint. A reoccurring beep also sounds. *Where am I,* I wonder?

"Will the baby be okay?" A male voice asks.

"We had to do an emergency C-section…"

The doctor's voice fades away and I'm transported to somewhere unknown.

Wait! I want to know about my baby!

When I resurface, I am in a meadow. Purple flowers sway all around me.

"Lex," a voice calls out. Spinning abruptly toward the familiar, relaxing sound I would know anywhere, my heart starts beating wildly.

"Ethan!" I call back.

"Be strong, beautiful. Fight for our daughter, and for me."

I keep spinning in circles, trying to find him. "Where are you?"

"I live inside you. Your heart to be exact. No promise me, you'll live. Live for yourself, for Kinslee, and for me."

He appears in front of me out of nowhere, dressed in his ACU's.

"Oh, Ethan!" I cry as I sprint in his direction, crashing into his arms. The feel of his arms around me feels real, feels right.

He draws back, causing a whimper of protest to leave me. Why can't I hold onto him forever?

Grasping my chin, he tilts my head up. *"You haven't kept your other promise, Lex, so I need to know you will keep this one."*

"I promise, Ethan," I vow, fighting back the sob wanting to break free.

"Good. Now, go live."

He vanishes just as he appeared, drifting away with the wind.

The beeping sound is back, but louder this time. The pain has returned with a vengeance, except it's a different kind of ache.

Warmth envelopes my skin. Cracking my eyes open, I groan when the light hurts my eyes.

"Alexis?" I know that voice, only it's not the one I was hoping for.

"She waking up?" Matt.

It takes me a minute for me to force my eyes fully open. Taking in the room, I notice I am in the hospital with Matt on one side and Brad on the other.

Brad makes me pause. Wasn't I with Ethan?

I open my mouth to speak, but I can form words. Brad reaches over and grabs a cup of what I assume is water, letting me take small sips. The water soothes my throat.

They both continue to stare at me, but I can only look at Brad. "Was I dreaming or wasn't I with, Ethan?"

Brad grimaces, dropping his head.

"Alexis," Matt says softly. "You weren't dreaming, baby girl."

I gasp as I struggle to sit up. "Then where is Kinslee?!"

The machine I am hooked up to starts going wild.

Both of them attempt to make me lie back.

"Alexis, she's fine. Please, lie back and relax," Matt assures me.

The nurses rush in, asking tons of questions. Brad explains what was said to make me panic.

One nurse leaves while the other one checks my vitals. "On a scale of one to ten, how is your pain?"

I want to tell her it's off the charts, but I refrain. She presses the button to administer the pain meds.

It isn't long before my eyelids grow heavy and I'm falling into the blackness.

When I wake again, Matt and Brad are gone. Glancing out the window, I notice it's nighttime.

I hear a light knock on the door, then Farris walks in. He smiles warmly and takes the seat Brad was in when I woke the first time.

"Kinslee is beautiful. You and Ethan did good."

I pick at the invisible lint on the blanket. "I still haven't got to see her and I don't even know if she is okay."

His smile brightens. "She is perfectly healthy, I promise. I'll see what I can do about getting her in here so you can see her."

"Thank you, Farris." Glancing down at my arm, I notice the wrap covering my hand and wrist. "What exactly happened to me?"

"I was actually going to ask you if you remember. From the details I've heard, you were involved in a hit and run."

I try to think back, willing my brain to remember the accident. Flashes of a truck ramming into my car appear. Then, I am trying to turn off the highway.

"A truck rear-ended me intentionally it seemed. I remember trying to get off the highway, but my memory is fuzzy after that." I breathe in deeply and slowly exhale. "I saw him, Farris," I murmur, hoping he doesn't think I am crazy.

"You saw who? Ethan?"

Nodding, I tell him about the flashes of him and Kinslee and all three of us. Then, I tell him how I saw him when I was unconscious.

"It was so real. I could actually feel his arms around me in the meadow. Does that make me crazy?"

Farris looks at me with tears in his eyes. Reaching out, I place my hand on top of his as I wipe away my own tears.

"No, it doesn't make you crazy, Alexis. He was watching over you. Now, back to the accident. Can you describe the vehicle for me? Do you have an idea of who it could be?"

I tell him all the details I can remember. The make, model, and color of the truck are vivid to me. "As far as who was driving, I have no clue. I mean, I've been meaning to talk to you about this stalker-"

"Stalker?"

I nod, fixing to explain when the doctor walks in. Farris leans down and hugs me before leaving the room.

The doctor explains my injuries to me. A stab wound in my left hand, a concussion, burns up my arms from the airbag, and some cuts and bruises.

The stab wound has me freaking out. Before I can analyze it any more, the doctor leaves and my parents walk in with Kinslee.

Mom and dad lean down and each kiss my cheek.

Finally, I get to hold my daughter for the first time.

Mom lays my new bundle of joy in my arms. The first thing I instantly notice is how much she looks like Ethan. All of her facial features resemble his.

My heart grows heavy as a weight settles on my chest. He should be here to enjoy this moment. With my good arm, I cuddle her closer as a gut-wrenching sob leaves me. Everything is suddenly hitting me all at once. It's hit me that Ethan isn't going to ever come home to us. He's really gone. My daughter will never get to meet her father.

This is our heart-breaking reality.

chapter forty-nine

Alexis

Fifteen days without him

After my parents left with Kinslee, I cried myself to sleep. I never wanted this for us. Never in a million years did I think I would lose the one man I love.

I'm slipping again. Life is beating me down, making me whimper in the corner. I'm also angry. A lot of 'should haves' are running through my mind. I wish I could've loved him longer.

Even though it's only been two weeks since he's been gone, it feels like an eternity. Ethan wanted me to live. He was my life, every breath I breathe. So no, I can't live without him. I don't even want to try.

Brad is suddenly crouched down beside the bed. He thumbs away my tears and I wish I had the heart to tell him to leave. Instead, I go with, "What are you doing here?"

He pulls his hand away from my face and places it on top of mine. "I had plans to meet Adam this weekend, but then he calls and canceled because you had been in an accident."

"Oh. Have they been here?" I don't remember them coming to visit me.

"Yeah, but you were asleep each time," he chuckles.

"You still didn't answer my question. Why are you here?"

He squeezes my hand gently. "Honestly? I have no idea. I just know I want to help you."

"Brad—" I start to tell him that I don't need his kind of help, but he interrupts me.

"Not in the way that you think. I'm not looking for a relationship with you and I'm certainly not trying to be Kinslee's father. I just want to help you until you get back on your feet," he explains.

Okay, not as bad as I was thinking. No one is going to take Ethan's place in my heart and definitely not taking on the fatherly role in my daughter's life.

"Fine, I don't care." My life is too messed up to care at the moment. As long as he doesn't think he will be a permanent fixture in our lives, I don't mind him being here.

Satisfied, Brad leans forward and kisses my forehead. I would have flinched away if I had the strength.

Adam and Kaylee come by a little while later, only I'm not in the mood to talk. My mother brought Kinslee by an hour before and Brad has been rocking her, spending time with her. I shouldn't let him, but the emptiness inside me is growing and I am unable to stop it.

Kaylee and Adam visit with Kinslee for a bit until the doctor makes a visit. He is keeping me a couple more days for observation and tells me I can't leave until I eat regularly. He also told me I have developed postpartum depression.

They all try to cheer me up when they come and give me a motivational speech, but what they don't understand is that Ethan walking through the door is the only thing that will bring me back.

Ethan not only took my heart with him, he is also taking a huge chunk of my soul with him. Without him, I feel lifeless, useless.

"Alexis, you have to eat something. You are losing too much weight," Matt chastens. He, Farris, and Brad have been taking turns sitting with me. My parents have come by every day with Kinslee. I signed her discharge papers a couple days ago, letting her go home with my parents. I can't bring myself to hold her. I'm scared I will let her down again. If only I had talked to Farris about my stalker sooner, maybe the wreck wouldn't have happened.

"I'm not hungry," I repeat for the tenth time. "Can I just be alone?"

Matt squeezes my hand and tells me he will see me later. Farris places his hand on my shoulder and tells me the same.

Brad leans forward and kisses my forehead. "Do you or Kinslee need anything while I'm gone?"

I shake my head, knowing if Kinslee needed something, my parents would have told me.

"Okay, I'll be back this evening."

With everyone gone, I close my eyes and beg for sleep to take me.

Every time I close my eyes, I dream of Ethan here with me and our daughter. I miss him so much.

The pain is not relinquishing, it only intensifies with every second that passes. Ethan, the man I love with my whole heart, is gone. The pain is so excruciating it has made me numb to everything. I can't feel, I can't do anything, but lie here and wonder how

Kinslee's life would be with her father. I imagine hearing Kinslee's clap and squeals as Ethan tosses her into the air. I imagine Ethan having a tea party with our daughter and her stuffed animals. I could go on and on with scenarios that Ethan will get to miss out on as a father.

My family, Kaylee, Julie…all of them try to comfort me, but it is no use. Nothing will take this hurt away. Only seeing Ethan again will heal me. This unbearable pain in my chest is making it hard to breathe.

Brad has been here, helping, too. I don't know how to feel about it. I just let him do what he wants since nothing seems to matter anymore. He has been trying to comfort me just like everyone else, yet I don't understand why. I broke his heart, I practically cheated on him with Ethan. I don't understand why is here, wanting to help me.

This time when I close my eyes, I hear his voice.

"I'm here, Lex. I just wanted you to know that. Our daughter is beautiful, just like her momma. When you open your eyes, I will be here, then we can go on with our lives as a family."

Oh God, I wish it was true. *"You were supposed to come back, Ethan. Why didn't you come back?"*

"Baby, I'm right here, open your eyes."

No, I can't! It would break my already broken heart to open my eyes and not see him. *"No, if I do you will be gone."*

I feel his familiar lips graze mine and I fight back the tears.

"Lex, baby, I promise you, I'm right here. Open your eyes, beautiful, I want to see them. Kinslee needs her momma and I need you. Please, Lex."

I feel the warmth of his touch on my hand. It feels so real that I take a chance and open my eyes.

chapter fifty

Ethan

I call a cab to take me to my apartment since no one came to pick me up. Where in the hell is everyone? None of them are answering their phones either. When I call Lex, it says her phone has been disconnected. What a welcome home this is.

When the cab turns into the parking lot of my apartment complex, I notice right away Lex's car is gone. I pay the driver and step out, throwing my bag over my shoulder. I unlock my front door and walk in, letting my bag fall down my arm to the floor. Her stuff is gone, there isn't a trace of Alexis in my apartment. I don't understand. I thought we were doing great? Did she realize she couldn't handle me being gone?

I turn back around and close the door behind me. I'm going to find her and we are going to talk about this. If she didn't want to be with me she shouldn't just shut me out.

The first place I stop is Lex's apartment which also looks to have been abandoned. Did she move back in with her parents?

I drive to my sister's, hoping someone will be home so I can know what is going on.

Adam's truck is sitting in the driveway when I pull in. I bang on the front door and wait for him to answer. The door opens revealing a jaw dropped, wide-eyed Adam. His face pales like he's seen a ghost.

"Dude, where is everyone and why didn't anyone come pick me up?" I ask when it's obvious he isn't going to speak.

"You're alive," he whispers in amazement.

Well obviously. "Yeah, I'm very much alive. Why would you think otherwise? You guys were supposed to pick me up today, remember?"

Snapping out of it, he finally says, "They came to your mom's and said you had been killed."

What the fuck? "Well, that explains it. Where's, Lex? Her stuff is gone from my apartment and hers." It kind of looks like she never existed.

Adam sighs heavily, running and hand roughly through his hair. "At the hospital, it's been a really long two weeks."

I take a better look at him noticing how exhausted he looks. What has been going on?

I'm on high alert now. "Why is she at the hospital?" She can't be having the baby already.

"Things have been downhill ever since we were told you were dead. Let me grab some things and we'll go." He disappears inside his house for a moment. When he returns he is carrying a diaper bag and backpack. "You can ride with me since I have tons to tell you. Kaylee and the twins are already up there."

Once we are in his truck and leaving his house, he starts to fill me in. "The only good news I have is that you're a father. She was born ten days ago weighing in at five pounds one ounce and she is twenty inches long." He pulls out his phone to show me a picture. My heart swells looking at my daughter. She's so beautiful. I can't wait to get to her so I can hold her in my arms. I've been waiting for this ever since Lex broke the news to me.

Adam runs his hand through his hair. "Now, for the bad news. Alexis has been staying with her parents for the last few months. Things have been happening around both yours and her apartment so she didn't feel safe at either one."

"What things?" I don't remember her telling me anything was going on.

"Several things have gone missing, her tires were slashed again, her car was keyed, notes were left… things like that. She even had to change her number because of the number of calls she was getting. Someone would call from a blocked number every day and all you could hear in the other line is breathing."

"Why didn't she tell me?! I could have talked to my Sergeant and worked something out."

"She didn't want to worry you. She thought it might hurt your military career. But, as much as I hate to say, it gets worse, and if I had known you were actually alive, I'd have called you.

"Alexis was involved in a hit and run accident ten days ago and they had to do an emergency C-section to get Kinslee out. Kinslee came out perfect, thank god. Alexis is okay physically, just a stab wound in her hand a concussion, some cuts from the glass, and a few bruises. Emotionally, she is a wreck. She's gone downhill, bad. She's held Kinslee one time. With the wreck, you supposedly being dead, and Kinslee looking like she was dug out of your butt, she's scared to touch her. The doctor has diagnosed her with postpartum depression. All Alexis does is lay there and stare at the wall. She doesn't eat, she doesn't talk, and she won't hardly drink. Alexis is pretty much nonexistent."

"Jesus." Guilt settles in from thinking my Lex had left me. I am just so afraid of losing her and Kinslee. Thank God they are both alive.

"Yeah, like I said. It's been a shitty two weeks. Mom and Dad have been helping out with the twins which has been a relief."

Lex promised me she would be strong if something were to happen to me. She also made a promise to me for our daughter.

Once Adam and I reached the labor and delivery floor, the first person I run into is mom. I hold my arms open for her and she runs into them. After holding her and reassuring her I'm okay, I finally walk the remaining steps to Alexis' room. I didn't know what to expect when I walked in, but this surely wasn't it. Alexis' mom, Georgia is rocking Kinslee while Lex is sleeping. Her eyes widen in shock when she sees me. She regains her composure and I hug her before taking Kinslee from her, thanking her. Georgia gets up and let me sit in the rocking chair.

Georgia places her hand on my shoulder. "It's so good to see you alive, Ethan."

"I'm going to find out what happened because none of you should have been going through all of this hurt."

Georgia nods in understanding. "From what I could tell, she was doing fine until the accident. I think it all just hit her at once, Ethan. Some mothers develop depression after giving birth anyway, but I don't believe that was the case here. If anyone will be able to bring her back it will be you. Take care of my daughter and my grandbaby."

"Don't worry, I will. Thank you for being here while I was gone."

She kisses the top of Kinslee's head. "Call us if you need anything or have any questions."

I nod and she leaves the room after kissing Lex on her cheek.

I rock Kinslee in my arms a few minutes, enjoying the little sounds she makes. She is so beautiful, just like Lex. Scooting closer to Alexis' bedside, I lean over to place a kiss to her lips.

"I'm here, Lex. I just wanted you to know that. Our daughter is beautiful, just like her momma. When you open your eyes, I will be here, then we can go on with our lives as a family."

A few tears escape her eyelids as she snuggles the blanket up to her face. "You were supposed to come back, Ethan. Why didn't you come back?" she murmurs in her sleep.

She thinks she's dreaming. "Baby, I'm right here, open your eyes."

Lex shakes her head. "No, if I do you will be gone."

I kiss her lips again, hoping she wakes up and sees this is real, that I'm really here. "Lex, baby, I promise you, I'm right here. Open your eyes, beautiful, I want to see them. Kinslee needs her momma and I need you. Please, Lex." I clutch her hand, squeezing it gently, urging her to wake up.

It takes a few moments, but finally, her eyes flutter open and she bursts into tears. I lean over the bed, gathering her in my arms, letting her cry on my shoulder as I try to comfort her.

Suddenly, she jerks backs and starts checking me for injuries. "Where are you hurt?" she sniffles.

"Lex, I'm perfectly fine. You told me to come back, and I did."

"I thought you were..."

"No, apparently there is a mix up somewhere. I'm going to make a call later and see what's up. Right now, I really just want to kiss you and spend time with you and our daughter, sound good?" The moment my lips brush hers, I know I am home. Lex grips my jacket like she is afraid I will leave.

Breaking the kiss, I brush away the tears that are coating her beautiful face. God, I hate that she has been through all this.

Kinslee starts crying so I retrieve her, cradling her closer. She quiets almost instantly.

"There, there. I'm here baby girl," I coo as I gently sway side to side.

"I didn't think I would get to see a moment like this. It hurt so bad to think my daughter wouldn't get to be held by you or be rocked to sleep by you. My heart broke for her just as much as it did me," Alexis murmurs, her voice cracking with sadness.

Sitting on the edge of the bed, I move Kinslee to one arm so I can wrap my other arm around Lex. Leaning down, I kiss her forehead, her cheek, then finally I claim her mouth. "You won't have to worry about any of that, Lex. As long as I am here, I will do everything I can for you and our daughter," I vow.

Lex lays her head on my shoulder, sighing contently. "I know you will, Ethan."

I lay Kinslee down in our lap so we both can admire her, love on her. I hope Lex isn't afraid to hold her now, not when me here.

"Do you want to hold her, Lex?" I ask softly.

She nods against my shoulder. "I was afraid to after I woke up because I thought I didn't protect her like I should have during the wreck. And with her looking exactly like you, it broke my heart all over again. I didn't think I deserved to love on her. Even now, I'm afraid to, but I want nothing more than to hold her, especially after seeing you with her."

I need to get Lex to quit talking like she is the worst mother in the world, because she is not, and I know she won't be. "Lex, Adam told me about everything. Why didn't you tell me that stuff was happening? I would have found a way to solve it. And, please, don't think you're a bad mother. You are far from it, baby. Kinslee is here, and she is healthy. She's perfect, Lex."

"I didn't tell you because I didn't want you to worry about us with you being on the other side of the world. I didn't want you to be so worried about us that you lose focus and something happen to you. Plus, I knew you would figure out a way to leave and I as much as I would have loved that, I didn't want you to hurt your military career."

"Lex, I would have found a way. You two are more important."

I pick up Kinslee, who fits perfectly in my hands, and place her in Lex's arms, carefully. When I place Kinslee in her arms, a tear rolls down Lex's cheek.

I pull out my cell phone and take a picture of my two girls, making it the background picture on my phone. It is hard not to capture the moment between them.

"Lex, baby, will you start eating again? I really want to take both of you home with me as soon as possible." She has gotten so thin.

Lex doesn't look at me, even when I try and turn her head in my direction she keeps her eyes downcast. She's so ashamed she can't even look me in the eye.

"Please look at me, Lex," I plead.

She finally looks up at me, her eyes full of shame. "I'm sorry I broke the promise I made to you, Ethan," she murmurs so low I almost don't hear her.

"I'm not upset with you or mad at you, babe. I just wish you would have told me and taken care of yourself. Kinslee not only needs you, but I do. You're my other half, my fighter. It's breaking me right now to see you like this because you are so strong willed-"

I am cut off by the door to our room opening. My eyes must be deceiving me because Brad is standing in the doorway. He stops when he see me. Of course, he thought I was dead, too.

I glance down at the bags he is carrying. It looks like stuff for both Alexis and my daughter. Looking at Lex, I notice she looks like a deer in headlights. I'm about to find out what he is doing here and nip this in the bud.

"Brad, can we talk, outside?" I ask as nicely as possible.

He nods and I swear I see him gulp. Good, be scared.

I place a tender kiss to Lex's temple and Kinslee's head before standing and following Brad out in the hallway.

I pull the door to and glare at him. "Start talking," I order.

"Look, Alexis needed someone, and since you were supposedly dead, I decided to step up and help," Brad replies, stating what I feared.

I ground my jaw. "So, you thought that since I was gone, you could sweep in like a white knight and take care of my daughter and steal my girl?"

"They were told you were dead. Alexis was in a bad place, and I still care for her. She needed someone to be there for her. Did I decide to do this just so I can get back with, Alexis? No, that was not my intention. If it happened, then, well, it would have happened." He

312

shrugs like it's not a big deal, but it is. Brad still wants my girl, yet he isn't going to get her.

"Brad, let me put this as nicely as I can. Lex, is mine, not yours. Kinslee is mine, not yours. I don't understand how you think you can just swoop in and take them from me?"

Brad shakes his head. "I wouldn't have done it if I had known you were still alive. All of us believed you were dead so you can't blame me for stepping up to help."

This conversation isn't getting anywhere.

Brad looks me dead in the eyes. "Just so you know, if the roles were reversed, I would have been okay with you stepping up to help when I couldn't."

He walks away without a word, leaving me stumped.

chapter fifty-one

Alexis

I don't know if my eyes are deceiving me or not, but I see Ethan sitting in front of me, cradling our daughter in one arm.

I blink rapidly to make sure it is really him, bursting into tears when I realize he is actually alive.

When he hugs me, I cling to him like he is going to disappear again. They told us he was dead, does that mean he was just injured instead? I jerk back, looking over for bandages, cuts...something.

Then he kisses me, and suddenly I feel like I can breathe again. I feel whole and full of life now.

He assures me he is fine, and then cradles Kinslee in his strong arms. Then he is sitting beside me, holding Kinslee in one arm, comforting me with his other arm around my shoulder.

That moment felt so surreal like I was dreaming again. I kept waiting to wake up and it all be a dream, not real.

Ethan hasn't mentioned Brad showing up since he walked back in the room. He has just been holding me while I hold our daughter.

I feel like the worst mother in the world. Kinslee needed me and I wasn't there for her.

The nightmare of not having Ethan in my life is gone, but the nightmare of someone wanting to harm me and my daughter is still there.

"Ethan, what are we going to do?" I ask in fear as I stare down at our gorgeous daughter.

Ethan grasps my chin and gently turns my head so I can look at him. "Don't you worry about it, Lex. You let me take care of it. I just want you to worry about Kinslee and yourself, okay?"

"Okay, I'm just scared that something bad is fixing to happen. I'm afraid whoever it is will not stop."

Ethan tightens his arm around me. "I'm going to find out who is messing with my girls and put a stop to it. I need you trust me to take care of it. You and Kinslee are my life, Lex."

I bury my head in his shoulder. "I love you so much, Ethan. I didn't think I would ever get to tell you how much again."

"I will love you until the end of time, Alexis Collins."

I sigh, feeling content. My family is together again, which is more than I could ever ask for.

True to my word, I started eating again. I hate that I let Ethan down, but I was so lost without him. I wasn't sure how I would be able to live my life without him in it. We just got together and then he left to go fight for our country. I prayed every day for his safe return. Ever since the Sargent's showed up at Julie's the sun has not risen. My life has been darkened by the pain of losing the man I love.

The weight of pain in my chest has lifted the moment I realized he was really in front of me. I am able to hold him, to kiss him, and to tell him I love him every day now.

Ethan steps outside to make a call, probably to figure out why this mess happened in the first place.

As I feed Kinslee, I begin to wonder where our family is going to go from here. Where will we live? I've been run out of my apartment and Ethan's because of the psycho that won't leave me

SHELBY REEVES

alone. I don't know what I have done to deserve this, but I wish it would cease.

I can hear Ethan talking in low murmurs to someone through the crack in the door. He must be standing off to the side because I can't see him.

The phone call must have taken longer than he anticipated because I am burping Kinslee a second time before he finally walks back in. Taking care of her with a wounded arm is tough, but I am starting to manage it.

He takes his usual spot beside me on the hospital bed. I am hoping I can go home this afternoon or in the morning, preferably today, though. We are just having to wait on the doctor.

"It turns out there are two Ethan Harper's, and they switched us somehow."

"Oh," I say sullenly, my heart cracking for the pain I know his family is feeling.

"Another thing. Has a detective come by to get your statement from the accident?"

Ethan is now in police mode now.

"I talked to Farris."

"Okay, well I arranged for someone to come take your statement, okay? And plus I have a friend coming to talk to you about what has been happening while I have been gone," he informs me.

Kinslee finally burped so I move to cradle her in my arms, but Ethan snatches her from me.

Well then.

In no time, an officer arrives to get my statement on the hit and run. I relay the information I remember from that day and everything that has been happening over the last year. He asks me question after question until finally he is satisfied and leaves.

"Why do you have two different people coming to talk to me when I could have just told him?" I ask Ethan when the first officer is gone.

"Because, the other officer coming is a real good friend of mine and I know he will put in more effort to find out who this person is that is messing with my family. Besides, if he figures it out before the other officer, then we know who the driver from the hit and run is. All the evidence will point to it."

Okay, I see what he is saying.

I should have known who is officer friend was, it should have clicked, yet it didn't until he walked in the room.

Farris breezes in the room with a giant smile on his face. "Long time no see, man! It was definitely a shock to get a call from you, but a damn good surprise! Come here and give your PIC a hug!"

Ethan hands me Kinslee then stands so Farris can bear hug him.

"It's good to have you back, Harper. I imagine the whole department has heard about it by now since I nonchalantly yelled it throughout the station," Farris exclaims happily.

I laugh softly at him while Ethan chuckles. "Knowing you, I'm sure the whole town heard you."

Farris nods in agreement. "I may have also ran to the chief's office and broke the news to him, and guess what, he actually smiled! I didn't think I would ever be able to get that hard ass to crack a smile."

Ethan shakes his head at his friend. "You are one crazy fucker you know that, Farris?"

Farris beams. "Yep, sure do, and I am proud of it. Now, let me hold the little angel while you tell me what the hell has been happening. On second thought, first tell me why you didn't call me?" he glowers at me, disappointed.

I drop my head in shame. "I just thought it would go away at first, but when it didn't I became scared. Remember when I texted you and asked if we could meet? I was going to tell you. Whenever I tried to tell you, something would come up."

Farris takes Kinslee from me as he shakes his head at my response. "Alexis, you should have reported it the second the mess started, no matter how small it may seem."

Ethan sits back down next to me. I curl into his side as he drapes his arm around me.

Farris takes the empty chair at the end of the bed. "Okay, when did this all start?"

"Last August."

Farris shifts Kinslee so he can pull out his notebook and a pen. He flips open the notebook and starts writing the information down. When he is done, he looks up at me. "Okay, I need you to tell me everything from start to finish, in order."

So, I dive into all that has happened over the last year, leaving nothing out, including my run in with Josh.

"Jesus," Ethan mutters when I am finished, holding me tight in the safety net that is his arms.

"Don't worry, Harper, I'm on the case. I should have this figured out soon since I've already got a prime suspect."

Ethan and I glance at one another trying to figure out who Farris believes is behind all of this madness.

"I believe its Kate," he explains.

Ethan's whole body tenses and his jaw ticks. "Why? Somehow I don't think it's her. She's crazy, but not that crazy. Now, Josh, on the other hand, should be a suspect."

"He can't be the suspect, Ethan, unless he is gay."

Some of the notes left rule Josh out or I would have thought it was him, too. Kate is the only one I know after my man. I agree with, Farris on this one.

"It's settled then, Kate is the first person I'm going after."

I nod into Ethan's chest. Ethan sighs heavily, his hand squeezing my shoulder. Why didn't I think of Kate all along? Maybe this could have been solved as soon as it had started if I had let Ethan handle it. Gah, it was stupid of me to brush it off and let it go on as long as it has.

Farris and Ethan build a plan on how to catch her and that's when I zone out. They need to handle this on their own.

Farris hands Kinslee back over to me and says goodbye.

"Farris," I call out, unable to let him leave without thanking him. He stops and turns, waiting.

"Thank you for being there for me after I called you. Without you making me keep fluids down, I would have probably lost Kinslee."

He smiles warmly and nods. "Anytime, Alexis. I'm just happy you are getting back to normal and that my boy is back alive and well."

Ethan chuckles next to me and kisses my temple.

With a parting nod, Farris turns and walks out of the room.

chapter fifty-two

Ethan

One month later

Things are slowly getting back to normal. Alexis is fully moved back into my apartment, so I get to hold both of my girls at night now. I took Lex car shopping the other day since hers is totaled. She picked out a black Dodge Journey. I scrunched my nose up at it, but she was dead set on it.

Lex and I take turns getting up in the night with Kinslee. She definitely doesn't sleep well at all at night.

I have given my retirement orders to my Sergeant and will be full-time at the police department. The army has changed me in a lot of ways, all for the better.

We are inching closer to nailing Kate. The bitch has sent a few texts since I found out everything. It still bothers me that Lex didn't tell me all of this was happening. I would have done everything in my power to solve this.

Mom is coming up this evening to watch Kinslee so I can take Lex out on a date. Lex and I need to make up for lost time. Two more weeks and we can *really* make up. I have something special planned for Lex tonight. Should I be nervous? Probably, except, I'm not. I'm anxious as hell, though. I love her so much and all the rough patches we have been through recently, prove how strong our love is. Watching Lex with Kinslee is a breathtaking sight to see. The way she cradles her, the way she talks to her, I couldn't dream up a more beautiful sight.

Sticking my head in our bedroom, I ask Lex, "Ready?"

"Just a second," she hollers from the bathroom.

Satisfied, I walk across the hall to check on my sleeping princess before I go. I haven't been out of the house much since I've been back. I took some time off from the department so I could give all my time to Lex and Kinslee. Tonight is my last night to spend with them before I go back to work.

Mom is leaning over Kinslee's crib, smiling down at her. "Thanks for watching her, Mom."

Mom looks up and beams at me. "She's so precious, Ethan. You know I'll watch her anytime for you."

"Lex and I are about to head out. Call us if you need anything."

Mom waves me off, silently telling me she knows what she's doing. Leaning over Kinslee's crib, I kiss the top of her head and tell her I love her.

Lex joins us and does the same.

Leaving Kinslee behind is tough, especially for the first time, but tonight is a special night.

Lex looks breathtaking in her sundress and sandals. Her legs look long and delectable.

"You look amazing, baby," I murmur then kiss her cheek.

The restaurant isn't far from our apartment so it isn't long before we arrive and are seated.

I haven't planned how I will ask her, I'm just winging it. There is no doubt in my mind she will say yes. I love this woman sitting across from me. Lex is the most amazing person I've ever met. It's like she was born for this. Crafted just for me. Her stubbornness, her sass, and her strength are what makes her perfect.

She is smiling at me now, and I can't wait a second longer.

Scooting back my chair, I stand to my full height and step around the table. Lex stares at me with a confused expression. She has no clue of what is fixing to happen.

Reaching into my pocket, I pull out the velvet box which contains the diamond I spent a week searching for.

My heart races as I drop to one knee. Why am I so nervous if I am confident she will say yes?

Lex lets out a gasp when she realizes what is taking place, her hands covering her mouth.

"Lex, baby, I know in the past I was stupid and kept pushing you away, and I regret it every day. The only thing I want now is to spend the rest of my life loving you. I'm so lucky you didn't give up on me. Will you put up with me for the rest of your life as my wife?"

Tears spill out of her eyes while I wait for her answer. "Oh, Ethan. Yes, I will marry you!"

My smile widens as I place the ring on her finger. Lex launches herself at me as the people around us clap. Drawing back slightly, I seal our engagement with a kiss.

This evening will go down as one of the best nights of my life. "I want to marry you as soon as possible, Lex," I murmur, my lips brushing hers.

"Yes, definitely," she agrees hastily.

Good to know we are on the same page.

Alexis

The wedding planning has been in full swing since Ethan proposed two days ago. Kaylee came right over with the twins the next morning after I called and told her the happy news. We have accomplished a lot in a short amount of time. My mother is over the moon excited and has been using some of her connections, too. She was shocked to learn I didn't want an over the top wedding. Kaylee's wedding was perfect, and while I don't want a beach wedding, just family and close friends will do.

Today, Kaylee, mom, Kinslee and I went shopping for a dress. I didn't leave with one, but I found one I really liked. Ethan and I are thinking of August the first as the day we become one. Ethan also suggested a destination wedding in the mountains, and while I love his idea, I'm not sure I can book the venue with it being so close the wedding date. More than likely, they will be all booked up.

Adjusting to motherhood has been a challenge, but a rewarding one. Kinslee is starting to sleep better at night now, thank goodness. Having Ethan here with me all day and night for the first month has been a blessing and fun. He is so good with her and at times I stand back and watch him. He tells her stories of his dad, her grandpa, she won't get to meet. It's touching to listen to him include his dad in her life when he can't physically be here to be a part of it.

Noticing it's almost time to leave, I begin packing Kinslee's diaper bag. Ethan had left a couple of hours ago to go workout before meeting us. I hate he works nights, but I remind myself it won't be like this forever. He will move to dayshift. I already don't sleep much when he is here, but I really don't sleep when he works.

Hearing a noise, I pause. My pulse starts racing when I hear a different noise. It almost sounds like people talking.

Kinslee. Running out of my bedroom, I race down the hall only to come to a halt right outside her room.

Kate.

"Breaking in, now? I didn't figure you'd stoop that low," I seethe. The last update I received, Farris is close to gathering all the evidence. If her breaking into our apartment isn't enough evidence, then I don't know what is.

She smiles wickedly. "Silly girl, I have a key." She holds up a brass key which looks exactly like mine. "Ethan, let me keep it this whole time. Did you know he was still calling me, texting me, asking me to come over before he left? Even now, he still chooses me."

She's lying. Her words won't affect me since I know the truth.

"Why bother with all the notes, the texts, and the vandalism for a man who doesn't want you?" I'm calling her out. She knows as well as I do all of it was her.

She scoffs. "Oh, he wants me all right. As soon as you're out of the picture, I'll be there for him and he will welcome me with open arms."

"Like hell you will. I'm not going anywhere. Ethan wouldn't run to you like you think he will."

Her devilish smile returns. "We'll see about that."

A sharp pain bursts through my skull, then my world goes black.

chapter fifty-three

Ethan

As I am pulling in the parking lot of the restaurant, I am meeting Lex and Kinslee at, my cell starts ringing. It's Farris.

"Yo, man, what's up?" I greet him as I park my truck.

"Harper, I figured it out. I know who has been harassing your girl. It's Kate *and* her brother Josh, which explains a lot. They are both crazy."

No way. "Are you fucking kidding me? Josh is behind this, too?"

Shit, this is messed up. And Josh, I'm trying to remember what he looks like.

"Harper, I will try and locate them. You just worry about your little family."

I need to call, Lex. I hand up with Farris and immediately dial, Lex's number, only to get her voicemail.

I try three more times and she doesn't answer. An unsettling feeling is gnawing at me, telling me something isn't right. I start my truck and back out of my parking spot. I speed through town, rushing to make sure my girls are okay.

I grab my phone and dial Farris' number. When he answers, I bark out, "She isn't answering her phone and I have a bad feeling. I'm driving back to the house now. Meet me there?"

"Sure thing, Harper. Give me ten minutes."

I toss my phone down blindly as I stomp down on the gas pedal some more.

I arrive at the house five minutes later. I jump out of my truck and race up the stairs, my heart beating hastily. I did notice that Lex's new SUV is still parked in the driveway.

The next thing I noticed, which was not good, was the door was unlocked. Turning the knob slowly, I open the door gradually and creep inside. The house is quiet downstairs so I tiptoe over to the stairs, clearing the room as I go.

As I ascend the stairs, I can hear murmurs. I go to reach for my gun, which is normally holstered to my hip, to remember I didn't get it out of my truck.

As I top the stairs, the voices get louder, more clear. A lone door is cracked open to my left, which is Kinslee's room.

Discreetly, I tiptoe forward, careful not to make a sound. Peeking inside the room, I can't see Lex, but what I do see has my blood boiling. Kate is cradling Kinslee in her arms while Josh is pacing back and forth with a gun fisted in his hand. I instantly recognize him, not only from trying to take advantage of Lex, but I went to Kate's once and saw him.

"Kate, what the fuck are you doing? We have to get out of here!" he hisses, a hint of worry in his voice.

Kate gives him a stern look. "Quiet, will you. It's not time to leave just yet."

Josh's eyebrows crease. "What are you talking about? The plan was to snatch the baby and leave, that's it. Now, you are changing it?!"

I have to fight the urge to barge in the room. Kate thought she could just steal my daughter from me?

Kate sits down in the glider with Kinslee and begins to rock her like she is her mother. "Josh, plans are made to be changed. Besides, how can I truly become her mother when the bitch is still alive? Ethan will be upset and vulnerable when he finds out the news, which is perfect timing for me to swoop back in and get my man back." Kate laughs devilishly.

I need to come up with a plan of my own before Kate or Josh kill one of my reasons for living.

With a plan in mind, I finally make my presence known. Kate's jaw drops when she sees me walk in. Josh straightens his stature, then changes his stance so that he is ready to fight.

I resist the urge to walk over and rip Kinslee from her arms. In my peripherals, I still don't see Lex, which worries me.

"Ethan," Kate acknowledges me when the shock of my walking in wears off.

"Kate, I wasn't expecting you," I reply, forcing my voice to stay even.

Kate gently rocks Kinslee like she knows exactly how to be a parent. "I know, but I have been expecting you though. I have been meaning to talk to you, E. I have been missing you so much here lately. When I heard the news a few months ago that you had died, I didn't think I would be able to go on with my life without you in it. But then, I heard the best news I could ever hear. Suddenly, there was light in my world again because you were alive. I had high hopes that we would get back together."

Swallowing the bile in my throat, I say the words that have me wondering why I didn't come up with a different plan. "I know, baby. You have been on my mind lately, too."

Kate smiles and tears well in her eyes as she stands and takes the couple steps toward me. "It's so good to hear you say that, E. I have wanted for so long for us to become a family."

More bile rises in my throat. "Me, too."

Just when I think I have fooled both of them, Josh gets between us and yells, "He's lying!"

Kate looks between me and Josh, wondering who to believe.

I give her a pleading look. "Baby, I'm not. I had to arrange some things first before I could surprise you." All of this is total bullshit.

Josh still isn't buying my lies. "Kate, don't listen to him! All he I trying to do is keep you from stealing his daughter and killing Alexis!"

Kate is still indecisive. I have got to try harder. "I don't care about, Alexis, Kate. I care about you." I take a tentative step closer to Kate, who is now placing Kinslee in her car seat. I have got to do something before she runs off with my daughter.

"Kate," I murmur as I take another step. "How about me, you, and Kinslee go away, just us three?" No, no. Vacation with her is the last thing I want to do.

She halts and straightens. Her face lights up.

Now, I just need to get my daughter in my hands. I walk toward her, but just as I am about to grab the handle of the car seat, Josh grabs me by my arm and jerks me backward.

"Not yet, not until I know for certain you aren't playing us."

I yank my arm free of his grasp and give him a hard look. "She is my daughter, who will always come first in my life. You cannot tell me I can't take her."

He holds his hands up defensively, retreating a couple steps. "The issue I have is I don't believe you are honest with my sister."

Dear God, I'm going to regret what I am fixing to do. *You are doing this to save, Lex and your daughter.*

I grab Kate's hand, pulling her toward me. When she is right in front of me, I lean down and kiss her on her mouth. It takes everything in me to not throw up on her.

When I pull back, I turn to Josh. "Does that answer your question?"

He gives me an approving nod, at least, I think that is what it is.

Kate launches herself in my arms again. "Oh, Ethan! I knew all along you still loved me!"

Unlatching her arms from around me, I flash her a smile then make another attempt to pick up the car seat Kinslee is currently strapped into.

This time, no one stops me. I crouch down to look at her first. "Hey, princess," I coo. Her coal eyes are wide at first, then she smiles at me, melting my heart.

I hear hushed murmurs behind me, capturing my attention.

"Where do you want me to dump her after I kill her?" I hear Josh inquire.

"Figure it out, I don't care what you do as long as she is gone," Kate replies in a hushed voice.

I catch Farris peeking around the corner through one of the toys with a mirror which is hanging off of Kinslee's car seat.

I catch his eye and give him a slight nod. Shit is fixing to go down. I pick up the car seat and move off to the side, looking for somewhere to hide my daughter so she doesn't get caught in the crossfire.

Just as I set Kinslee down in the corner of the room, all hell starts breaking loose.

Farris bursts in the room, gun raised. "Well, well, it looks like it's game over for the insane siblings."

Kate lets out a shriek which almost makes my ears bleed. Josh, however, moves to attack Farris so I sling my arms around him from behind, keeping him from touching my friend.

I throw Josh to the ground and climb on top him, pinning him to the floor with Farris' help. Farris hands me a pair of handcuffs and I snap them around his wrists.

Feeling pleased, I stand, preparing to arrest Kate. All the color drains from my face when I realize she has disappeared. I whip my head back to the corner and I placed Kinslee in to find the space empty.

I turn to Farris. "Interrogate this lowlife until he tells you what they have done with, Lex. I'm going after my daughter."

He gives me a quick, hard nod then I race out the door and back down the stairs. As soon as I run outside, Kate is peeling out of the driveway.

For a split second, back in my daughter's room, I felt torn between who to save, my daughter or the girl who makes my world spin on its axis. But, I knew right away Kinslee would be the one I run after. Besides, Lex would beat my ass if I didn't.

I am on the pavement within seconds, pushing the pedal to the floor, trying to catch up with Kate. I'm on my phone the next second with the dispatcher explaining what's happening.

My breath catches when Kate starts weaving in and out of traffic. *Please don't wreck.*

I'm wracking my brain on how to get Kate to stop without hurting Kinslee.

Then, cruisers fly past me and surround Kate's car, one in front and one the left side. She's still speeding down the highway, showing no signs of slowing down. The scenario I see playing out is not how I want this to end.

One of the cruisers hits his brakes, causing Kate to slow down, but she doesn't fully stop. She tries to go around the cruiser in front of her by driving on the shoulder of the pavement. The officer in front turns to block her path while I help by driving up on the right side of her car, effectively blocking her in. She can't go anywhere. Leaping out of my truck, the first thing I do is retrieve my daughter, relieved to see she is sleeping. Holding her against my chest, I vow to protect her from everything I possibly can.

Leaving the other officers, who I learn are Sanders, Ross, and Stratton, to arrest Kate, I buckle Kinslee back in her car seat and transfer her to my truck.

Once she is safely strapped in, I search for my phone to call Farris.

"We found her, Harper. She's shaken up, but otherwise, she's fine," he informs me as soon as he answers.

Relief floods through me. "Good, tell her I love her and I will be there soon. Kinslee is safe with me and Kate is cuffed so I'm coming home."

I hear Farris saying something to someone, then he is back. "I'll tell her for you."

"Thanks, Farris. I owe you."

Farris chuckles. "Don't sweat it. You would do the same for me."

The thought of having lost Lex is unbearable. I pretty much felt like Lex did when she thought I was dead.

Lex is sitting on the steps when I pull in the drive. When she sees me, she takes off running towards me. I catch her when she leaps into my arms.

I kiss her hard, then set her back down on her feet. I retrieve our daughter and hand her to Lex who starts bawling the moment I hand her over.

I wrap my arm around, Lex and place my hand on Kinslee. Lex lays her head on my shoulder and I kiss her hair. "It's over, Lex."

Now that Josh and Kate are caught, Lex and I can move on together with our daughter.

epilogue

Alexis

The sun is shining bright this afternoon. The weather is hot, but not unbearable. The mountains are beautiful, which makes me glad Ethan and I chose this place for our wedding.

I haven't seen my man in almost twenty-four hours, but that's about to change. In a few moments, I will be walking down the aisle to him. He will take my hand and vow to love me for the rest of his life.

Since Kate and Josh are not bothering us anymore, life has been bliss. Kinslee is growing so fast on me and I wish time would slow down.

Dad pats my hand, which is grasping his elbow. "You ready?"

"More than ready." There are no nerves, only excitement and happiness.

The moment I see him, I refrain from running to him. *One foot in front of the other*, I think to myself.

His smile is wide, mesmerizing.

How did I get so lucky? I never gave up on us because I knew, Ethan and I, we were meant for each other.

Love is risky and rewarding.

Love is bliss and beautiful.

Love is sometimes hard, yet it's everlasting.

And it is always raging in your soul.

From this day forward, I will be Mrs. Ethan Blake Harper and I can't think of a better way to spend my life. Whatever bumps in the road Ethan and I come across, I know we can work through them.

"I love you," I mouth to him.

Then, my heart soars when he says, "Until the end of time."

ABOUT THE AUTHOR

Shelby lives in Alabama with her loving husband and their energetic son. When she is not writing or working, Shelby enjoys reading, spending time with her family and friends, and traveling.

You can follow Shelby and her writing journey on
Facebook: www.facebook.com/shelbyreevesauthor
Twitter: www.twitter.com/shelbyreeves92

Other books by Shelby

Pieces Series
Picking up the Pieces
Healing the Pieces

Saved Series
Safe with you

What's next?
Saving you (Saved, #1.5) – Spring 2016
Breaking Free of the Pieces (Pieces, #4) – Summer 2016

Made in the USA
Charleston, SC
06 January 2016